W9-DGN-319

1 /18

T-14

2014-10

L - 5/18

12-19(16)

DON'T EVER LOOK BACK

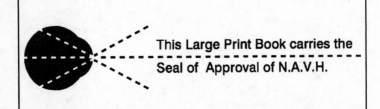

DON'T EVER LOOK BACK

DANIEL FRIEDMAN

THORNDIKE PRESS
A part of Gale, Cengage Learning

GALE
CENGAGE Learning·

Farmington Hills, Mich • San Francisco • New York • Waterville, Maine
Meriden, Conn • Mason, Ohio • Chicago

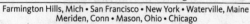

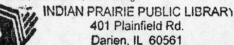

Copyright © 2014 by Daniel Friedman.
Thorndike Press, a part of Gale, Cengage Learning.

Thorndike Press® Large Print Mystery.
The text of this Large Print edition is unabridged.
Other aspects of the book may vary from the original edition.
Set in 16 pt. Plantin.

LIBRARY OF CONGRESS CATALOGING-IN-PUBLICATION DATA

Friedman, Daniel, 1981–
    Don't ever look back / by Daniel Friedman. — Large print edition.
        pages ; cm. — (Thorndike Press large print mystery)
    ISBN 978-1-4104-7004-1 (hardcover) — ISBN 1-4104-7004-0 (hardcover)
    1. Older men—Fiction. 2. Ex-police officers—Fiction. 3. Jewish men—Fiction. 4. Large type books. I. Title.
PS3606.R5566D64 2014b
813'.6—dc23   2014011754

Published in 2014 by arrangement with St. Martin's Press, LLC

Printed in the United States of America
1 2 3 4 5 6 7 18 17 16 15 14

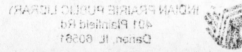

For Buddy and Marget Friedman,
Sam and Goldie Burson,
and Aunt Rose Burson

ACKNOWLEDGMENTS

I'd like to thank my agent, Victoria Skurnick, and foreign rights manager, Elizabeth Fisher, who is largely responsible for Buck Schatz's wildly successful invasion of Europe. I'd also like to thank my editor, Marcia Markland, for championing these books, her former assistant Kat Brzozowski, publicity manager Hector DeJean, Laura Clark, Lauren Hesse, Quressa Robinson, Thomas Dunne, and Andrew Martin. I'd also like to use this space to remember St. Martin's Press publisher Matthew Shear, who died in August 2013. His loss was deeply felt.

I'd also like to thank my mom, Elaine Friedman, my brother Jonathan Friedman, Grandma Margaret Friedman, and Bubbi Goldie Burson for all their love and support. Thanks as well to Rachel Friedman, Sheila and Steve Burkholz, Carole Burson, David Friedman, Skip and Susan Rossen, Stephen and Beth Rossen, David and Lindsey Rossen, Martin and Jenny Rossen, Scott Burkholz, Rachel Burkholz, Claire and Paul Putterman, Andrew Putterman, and Matthew Putterman.

Finally, a special recognition: In chapter 10 of this book I used an extraordinary story about a failed 1919 attempt to integrate the Memphis Police, to justify Buck's hesitance to divulge information he knows about a Jewish criminal to the department that employs him.

I learned about this obscure event from an exhaustive history of the Memphis Police, commissioned by the department and written by Eddie M. Ashmore, with research from Joseph E. Walk. I attempted to find a second source for this story, and could not; I suspect Mr. Ashmore found this information by delving deep into primary sources.

I contacted Marcia, my editor, and asked her whether I needed to include a citation or a footnote in order to retell this story in my own words, since it was only documented in a single place. We decided that the anecdote did not require a citation, as a footnote would be aesthetically jarring for readers, and facts are not proprietary, and are routinely included in fictional works without sourcing.

However, I believe the work of Mr. Ashmore deserves some recognition here. Eddie Ashmore was an ordained minister, an academic and a historian of local police departments in Tennessee. He died in 2007. His careful work documenting the histories of local police departments is probably obscure, but not unappreciated.

1
2009

In my misguided youth as a Memphis police detective, I wrecked a fair number of motor pool cars. I damaged more than my share of property. I violated a lot of people's constitutional rights, often with a rolled-up phone book. So getting taken to the woodshed by somebody in an official capacity was not a new experience for me.

Used to be, I could just sit quietly and think about football while my superiors yelled and vented their anger. Then, I'd make some token gesture of contrition and head back out to resume whatever I had been doing before. Nobody ever stayed mad at me for long; I'd always bring a nasty criminal to a messy end and my various excesses would be forgiven.

But I wasn't sure how I could placate Vivienne Wyatt, the director of resident relations for the Valhalla Estates Assisted Lifestyle Community for Older Adults. She looked really pissed.

I draped an arm over the back of the chair I was sitting in and threw a sort of raffish half grin her way. "What can I say? I'm a maverick. I play by my own rules."

By my standards, that was pretty close to an apology.

Unimpressed, Viv scowled at me. This one, apparently, was immune to my charms. "Mr. Connor says you went after him with an axe."

"I didn't go after him."

"But you had an axe, Mr. Schatz."

"Call me Buck, sugar."

"He thought you were going to kill him, Buck. And please call me Ms. Wyatt."

I snorted. "When I decide to kill Connor, Ms. Wyatt, I promise I'll be unambiguous about it. I just needed the axe to bust up that damn rocking chair of his."

"That chair was very dear to Mr. Connor. It was one of the few remnants he was able to hang on to from his life before he joined our community. Think about how difficult the transition was for you, and try to understand why your actions are so hurtful."

I hunched my shoulders and didn't say anything. I'd come here in a wheelchair, recovering from bullet wounds and crushed bones. I'd needed help moving around, help getting out of bed in the morning, help getting in at night. Help in the bathroom.

I was despondent over the loss of my independence, and over the loss of the home I'd lived in for half a century. Most days, I woke up wishing more than a little bit that I'd let the man who hurt me so bad finish the job.

I knew that, if I'd taken the easy way out, I wouldn't have had a chance to kill Randall Jennings, and I'd really enjoyed splattering that bastard's brains all over the walls of my hospital room. But getting better was hard work; it took nine long weeks of physical therapy before I was strong enough to piss standing up. Even then, I still needed to hold on to the assistance rails that were bolted to the walls next to the toilet, which had made it difficult to aim my stream. And the first time I got down on the floor to wipe up the splatter, I couldn't stand back up, and I had to use the remote control button to call for the staff to come help me.

I was better than I had been, but I was still weak. I couldn't really even swing the axe properly. My shoulder wouldn't rotate. My body wouldn't twist right. My legs were weak. I'd managed to hack off one of the rockers and an armrest and gouge at the seat a little bit, but when I was done, I was

13

glazed in sweat and breathing ragged, and the goddamn thing still looked like a chair.

Six months ago, I could have smashed it to kindling.

I considered the fact that Vivienne Wyatt knew all of this, and I undraped my arm from the chair and stuck my hands in the pockets of my windbreaker.

Regardless of the various indignities I'd endured, I couldn't find common cause with Dwayne Connor. I hated everything about my one-legged redneck neighbor. The man's skin had the same texture as a pair of boxer shorts left to dry and crust up in the sun after spending a hard three-day ride wedged in a cowboy's ass crack. And his personality matched his looks.

"Why did you feel the need to destroy Mr. Connor's rocking chair with an axe, Buck?"

"My friend Crazy Mack came to visit. Mack is —" I paused. "Mack is like you."

Ms. Wyatt arched one eyebrow. "You mean he's black?"

"Yes. And Connor has some problems with that."

Connor had called Mack several different names; shouted the kinds of words that make my grandson flinch, even when there's no colored people around to overhear. But when I explained this to Ms. Wyatt, all she

14

said was: "You can't go smashing people's chairs up with axes. Why do you even have an axe?"

"For situations like this one," I said. "When stuff needs smashing. Aren't you people supposed to get more upset when folks like Connor say stuff like that?"

"We people aren't supposed to do anything," she said. "If I started worrying about what every ignorant old white man in this place was thinking or saying, I wouldn't hardly have time in the day to do anything else. You alone would probably take up my whole morning, Buck."

I didn't particularly like that implication. "Well, I'm upset about it. He was rude to my guest. There's no excuse for that."

She picked up a folder off her desk. "Look," she said. "I'm really not supposed to talk too much about specifics of our residents' circumstances, but I want to give you an idea of what the last few months have been like for Mr. Connor. He came here because he can't be on his own anymore. His son went looking for him when he didn't answer the phone; found the old man lying on the floor of his house. He'd been there for days, in a pool of his own mess. The smell was terrible. When Mr. Connor got into the emergency room at

15

Baptist Hospital, a doctor discovered that a large clot had cut off all the blood flow to his femoral artery. His leg was dead and the flesh was rotting off the bones. They had no choice but to amputate."

"The mean old bastard had it coming," I said. "You can't talk like he did to my friend. Crazy Mack is kind of emotionally delicate, on account of his schizophrenia."

Viv leaned forward, toward me. "Buck?"

"Yes, Ms. Wyatt?"

"Did you bring a schizophrenic black man up to your floor to antagonize your racist neighbor?"

"Of course not," I said, grasping the arms of my walker to help me rise out of my chair a little bit, so my eyes were level with hers. "Mack came by to show me some photos of his grandchildren. He has been my friend for more than fifty years."

A trace of a smile from her. "Where did you get yourself a schizophrenic black friend, Buck? I think I need to hear this one."

"Back in the prehistoric days, when I was a young patrol officer, I responded to a noise complaint, and I found Mack up on the roof of a low-rise apartment house wearing nothing but tinfoil, waving a big knife and screaming. Circumstances like that can easily escalate into a tragedy, but I kept a cool head and I was able to defuse the situation."

"How'd you do that?"

"I shot him in the neck."

Both her eyebrows went up. "You shot the black man?"

"The doctor who treated the gunshot wound also put him on chlorpromazine," I said. "That helped him a lot with his episodes."

The corners of her mouth turned downward. "And he's your friend now?"

"Of course he is. He says I'm the man who gave him his medicine, which I think is pretty close to true. He's very polite, my friend Mack; sends me a card every year at Christmastime. You know, I've shot thirty-one men and he's the only one who ever had the common courtesy to thank me for it, even though all of them sorely needed shooting."

There was a long pause while Vivienne Wyatt thought a bunch of things and then decided not to say any of them. Instead, she asked: "You shot thirty-one people?"

"Eighteen of them died, so I suppose they get a pass. But the rest were just rude."

Viv kind of shook her head. "What's going to happen when I send you back upstairs to your unit, Buck?"

I shrugged. "It's almost time for *Fox and Friends,* so I'll probably watch that."

I could tell she was beginning to lose patience with me. "What's going to happen between you and Mr. Connor?"

"I think you should send him home to Mississippi, where he can resume the slow process of decomposition."

"I'm not going to be doing that. And I hope I won't need to call the police up here over your feud."

"I hope you do," I said. "Rose just loves having visitors."

Viv rubbed her temples with her index fingers. "You're on thin ice, Buck Schatz," she said. "I'm keeping my eye on you."

I gave her a little salute as I hauled myself slowly to my feet and unfolded the walker. "Thanks for letting me know, Ms. Wyatt."

I hobbled out of her office, leaning on my walker and favoring my left leg. I crossed the lobby, where a few of the residents were draped across the cushy sofas and easy chairs. One or two were staring at nothing, and the rest were asleep. I checked my watch; it was seven thirty in the morning, which meant it was just about breakfast time. I guessed that's what these folks were waiting for. That, or death.

The walker I used was lightweight, made from hollow tubes of anodized aluminum. My doctor had recommended a newer model of "mobility aid" with four wheels instead of legs, but that thing felt unsafe to me. It had a little bicycle handbrake, which was supposed to assure it wouldn't roll out from under me, but the fact that it needed a brake at all suggested that the risk of it getting away was something I should be concerned about.

I opted instead for a regular one with wheels on the front two legs and rubber feet on the back. I could push it in front of me instead of lifting it up and setting it down with every step, and it felt stable. I was pretty sure it couldn't move on its own, though I sometimes watched it through squinted eyes when it thought I wasn't paying attention, just to make sure it wasn't going to try anything sneaky.

I made my way to the cafeteria-style dining room. Rose was a late sleeper, and wouldn't be up until at least eight thirty, so I usually ate breakfast alone. That morning, they were serving eggs and whole wheat toast and underripe cantaloupe, still greenish around the rind.

Whoever said that life in assisted-living facilities lacked variety clearly never had breakfast at Valhalla. A single plate of scrambled eggs could have burnt bits, cold places, and runny parts.

I'd situated myself at the farthest table from the other residents, so they'd leave me alone. But somebody came and sat down with me anyway.

He wasn't as old as I was, but a man can be a lot younger than me and still be old. He had a thin pencil-line of a mustache and short, neatly combed white hair. He hadn't brought any breakfast to the table.

"Hello, Baruch," he said.

I paused; drummed my fingers on the plastic tabletop. I'd been ambushed, and flight was not an option. Physically, I couldn't bolt for cover. I'd folded up the walker before I sat down, and even if I hadn't, it wasn't a mode of transport conducive to quick getaways.

I hadn't been paying attention to him as he approached; I'd been too busy poking at my eggs. Now that he was sitting, I couldn't see how his jacket was hanging, so I couldn't figure whether he had a piece under it.

He had me at a considerable disadvantage. I decided to be friendly.

"Hello, Elijah," I said. "It's been a while."

"I wasn't sure you'd recognize me."

"I know who you are."

"Are you surprised to see me?"

I was, a little bit. But I wouldn't give him the satisfaction. "Nothing surprises me anymore," I said.

"The last time we spoke, you promised me something. Do you remember what it was?"

I stabbed my fork into the plate and shoveled a glob of egg into my mouth. "I said I'd kill you if I ever saw you again."

"Precisely. I have visited you as a courtesy. If you intend to make good on your threat, you'd best do so immediately."

"Why's that?"

"Because, whether you kill me or not," he said. "I shall be dead in forty-eight hours."

Apparently, nobody I have ever met can die without bothering me about it.

2
1965

I glared at the little European and said, from between teeth clenched around a cigarette: "I heard you been looking for me."

"Indeed, I have been, Detective." He gestured for me to take a seat across from him. His fingers were long-jointed and delicate, like a pianist's or a stage magician's. "I want to talk to you."

I sized him up. Dark eyes and dark skin; a waxed pencil-line of mustache beneath a prominent nose. He wore a gray Savile Row–style suit with white chalk stripes. The jacket was cut slim; tailored close enough to his body that I could see he didn't have a gun underneath it. This was a man I could break six different ways, using just my hands.

But if he didn't look like a tough, the fellows he ran with certainly did. There were five of them with us in the dingy basement barroom, and each was as big across as a beef steer. Other than the European's entourage and a nervous-looking bartender, the place was empty, and one of the goons had settled his bulk in front of the door to make sure it stayed that way. I looked around for another way out, but there wasn't one. If I needed to escape, I would have to go through that man, and he was awful thick.

"Talk, then," I said.

His heavy eyebrows knit together. "I understand you refused to surrender your weapon as my associates requested."

I unbuttoned my own baggy American off-the-rack suit jacket and opened it, so he could see the .357 Magnum hanging at my side.

"I ain't accustomed to complying with requests from folks like your associates. And I didn't survive this long by walking unarmed into basements with men like you. A while back, a real smart fellow told me I should always hang on to my gun."

"And yet, surely, you recognize that the fetish object to which you cling affords only illusory protection. That weapon will be woefully insufficient to dispatch us all, should our conversation devolve into gunplay."

I didn't like his smugness, and I didn't

like his condescending tone. But what I liked least of all was the fact that his observation carried an implicit threat. We were down near the river, on a mostly deserted block. If things got sticky, nobody would be coming to help me. Luckily, I was the self-reliant sort.

"This gun carries a pill for each of you, by my count, and the first is yours, Slick. Illusory or not, your friends would have to be preternatural quick to put me down before I get a shot off. I reckon my fetish object will afford me a fine opportunity to make your evening pretty unpleasant, should our conversation, as you put it, devolve," I said.

"I have no doubt of that, Baruch, and I have no desire to test the extent of your dangerousness. People say you are a man who has been through Hell and come out meaner for it, and looking at you, I know what I have heard is the truth. You have the eyes of a feral dog. But I would caution you: I am, in my way, just as unyielding as you."

I weighed that, to decide whether to take offense. "You spit out a lot of words, to say a whole lot of nothing, and I ain't got time to listen to you make noises to amuse yourself. Who the hell are you, and what do you want?"

"I apologize, most sincerely, if I have been

circumspect. I am called Elijah, and I am a gentleman of fortune. I want to offer a proposition to you."

"If you heard I take bribes, you heard wrong," I told him.

"I didn't go to all this trouble to offer a bribe," he said. He punctuated this with a nasal, chirpy laugh. "I wish to engage your participation in a rather elaborate and highly lucrative criminal conspiracy."

"You want me in on a job you're doing."

"Yes."

"What kind of a job?"

He smiled at me, showed me the only thing about him that wasn't neat. His soft, purple gums were badly receded, exposing the brown roots of his jagged teeth. I'd seen mouths like his before, but never in America. Not even on hopheads. Hell, not even in Alabama. Those gums told a story of a man who had survived an extended period of severe malnutrition. Elijah had been through a hell of his own.

"I can't divulge the particulars until you're inextricably committed to the enterprise," he said. "Otherwise, perhaps Detective Schatz will arrest me." He chirped at me again.

I got real still for a minute and just looked at him; a feral dog catching the scent of a cottonmouth snake.

"I ain't interested in your offer," I said. "As far as arresting you, I'll keep my options open." I stood up, and my chair scraped across the floor as I pushed it back. "No hard feelings, Elijah, but this dog prefers to keep his nose clean." I moved toward the exit. The man at the door didn't look like he was planning to let me pass, so I stuck my hand inside my jacket.

"Baruch," said Elijah. "You are a warrior. You have killed and imprisoned the enemies of your sovereign. For your labors, you're rightly owed a prince's reward, and yet your wife, Rose, and your son, Brian, are deprived of even modest comforts."

This wasn't a sales pitch; it was a threat. This was his backhanded, Continental way of telling me he would hurt my family. I had killed men for less, on his continent and on mine, and I wasn't averse to doing it again. My hand closed on the grip of the .357.

He continued. "And all the while, the men who shape society's strictures so as to funnel wealth to themselves grow fatter and richer with each passing day, while you protect their hegemonic rule and beg them for scraps. How can you say this is clean? How can you believe this to be just?"

"I'm getting by," I said, not taking my eyes off the hulking form in the doorway. The big man's face looked like a boiled ham.

"Please, let me show you something." Elijah laid a hand on my shoulder. I dropped my cigarette on the floor and whirled around to face him, drawing the gun from my holster. I had not realized he'd left his seat at the corner booth in the back of the room; he'd moved without making any noise.

The five thugs all drew down on me, and we had a nice little standoff.

"Gentlemen, put away your guns," Elijah said, keeping his voice soft and even. The men obeyed. He turned toward me. The .357 was pointed at his nose. "I'd appreciate it if you would as well, Baruch. It's only polite."

I thought about just going ahead and blowing his sleek little head apart. The five gunmen would probably ventilate me pretty good, but that might be less unpleasant than listening to more of his monologues. It wouldn't be right, though, to leave Rose a widow. Not with the kid wanting to go to college. I felt I owed it to them to make a reasonable effort to avoid getting myself killed. I holstered the Magnum.

"Thank you, Baruch," Elijah said with a

gracious nod as he smoothly slipped out of his suit jacket. He folded it once and draped it over the nearest chair. Then he rolled up the left sleeve of his crisp, white dress shirt and showed me his forearm. Near the inside of his elbow, tattooed in blue ink, was the serial number *A-62102.*

"A souvenir from the place my childhood ended," he told me. "And a constant reminder of the lesson I learned there. Society's veneer of civility and order is false and fragile, and a Jew's position is always precarious. My parents believed they could be professionals, put down roots, join the community. Their miscalculation was punished, rather severely."

"I know who you are. I've heard of you." It had been a bad couple of years for people who owned safes full of cash and the people who insured them, and a few of my better-connected snitches had heard whispers that someone called Elijah was the reason for that. Word was: He'd emptied more banks than the panic of 1929. They said he didn't know fear, and could move in and out of a place like a ghost. No law enforcement agency had ever gotten close to even proving he existed. And here he was, with his neck within easy reach of my hands.

He smiled his damaged smile. "A strong,

28

capable Jew shouldn't be beholden to the goyish establishment. We are society's eternal outsiders, so what is our stake in social stability? We are imprisoned and executed even when we follow the rules, so why shouldn't we transgress?"

He was taking a big risk trying to recruit me. Or maybe he wasn't. Maybe this was how he worked. Maybe he had a whole network of disaffected Jewish cops working for him. Maybe that's how he stayed so far ahead of the law.

"I'm sorry about how things worked out for your people," I said. "But I'm an American. I bled for this country."

"You sound like the German Jews who fought for the Fatherland in the Great War. They marched, in proud military lockstep, into the ovens." He spit on the floor.

"My answer is no."

Elijah's dark eyes narrowed, and the corners of his thin mouth turned downward. "When I look at you, I think we are kindred souls. It pains me that we will not stand side by side."

"Well, that's the way it is. And here's a fair warning, since I reckon you've seen your share of suffering. Don't pull any jobs in my town. Because, if you test me, I'll kill you, kindred soul or not."

"Then we shall be enemies." He gave a nonchalant shrug as he pulled his jacket over his shoulders. "I shall be hunted by the feral dog. This outcome disappoints me, but I find it acceptable. Your pursuit will make my work here more interesting, and when I humiliate you, Baruch Schatz, it will burnish my legend."

Something about the way he said that made the hairs on the backs of my hands stand on end. I wondered what sort of monster he kept hidden behind his own fragile veneer of civility. But the circumstances weren't right for finding out; I was outnumbered and outgunned. So I turned my back on Elijah, to face the slab of muscle still blocking the exit.

"Get the fuck out of my way," I said.

The big man looked over my shoulder at his boss, who must have gestured approval. He moved aside, and I pushed past him, out into the cold and the dark. The door slammed behind me. Startled by a shadow in my peripheral vision, I spun on my heel, drew my gun, and pointed it back toward the narrow entryway, in case somebody was coming out after me.

Nobody was.

3
2009

Morning wasn't such a bad time at Valhalla Estates. The dining room had big plate glass picture windows overlooking the facility's rear lawn, which was lush and sunny and big enough to play a game of touch football on, if anybody had the desire or capacity to do so.

I was not pleased that this specter from my past had arrived to spoil my breakfast. Breakfast was one of the better parts of my day. I wanted to enjoy it, because later, I'd have to do physical therapy. That was always unpleasant.

"You didn't need to make a special trip out here to tell me you're going to die," I said. "You could have just sent a save-the-date for the funeral, or something."

He cringed a little. There was a sagginess, a pouchiness to the various bulges of his face. Elijah might have been a legend, but he was made of flesh, and he was decaying

31

like everything else.

"I thought you might want to do something about it," he said.

"I don't want to kill you anymore," I said to Elijah. "I don't care a whole lot what happens to you, one way or the other."

"There are many words I'd use to describe Buck Schatz, but 'indifferent' would not be one of them."

I stuck my fork into the eggs and stirred them around on the plate. I was hungry, and I was used to eating around this time, but I didn't think I could choke down this slop with him watching me.

"I was a cop. Now I'm not anymore. I haven't been a cop for a long time. I've been retired for more years than I spent working. I used to get paid to care about what people like you did, and what happened to you. Now somebody else has that job. If you need to talk to the police, I don't suppose it's too hard to find their number."

"So, if you are no longer the police, what are you now?"

"The way I get through most days is by not asking myself that question," I said.

He bared his teeth, and I saw they were straight and white like fresh-scrubbed kitchen tile. There was no natural way to make that out of what he'd had in his mouth the last time I saw him. The legendary thief was wearing a full set of dentures.

When he didn't say anything for a minute, I asked him: "What is it you really want?"

"Help." He clenched and unclenched those long pianist's fingers. They were knottier than they'd once been, but the motion of them was still smooth and assured. "I need help."

I shoveled some eggs into my mouth. I chewed for longer than eggs ought to require chewing — out of necessity, not for effect — and then I reached across the table to grab the plastic saltshaker. I shook it vigorously over my plate until the gelatinous yellow-white scrambled mass was coated with crystalline flakes. I took another bite, and this time, it was kind of crunchy. My doctor had warned me about my sodium intake, but salt was one of the only things I could still taste.

"And you came looking for me? To help you?" I asked.

He nodded a curt, European nod. "I asked for your help once before, and you refused. I thought, perhaps, this time might be different."

"That line of reasoning runs into three problems that I can see. First, I'm eighty-eight years old. Second, I'm damn near crippled. And third, I don't like you."

"Baruch," he said, lowering his voice to a near whisper. "Look at this place you've come to live in. Is this where you thought you'd end up? Is this what you wanted for Rose, your wife? The last time I saw you, you were violent and irrational and deeply misguided, but you were fierce and proud and full of dignity. There is no dignity in this place."

I set the fork down. "What's that got to do with anything?"

"I know you're here because you need access to nursing care, due to your failing health. If you help me, I'll pay you enough that you can hire a full-time nurse and buy a fine house outfitted with all the fixtures you need to ease your slide into decrepitude. I know about the fortune you lost, Baruch. If you make a friend of me, I can replace all of it."

"Maybe I don't want to be your friend. Why do people have such a hard time understanding that I ain't friendly?"

"If you won't help me, then kill me, damn you," said Elijah. "At least deprive my pursuers that satisfaction."

I hesitated, long enough to think about the kind of damage I could do with my fork. I considered the pale blue bulge of his

34

jugular vein, throbbing beneath the loose flesh of his jaw. I wasn't sure, though, whether I was fit enough to lunge across the table, and I didn't want him bleeding all over my eggs. "What kind of help do you want from me?" I asked.

He stared straight into my eyes, without a trace of a smile, or I'd have thought he was putting me on. "I need you to keep me safe for as long as you're able, and if I am killed, I want you to rain vengeance upon my enemies."

"I don't rain a lot of vengeance on people these days. Sometimes I dribble urine down the front of my pants, but that's as close as I get."

"I saw you on the news a few months ago. You blew a man's head apart at close range with a pistol. You're the meanest son of a bitch I ever met, Baruch. You're mean in a way I never learned to be, no matter how bitter I became. You're meaner than the soldier who shot my mother in the head. He looked pale and scared. You never looked scared. You never looked uncertain. Mean doesn't weaken with age; it just curdles and gets more pungent. And, today, I need mean on my side."

I always enjoyed hearing about my more attractive traits, but: "If you're in danger, call the police."

"I do not lightly subject myself to the coercive power of the State. I don't know those people. They aren't Jews."

"Bullshit," I said. "You don't want to call the police, because you are a criminal, and you need help with some kind of a crime."

He leaned forward and bared his teeth again, as if he were shocked by the very suggestion. "I am reformed," he told me. "I've become a philanthropist. I administer a charity that has helped hundreds of Jewish refugees immigrate to Israel."

I would have thought he was lying, except that a charitable foundation was probably a great way to launder stolen money.

"Why don't you ask Israel for help?" I said, liking the idea of Elijah going halfway around the world to a place where I wouldn't have to deal with this.

"I'm not going to run, this time. I'm too old to run."

"Philanthropists don't usually get into the kind of trouble you say you're in."

"Not everyone wants Jews to get rescued."

That sounded like a load. I ate some more of my salty eggs. They tasted like the sea, if the sea came from inside of a chicken. "And I'm too old to help you. I got nowhere to hide you, and no means to protect you. If you want to be safe, you have to go to the police."

He sank into stylish, European reverie as he considered his options. I ignored him and focused on the eggs. I was thinking about going back through the chow line to get a bagel. The staff at Valhalla had an amazing way of cooking them, so they came out burned on the bottom but still frozen in the middle.

"If I go to the police, will you wield your influence to assure that I am protected? Will you make my safety your personal responsibility? Will you see to it that the danger I am facing is taken seriously, and that I am not subject to persecution?"

"You'll have to admit to whatever you're involved in. You'll have to confess to everything you have ever done, and you'll have to tell the officers about these people who are after you."

He sat, contemplating his options, while I chewed. "That's acceptable," he said at last. "But I am not depending on the police. I am depending on you. I want you to assure my safety, and if I am killed, I want my vengeance to be a matter of honor for you."

"Whatever you say," I told him. "If you're going to turn yourself in, I'll broker your surrender. You ought to get a lawyer first."

"I'll look into that."

"Well, you might want to hurry, since you're going to be dead soon," I said. "Or, don't. If you wait long enough, the problem will most likely solve itself."

Something I Don't Want to Forget:

Early in my career, I responded to a domestic disturbance call, involving a man in a leather coat who called himself Liminal Doug. He stood in the doorway of his shitty duplex and explained to me that, when a pimp truly loves a bitch, he sometimes needs to go upside her head.

I leaned sideways a little, so I could look over his shoulder and into the residence. I saw a woman lying on the floor, weeping and clutching at her face.

"So, I guess I must love you a whole bunch," I said to Liminal Doug. Then I caved his goddamn skull in with my police baton.

The stick I carried around in those days was a blackjack truncheon; a ball of lead the size of a child's fist wrapped in leather and mounted on a coil of stiff spring. A lot of officers were switching over to the side-handled nightsticks, persuaded by arguments that the new design was superior for defensive purposes. Since you had to swing the thing sideways, it kept your arm raised in a blocking position, and since the stick extended along the forearm past the grip, it provided some protection against a knife-wielding attacker. The nightstick was also supposed to be more difficult for an assailant to strip away during a struggle.

I wasn't impressed by such practicalities, however, because I did not generally make a habit of trying to block knives with my arms. If somebody came at me with a knife, I did the sensible thing and shot him. And the sideways swing of a nightstick just felt counterintuitive to me. The blackjack felt like an extension of my fist, and I had a deep affection for the softness of the leather around the lead weight and the give in the spring. I liked the way the bludgeon would bounce off an offender's head. I liked the sound it made.

I called the blackjack "Discretion," and I exercised my Discretion liberally.

The district attorney refused to pursue assault charges against Liminal Doug, on account of what he deemed an excessive use of force on my part, but then somebody from the federal prosecutor's office interviewed the girl at the hospital, and then charged Doug with a Mann Act violation: transporting a minor across state lines for immoral purposes. That got him three years up at the federal farm.

And nobody ever called him Liminal Doug again after I busted his head open. People called him Doug Drool, on account of one of the more embarrassing side effects of his brain injury.

He also suffered from eye twitches and occasional seizures.

4
1965

People who learn most of what they know about police work from television programs and detective novels are always surprised by how much cops rely on dumb luck. We don't solve crimes with brilliant deductions and minute observations. We don't outsmart the bad guys most of the time. If we were smart, we wouldn't be working jobs that involve getting shot at on a regular basis.

Actually, it's hard to get away with crime. There are always witnesses. I saw a TV show where the cops found a body in the street, so they called in some white-coat scientist guys from the crime lab. The techs found some synthetic fibers near the corpse. Then they identified the killer by comparing the fibers to some kind of database that knew what kind of carpet everybody had.

That seemed fake to me. As far as I know, most carpeting is pretty much the same, and most people don't have bits of their rugs sticking to them when they leave the house to go kill somebody. But if there's a body in the street, and you send guys out to knock on every door in the neighborhood, a good percentage of the time, somebody will just tell you who the killer is.

The reason cops cruise around neighborhoods or walk the beat is that, more often than most people realize, you catch the bad guys by just being in the right place at the right time to observe suspicious activity.

I wasn't looking, specifically, for Paul Schulman when I went to the synagogue. I wasn't even at the synagogue on police business. My son had been going two afternoons a week for bar mitzvah lessons with Abramsky, the new assistant rabbi, and I was just there to pick him up. Brian and Schulman and the rabbi were coming out the front door when I turned onto the street.

Abramsky was supposed to be a "Modern Orthodox" rabbi, which, as I understood it, meant he shaved his beard but still kept his sidelocks. With his ridiculous haircut and his pudgy round face, he looked a lot like a giant toddler, and I disagreed with most of his ideas. Still, I liked him a little better than the senior rabbi, who believed cotton clothing was unkosher and wore black wool suits year-round. Even before there was allegedly global warming, Memphis, Tennessee, was not a good place to wear wool in the summertime, and between late April and mid-November, the old rabbi smelled like a pile of dirty gym socks.

Paul Schulman was the right age to have served in Korea, but he'd never joined up. You could get designated 4-F if you were deemed unacceptable for military duty on physical, mental, or moral grounds, and Schulman was disqualified all three ways.

He stood five feet and eleven inches and weighed 210 pounds, but with all that size, he still managed to seem like a small man. Part of that was because of his face; he was bucktoothed and jug-eared, and his jaw receded timidly into his neck. He also had a habit of tucking his elbows against his torso and folding his limp hands in front of his chest, which made him seem submissive and weak. And he had an ungainly, flat-footed way of walking.

Even a peaceable man would have had a hard time not punching Paul Schulman, and I'd never been a peaceable man. So it was a good thing that he was a scumbag and I was allowed to beat the shit out of him whenever I felt like it.

He was small-time, mostly: he ran little scams, bilking widows out of pension checks and selling bogus investments to credulous Negroes. But occasionally he overcame his numerous defects and managed to worm his way into a crew working on an elaborate con, or planning some kind of heist.

He wasn't a thinker, and he wasn't much good as muscle, but he had nimble fingers and a certain degree of facility when it came to opening doors or cheap safes without using keys. If you were looking to break into something, Schulman was the sort of guy you went to if you couldn't get a first-rate safecracker. Fortunately for him, a lot of valuables were protected by third-rate locks.

Paradoxically, his capacity to involve himself in these larger crimes was what had kept him from serving any long stretches in prison for his petty offenses. Detective work was kind of like fishing: it was sometimes a good idea to throw the little ones back, so that you might reel in some big ones later on. And Schulman was a strong candidate for catch-and-release because he could be counted on to spill whatever he knew, anytime I roughed him up a little. There are few things more valuable to a detective than a reliable snitch.

But on that particular evening, at the synagogue, Schulman saw my car and he took off running.

Like I explained, there's a lot of luck involved with police work; and knowing how to capitalize on that luck solves more cases than a capacity to make obscure deductions or a good eye for tiny clues.

A crime novelist gave a speech a couple of years ago at the Jewish Community Center, and he said coincidence is anathema in a mystery. He said that all crime stories are about how the universe is fundamentally an orderly place, and how disorder, in the form of crime and corruption, is systematically expunged. Therefore, the story must also have order; everything must follow logically. Everything must fit together neatly.

I don't know much about narrative structure or overarching themes of order and disorder, but I know a bit about crime and how it gets punished. I worked plenty of cases that got messy, and I've seen more than a few that broke on account of coincidence.

If my son hadn't been studying at the synagogue with the rabbi, I wouldn't have been there to pick him up. If Schulman's father hadn't died that year, he wouldn't have come to the evening Maariv service to say Kaddish. If he'd kept his cool, I probably would have ignored him; I wasn't particularly interested in him that day. And if I hadn't chased him down, I might never have found any kind of lead on Elijah.

But I was there, and he was there, and he ran when he saw me. And if somebody thinks they have a reason to run away from me, I assume I must have a good reason to chase them. Thus, I pursued.

When Schulman bolted, I was halfway into a parallel space on the street, so I cut the wheel and worked the shifter, and the Dodge lurched back into the road. My son was shouting something at me, but I couldn't hear what it was over the sound of the engine. I popped the clutch and the car jumped forward. I caught Schulman at the end of the block and drove over the curb and onto the sidewalk to cut him off. He was running as fast as he could, leaning forward and off balance. I think he'd been planning to try to dash across the intersection through oncoming traffic and lose me that way, but he wasn't fast enough.

He put a hand on my car to steady himself and turned to try to run away in the other direction. But I had more experience catching bad guys than he did in fleeing from cops. Before he could pivot and dash off, I kicked my door open and caught him in the back of his legs with the corner of it. He pitched forward and staggered a couple of steps, which gave me enough time to jump out of the car and and smash him between the shoulder blades with my Discretion.

The flesh and bone rippled under the weight of the lead, and the spring flexed, so the club bounced off his back with a satisfying, hollow sound. Hitting somebody with the blackjack felt like banging a bongo drum with a hard rubber mallet. The impact of the blow spiked Schulman straight to the ground. He didn't even have a chance to get an arm underneath his face before it hit the pavement.

"Seems like you have something you want to tell me, Paul," I said.

He spit a big wad of wet stuff onto the sidewalk, and I saw there was some blood in it. "I don't. I swear."

"If you lie to me, I might get angry with you. And if I get angry, you'll get hurt."

"Oh, God. Please don't."

"If you have nothing to hide, why'd you run from me?"

He paused just long enough to anticipate the consequences, before he said: "My current circumstances entirely justify that decision." Then he braced a little, in case that caused me to hit him.

"You think you're real smart, don't you?" I said.

"I wouldn't mind being a little dumber, if I could also run a little faster," he said.

"It ain't the weight of your brains slowing you down, Paul." I pushed the toe of my boot into his soft belly, and he curled himself up into a fetal position.

"It feels like something is grinding inside of me."

"Those are your ribs. I've gone and broken your damn ribs. And if you don't start talking, I will break something else."

Schulman didn't respond, but his gaze fixed on a point behind me. I glanced back and saw that my son had caught up with us.

"What are you doing, Dad?"

"Get in the car and shut the door," I said.

"Why did you hit Mr. Schulman?"

"Get in the car and shut the door."

"It's okay. Your pop and I are just having a little chat," said Schulman.

"Don't talk to my kid," I told him.

Brian crossed his arms. "This is wrong."

"Give me something, Paul," I said. "I don't necessarily want to beat you in front of the boy, but I've got a real bad temper and I might just lose it." I raised the club and he winced. Usually, it took very little persuasion to get a low-rent scumbag of this caliber to squeal. The list of people who

49

could clam Paul Schulman up like this was short.

I knelt next to him; got my face close to his. I looked in his eyes, and I could tell if he was deciding whether his fear of me outweighed his fear of whoever he was protecting. I made a quick calculation. "Tell me what you know about Elijah. Are you in on this job he's lining up?"

I tightened my grip on the club. He looked at me for about ten seconds, while I loomed enormous and occupied his entire field of vision, and he realized that I was all-knowing and all-seeing and terrible in my wrath.

"I'm on the outside of this thing," he said. "I know a little, but not much. Please, Buck, don't hit me again."

"Give me what you have, and we'll see how much mercy it buys you."

He shuddered, and then he cringed, because shuddering shifted his cracked ribs. Then he screamed a little, because cringing just made it hurt worse. "Ari Plotkin has a piece of it, but he says Elijah don't trust me. I heard the job has got something to do with the colored boys striking down by the river. That's all I know."

I stood silently over him for long enough to see if he had anything else he wanted to

say. But it didn't look like there was anything else for me to get out of him, except
for tears and drool.

"I ought to arrest you, Paul. I know damn
well you've been up to something lately that
should earn you six months upstate. But
I'm off duty, and I'm feeling charitable," I
said. "When you think about what happened here tonight, think about how nice I
was to you. Next time you make me chase
you, I will be a lot less forgiving."

I rose to my feet, which brought me eye-
to-eye with Abramsky, who was standing
with one protective arm draped over Brian's
shoulder.

"This is a place of prayer, Detective," he
said.

I glanced down at Schulman, who was
quivering on the sidewalk. "I guess Mr.
Schulman should have prayed a little
harder."

The rabbi pinched his features so hard,
his lips turned white. "These are your own
people. How can you do this to your own
people?"

"Pretty easily, it turns out," I said. I
pointed at Brian with the club. "Get in the
car."

But my son just stood there and balled up
his fists. "I want to hear a real answer to

that question." In some ways, he was a lot like his mother.

I looked at the rabbi. "Isn't there a commandment about how he's got to do what I say?"

Abramsky crossed his arms. "He's almost a man, and a man can't just look the other way when he sees something like this. I think you had better try to justify yourself."

I was surprised by this show of backbone from such a soft, childlike man. I said to Brian: "Paul Schulman is a scumbag. He is not our people. We are nothing like this man. That isn't what we are."

"You may have a big stick, but you are still a Jew, and one day you will learn that," Abramsky said. "I hope, for the boy's sake, that lesson doesn't come at too great a price."

"If you feel like doing a mitzvah, call an ambulance for this schmuck," I said to the rabbi. Then I turned to Brian: "Get your ass in the car. We're done here."

5
2009

I was lying flat on my back on a soft mat in a windowless interior room, staring up into the fluorescent lights. Getting myself down to the floor had been accomplished with great difficulty, and not without assistance. Getting up would be painful.

"Let me see you do two more sets of leg lifts," said Claudia, who was a physical therapist or a rehab specialist or something like that.

"I think I've had enough for today," I said.

"If you can swing that axe, Buck, you can give me a couple more leg lifts." She pronounced her name "Cloudy-ah." Her people were from someplace in Central America, and if she ever went back there, she was well qualified to work as a torturer for an autocratic governing regime. I'd had hurt put on me by some of the best, and this girl could hang with any of them.

"I'm all worn out from the axe. The axe

was a hell of a workout. I think it earned me a day off."

"There are no days off. There are just days when you get better, and days when you get worse."

This was the ninety-second day I'd done rehab therapy. This was the ninety-second day I'd spent paying the price for going after an old enemy and tangling with bad guys.

I'd already done fifteen minutes of slow pedaling on the stationary exercise bicycle, and three sets of an exercise that involved pulling on a rope, which was supposed to help my core muscles. My core muscles were a mess. It turns out that getting shot in the back is real bad for the core muscles.

Rose arranged to move us to Valhalla Estates while I was still in the hospital. It was a decision I wouldn't have approved, but there was no choice, really. The house wasn't accessible to me anymore. We had no grab bars or seats in the bathtub. We didn't have a toilet I could slide onto from a wheelchair. The hallway leading back to the bedroom was now too narrow for the chair to maneuver, and even after all my therapy, I still needed somebody stronger than my wife to help me out of bed in the morning.

Rose picked this place over a couple of

less-expensive options, in part because it had an on-site rehab facility and a physical therapist on the staff. Using the same criteria, she could have just moved us to the prison at Guantánamo Bay; I hear they've got room there, since that Kenyan president turned all the terrorists loose.

"You know, I've studied the biomechanics of walking," Cloudy-ah said. "The human gait is a kind of negotiation with the gravitational pull of the Earth. The planet is always trying to pull you down toward its center, and your body has adapted itself to use that very force to propel you along the surface."

"Until one day, it doesn't, and then you get buried," I said.

"That's why we have to work to keep all those muscles in good condition. If just one of these complex systems goes out of whack, the whole machine breaks down."

My machine was a heap of junk; I was made of ground-down gears and worn-out belts, with load-bearing beams held together by spit and Spackle, and that was before I'd gone and got myself shot.

For the elderly, healing is complicated. The doctors' primary concern was something they called decompensation: essentially, I had become so fragile that the stress of a trauma could cause a cascade of organ failures that would most likely kill me.

The way my doctor had explained it: "With patients in advanced old age, an incidence of a fall or a trauma signals that a subsequent fall or trauma within the next six months is highly probable, even if the injury sustained in the first fall appears minor or superficial. Where we have two injuries within a six-month period, we see a dramatic increase in the probability of death within the subsequent twelve months, relatively speaking."

"Relative to what?" I'd asked him.

"Well, mortality rates are already quite high within your age cohort," he said.

He always knew just what to say to make me feel better.

After two weeks immobile in bed, the best someone my age could hope for was irreversible muscle deterioration, but more likely, my legs would just fill with blood clots, which would turn into embolisms and kill me. That particular serious mortal risk was compounded by the fact that my blood thinners had to be discontinued for a while to allow my wounds to start healing.

So, they'd sent somebody in to start the rehab while the gunshot wound in my side was still seeping; just days after they set my broken leg in a cast. They had me raising and lowering my arms, lifting and bending my good leg.

Several times a day, they hauled me out of bed just to make me sit in a chair, even though it hurt like hell to be upright. I was discharged from the hospital after two weeks, but I spent another month in a wheelchair while I waited for the bones to knit. The cast was too heavy to drag around, and crutches or a walker would pull open the stitches in my side.

Despite the effort, when the cast came off, the leg still wouldn't support my weight. I tried to use the walker, but Rose thought I was unsteady on it. So I went back into the wheelchair for another three weeks while Cloudy-ah made me do lifts and bends until I was stronger.

"I'm ready to stop now," I said.

"Just give me eight more."

I looked up at her. She was big without being fat; healthy-looking without being especially pretty. She had broad, flat features, and shoulders and limbs that seemed too big to fit on a woman's frame. Sometimes, when I stumbled, she caught me with one arm and propped me back up. If I had to describe her with one word, that word would be "sturdy." That was what she was: sturdy. Like a piece of furniture.

Thinking about furniture made me think about Connor's rocking chair again, so I laughed. Hacking that damn thing up had hurt like hell and worn me out, but it was worth it.

"What's so funny, Buck?"

"Nothing important."

"Is it really nothing important, or did you already forget what you were laughing at?"

Monitoring my mental state was part of my rehab regimen. I'd already exhibited several symptoms of mild cognitive impairment before I got hurt, and my mind was one of those systems that could potentially decompensate as a result of my injuries.

"I didn't forget anything. I just don't feel like talking."

I lifted the leg again. The leg hurt. My side hurt. My core muscles hurt.

Even after three months of work, I was still so tired some days that I went back into the wheelchair after my therapy sessions. The whole situation made me grumpy, even relative to my age cohort, among whom grumpiness rates were already quite high.

This was actually something of a problem. When I got angry, I got sullen, and when I got sullen, I got uncommunicative, and being uncommunicative was supposed to hasten the progress of my dementia.

My doctor gave me a lengthy lecture about this particular subject, and at the end of it, he wrote something on his pad for me. His handwriting looked indecipherable, so I took the paper to my pharmacist, who told me that my asshole doctor had prescribed a "positive outlook."

I cursed a few times about the waste of a trip to the Walgreens, but I bought two cartons of cigarettes while I was there, so it wasn't a total loss.

My previous doctor had been a little more helpful. After my son died, he'd sent me to a psychiatrist, who had written me a scrip for an antidepressant. I still had some of the pills in my cabinet, but I didn't like taking them. I wasn't myself when I was on anti-depressants.

"What are you thinking about, Buck?" Cloudy-ah asked.

"Doesn't matter."

"Does it not matter, or did you already forget what you were thinking about?"

"Have I ever told you that I don't like you?"

"Not since yesterday."

I remembered that. I did. Really.

"While you do your leg lifts, repeat this list to me," Cloudy-ah said. "Chair, bird, truck, bush, hat."

"That's not a list," I said. "It's just some things that have nothing to do with each other."

"That's the point. It's just a test of your short-term memory. We've done this before. Do you remember doing this before?"

"Of course I do."

"Then you know the drill. Repeat the list back to me."

"I don't want to. I've got other things on my mind." I was thinking about Elijah. Maybe I should have stopped him from leaving, although I didn't know how I could have accomplished that. It wasn't as if I was going to chase the man down on my walker.

Was he really out finding a lawyer? Did he really plan to turn himself over to the police? There was a good chance he'd come to Valhalla looking for a kind of help I hadn't been able to offer, and if that was the case, I'd never hear from him again. Maybe when he saw what I had become, he'd decided I wasn't in any shape to provide whatever it was he needed from me.

I was also aware of the possibility that the whole scenario might be a trap. Elijah and I had not parted on friendly terms. It's never a happy occasion when old nemeses show up after fifty years. Only a few months earlier, I'd walked into a place not unlike

60

Valhalla, looking for an enemy from my own distant past, and my intentions toward him had not been benevolent. It was not unthinkable that Elijah was on a similar trip.

Except I had a lot more reason to hate him than he had to hate me; he'd got away from Memphis mostly intact and left a hell of a mess in his wake for me to clean up. You don't come looking to settle up when you're already in the black.

In any case, he'd probably never call. And if he never called, I knew I'd be better off. I didn't need trouble. But I liked trouble, and I wasn't sure how many more opportunities I'd have to get into trouble.

"The list, Buck."

"Chair, bird, truck, mat . . . goddamnit."

"Come on. I know you can do this."

"Chair, bird, truck . . ."

Silence. Five things that had nothing to do with one another. Who could remember a list like that? Nobody. Rose came along sometimes to my sessions with Cloudy-ah, and she said she couldn't remember the lists, either.

"Okay, time for a smoke break," Cloudy-ah said, so I wouldn't have to humiliate myself by admitting what was obvious to both of us. "I forgot mine. Can I borrow one of yours?"

I had never seen Cloudy-ah smoking with any of her other patients, but I liked that she knew not to bother me about my bad habits. My bad habits were just about all I had left.

"I smoke the unfiltered kind," I said.

She laughed. It was not a girlish laugh. "I think I can handle it," she said, as she cradled a thick arm beneath my back and lifted me to my feet.

"I suppose you can."

I gripped the rubber handholds on the top of my walker, and Cloudy-ah slowed down to keep pace with me as we left the physical therapy room and walked down the fluorescent-lit, medical-smelling hallway where the nurses had their offices. She held open the side door while I made my way through it, and she held on to my arm as I navigated the two low concrete steps on the other side of it.

I fished the pack of Lucky Strikes out of the pocket of the hooded sweatshirt my grandson had sent me from NYU, and she flicked the lighter for me. I inhaled, and held on to the smoke for as long as I could. I leaned on the walker and tried to enjoy the view of the employee parking lot. When this was done, I'd go back to my room and sit in front of Fox News until I fell asleep, and she'd go back to her office and fill out a form. And in three or four weeks, I'd have an appointment with a neurologist.

Unless Elijah called, and then maybe something unpredictable would happen. I hoped to God Elijah would call.

Something I Don't Want to Forget:

"Take a look at this graph," said the man in the suit, on my television screen. "This is a chart of the performance of the S&P 500 over the course of the last fifteen years."

"Right," said the host, jabbing his finger at the chart. He was wearing shirtsleeves and a tie, but he looked kind of rumpled. Ever since I'd gotten one of those new flat televisions, all the people on cable news looked worse. All pores and sweat and Pan-Cake makeup.

I didn't have much room to criticize him, though; the last few years had not been kind to my looks. George Orwell said that, by the age of fifty, every man has the face he deserves. What he failed to mention is that, by the age of eighty, every man has a face that nobody deserves. I looked like a wax dummy of myself that somebody had melted partway with a blowtorch.

"You can see the tech bust, right here," said the man on the television. "You can see the 2001 recession."

I could see acne scars. I could see a patch of stubble along his jawline that he'd missed with his razor. I rubbed at my face and felt a couple of similar spots on my own cheeks. I'd been having trouble shaving lately. It was hard to see what I was doing, even with a magnified shaving mirror.

As recently as a few years ago, I shaved every morning with a straight razor, which is the only way a man should shave. Clean and close, every time. But my hands had gotten a lot less steady. I hadn't cut my face with it, but I had sliced the hell out of a couple of my fingers trying to change out a blade, which caused a real mess because of my blood thinners, and we wound up visiting the emergency room. That was enough for Rose to insist on me switching to an electric shaver.

"And here at the end is this mess we're in now," said the guest.

"Why are we looking at this?"

"You see how this line looks jagged. Lots of ups and downs. Unpredictable, right?"

"Right."

"Wrong! That's how a sucker sees the stock market." He took a fat blue marker and drew a diagonal line through the middle of the chart. "In a college math class, we'd call this line a regression to the mean. That means the extreme nature of all these up-and-down data points is really just noise. And that noise obscures the essential story of this data, which is that America's fundamentals are strong, and while things can be volatile in the very short term, a diverse portfolio of American stocks is always going to go up, over the medium and the long term."

"Okay, but here at the end, beginning in 2008, your regression line keeps going up, but the line showing market performance drops way down."

"That's still noise. The effects of a market correction are always exaggerated by the panic selling of unsophisticated investors. In the long term, the market is going to move back to the regression line, and the regression line is going up! I don't want to start talking about technical stuff like price-to-earnings ratios, but fundamentals are rock solid, and there are a lot of great buys out there right now. Don't fall victim to panic! Don't be a chump! Day-to-day, you can't time the market and play all these ups and downs unless you're an expert in the industries and the companies you're investing in. Leave that stuff for the professionals. Just buy blue-chip companies for the long term, and hang in there."

"And of course, it's always smart to diversify your portfolio by investing in precious metals."

"Well, that goes without saying."

I hit the clicker. I was, I realized, like the stock market. My day-to-day progress in rehab, and any healing I'd done since my injury; all of that was just noise. Nothing but temporary victories obscuring my regression line: a steady downward slope of permanent compromises. I'd given up driving at night, and then given up driving almost entirely. No more smoking in front of the television; no more smoking indoors at all. No more eating the foods I liked. No more walking up staircases.

Everything I had was just something I could lose. My son. My house. My mobility. My mind.

The door of the unit opened, and Rose came in. She'd joined a mah-jongg club that met in the main sitting area every afternoon, during the time I usually went to sleep for a while, after rehab. As far as I knew, she had never played mah-jongg before we moved to Valhalla, and she'd never shown any interest in games of that sort, so I suspected she was just using it as an excuse to get away from me for a while.

She looked at the television: "Is there any good news?" she asked.

"Is there ever?"

6
2009

At two in the afternoon, the phone rang and woke me up. Nobody calls me at two in the afternoon. Courteous people show some goddamn respect for naptime, and anyway, not that many people call me to begin with. Mostly just my daughter-in-law, who calls once or twice during the week to check in, and my grandson, who calls every Sunday, just before dinner.

I yelled at Rose to pick it up, but she wasn't in the apartment, so I grabbed the cordless handset off the nightstand and pushed the talk button.

"What is it?"

Instead of a response, I heard a dial tone, and somewhere else in the room, a phone was still ringing. I was briefly confused, and then I realized that call was coming in on my cell.

I never got calls on the cell; that phone was just for emergencies. Except, I'd given that number to Elijah. I didn't want him to call on the regular phone, because Rose might pick that one up. I'd meant to put the cellular someplace I could get to it easily, but I was tired and angry after having such a poor session at rehab, and I forgot. I left the damn thing in the pocket of my pants, which were now draped over the recliner chair, all the way across the room.

I'd never be able to pick it up in time, and I didn't know how to call him back. The cell held on to the numbers of recent missed calls, but Elijah was likely to be calling from a pay phone or some other untraceable location. I didn't have much of an understanding of how these machines worked, but I knew that he wasn't the sort of man who could be reached by hitting the redial button.

Ninety-two days, I'd been doing my rehab. Hurting myself and pushing my body to the point of total exhaustion. If I couldn't get out of bed to pick up the phone, what was the point of any of it?

It was only a few weeks previous that I'd managed, for the first time since my injury, to get out of bed without any help, and it seemed like a huge triumph after three months of having to call building staff into the unit every day to lift me upright. But the process still took me several minutes, including a couple of brief rests to catch my breath. The phone would ring for maybe twenty seconds.

Rushing this was not a great idea. If I put too much weight on my legs all at once, they might give out, and then I'd fall and hit my head on the floor and die like an asshole. A needless risk to get a phone call that I shouldn't even be taking.

But sooner or later, I was probably going to die like an asshole anyway.

I slid my left leg onto the floor and reached for the stability rail on the wall. With my other hand, I grabbed on to the walker, which I'd parked next to the bed.

Thus secured, I slid my right leg to the floor, clenched my teeth, and attempted to sit up. The motion strained my weak core muscles and yanked at the tight scar on my lower back where I'd been sewn up. This simple task was the thing I'd been working so hard to be able to do, and I could still barely achieve it without help.

My vision went white, and my side was all fire. I yelped in pain and let go of the wall. Now my weight was on my legs, which was exactly where my weight was never supposed to be. My thighs shook, and I felt my knees begin to give out, and my body started to pitch forward, but I managed to splay my arms across the top of the walker and regain my balance. Before I pulled myself fully upright, I took a couple of deep, ragged breaths.

And then the phone stopped ringing.

"Aw, shit," I said to the empty room, because I was feeble and senile and miserable and broken.

And then it rang again. He must have hung up and called back. I pushed the walker across the room and fumbled the device out of my pants in time to answer.

"Hello, Baruch."

"Elijah."

"I thought maybe you had decided not to help me."

"I ain't helping you. You said you'd turn yourself in, and I said I'd be there."

"Very well. I have obtained the services of a criminal defense attorney, and I am prepared to surrender, if the authorities can protect me."

"Go to the Criminal Justice Center at 201 Poplar, and I'll meet you there."

He laughed. It was still a chirpy sound, but now it had some gravel in it. "Didn't I tell you that I am in danger? I did not come looking for Baruch Schatz so that I could walk through the front door of a building full of police and criminals. You know as well as I do that men who carry badges may serve many interests other than that of justice."

I hated a lot of things about Elijah, but I hated the way he talked most of all. "So what do you want me to do?"

"Well, since you are famously incorruptible, I would like you to make arrangements with a police contact you trust. I will surrender to that officer at a place of my choosing, and you and he will arrange for me to be taken to a secure location."

"You want some kind of witness protection program?"

"I would like to not be murdered today."

"You have to tell me what you've got yourself into."

"I will tell the police. You are not the police. Not anymore. Your task is a simple one: You are to put me into contact with men to whom I can entrust my safety. Are you capable of this?"

"I know a guy," I said.

"Very well. Get in touch with this man. I will assume you can reach him in the next hour. At that time, I will call again and tell you where we will meet."

"I don't like this," I said. But the line had already gone dead.

7
2009

I retired from police work in 1976, so all my friends on the force were retired, and very few of them were even alive anymore. I had only one real police contact left, a twenty-six-year-old colored kid named Andre Price. He and I were not friends, on account of I shot his mentor, homicide detective Randall Jennings, in the face with a .357 Magnum revolver.

Jennings had it coming; he was a scumbag who killed four people and shot me in the back with a deer rifle. But killing him was still a sore point with Price, who had been the only policeman in attendance at Jennings's funeral. He gave the eulogy.

There's nothing to be gained by showing up to bury a disgraced man. There was nobody there for him to ingratiate himself with; no angle to play. Attending that funeral invited scrutiny from Internal Affairs and made any mark on his record look like something to dig into. If he couldn't stand some heat, he wouldn't have gone, and even if he was squeaky clean, he was still making trouble for himself that most cops could happily live without.

I respected Price for eulogizing his scumbag friend. It showed real integrity. Real backbone.

When I called him on the phone, he hung up on me, which was also an honest thing to do.

I called him back.

"Old man, I know you ain't got nothing to do all day, but I am busy," he said. "I've got no time for you."

"Have you got time to be the guy who finally closes a string of bank robberies that have been unsolved for fifty years?"

"Dude, if you were going to catalog all the things that exist in the world and choose the single Platonic ideal of shit I don't give a fuck about, a bank robbery from fifty years ago just might be it."

"Watch your language."

"I'm busy dealing with crimes that happened yesterday. We had half a dozen drug-related killings in the last two weeks, and no arrests yet in any of them. Some robbery from fifty years ago ain't my problem."

This was, of course, an eminently sensible

response from him. But he didn't hang up, so I told him about Elijah, and about my strange breakfast meeting at Valhalla, and the thief's plea for help.

"He's playing you," Andre said. "Setting something up."

"Could be he's backed into a corner, and this is his only way out."

"That's greedy thinking. You want this, so you're ignoring all the facts you don't like. It's a near certainty that he's planning some sort of trap or double cross."

Greedy thinking. A good way to put it. The entire situation stank. Elijah's caginess and his secrecy were reasons to distrust him, and if he really wanted to turn himself in, he didn't need me as an intermediary.

If he was afraid to walk into a police station, he could have had the police come get him at his lawyer's office. And if he was worried about his enemies having corrupted members of the police force, the lawyer could probably have steered him toward an honest cop as easily as I could have. More easily. Criminal defense lawyers dealt with cops every day. I was a crippled retiree living in a rest home.

Elijah was messing with me, and I knew it. Andre knew it. And I was dragging him into a mess anyway, for one reason:

"When a legendary thief offers to turn himself in, you don't tell him to take a hike. This is like catching the Zodiac Killer or the Unabomber. This is the kind of thing people write books about."

I'd never thought of myself as the kind of man who'd spend a lot of time thinking about his legacy, but I'd become pre-occupied with the idea of losing my mind, losing myself. For a couple of days while I hunted for the Nazi fugitive Heinrich Ziegler and his cache of stolen gold, I'd felt like the man I remembered being, back when I packed heat and chased bad guys every day. And then I'd gotten hurt and ended up more decrepit than ever. I wanted to be myself again, even if it meant rushing into a trap. Even if it meant dragging Andre Price into it with me. How bad could things turn out, really?

"I don't need any books written about me," Andre said. "I don't need to be getting myself backed up into any corners, either."

"Some things are worth a little risk," I said.

"I know all about you, Buck. I know you've walked into a lot of situations you had to shoot your way out of. You and I are very different. I don't like shooting people, and I really don't like getting shot at."

"This guy is worth taking a look at. Whatever Elijah is after, I don't think it is a gunfight. If the situation looks bad, we can just leave, but it's at least worth taking an hour to maybe solve a famous crime."

"I can't believe I am actually considering this," Andre said.

"Come pick me up at Valhalla, and I'll set up the meeting."

"You expect me to give you a ride? Do I look like Morgan Freeman to you, Jessica Tandy?"

"Do you want me to try to drive myself?"

"Fuck." He paused. "Be waiting for me, because I don't plan to wait for you."

Almost as soon as I hung the phone up, it rang again.

"There is a Jewish cemetery off of South Parkway," Elijah said. "I will meet you and your police contact there. Do you know this place?"

"I know it. Why do you want to meet there?"

"It is close to my lawyer's office. He recommended the location, when I told him I did not want to be cornered indoors when you came for me. There is little traffic, and no surveillance. It is adjacent to a railyard, so there are no tall buildings nearby. There is good visibility in every direction. If you are followed, I will see the tail. If there is an ambush, I will see it coming. If I don't like the look of the men who accompany you, I will have routes of escape."

"I guess that makes sense," I said.

"Do you have a problem with this place?"

"No." I saw no need to tell him my son was buried there; he almost certainly knew it already.

8
2009

Valhalla was built in 2003, but the front entrance had an old-fashioned wraparound porch built onto it, with rocking chairs where residents could sit on warm days and enjoy a nice view of the cars in the lot and, beyond that, six scenic lanes of Kirby Parkway.

When Andre arrived, I was sitting in one of the rockers and smoking a cigarette. He parked in the fire lane and flicked on his hazard lights, and then he climbed out of the car.

"Is that your walker?" he asked.

"You see anyone else out here?"

He laughed. "It suits you. I like the chrome finish."

I lifted myself painfully out of the chair. There were three steep steps to the sidewalk from the porch, and Andre didn't disguise his amusement as he watched me navigate them. There was a ramp around the side of the building that I could have used, but I felt like avoiding the steps would have made me look weak.

I opened the passenger's-side door and started folding up the walker.

Andre was driving an unmarked police car. An unmarked car is exactly what the name suggests; a patrol cruiser, but without the markings. It doesn't have a black-and-white paint job, and it doesn't have an array of flashing lightbars mounted on the roof, but it's still a cop car; a four-door American sedan like a Caprice or a Crown Victoria. Often, as was the case with Andre's ride, an unmarked car will come complete with a perp cage in the backseat and a radio antenna.

"What is that you're wearing?" Andre asked.

"I don't know," I said. "Clothes."

"That's some vintage shit." He walked around the car to get a better look at me. I was still wrestling with the walker. He didn't seem inclined to help. "Is that a Members Only jacket?"

I didn't say anything.

"That is totally a Members Only jacket. It's got the epaulets and everything."

"It was a gift from my son."

"When? In 1985?"

I stopped what I was doing with the walker. "1986," I said. "It was for my sixty-fifth birthday. My son and his wife took Rose and me to the Folk's Folly steakhouse. I got the rib eye. Ordered it medium-rare, but they cooked it to medium-well, and I ate it anyway."

I could remember that, but I couldn't remember Cloudy-ah's list. Funny thing, memory.

"It's almost July, Buck. Isn't it a little warm for a jacket?"

"I got bad circulation."

"Why don't you let me hold that coat for you?"

"Why?"

He wasn't smiling now. "Because I want you to take it off."

"Leave it alone," I said.

"We ain't going anywhere until you take off that jacket."

I stared at him and considered my options for a minute. Then I flicked my cigarette onto the asphalt and unzipped the jacket. Underneath it, I was wearing my .357, tucked under my arm in a shoulder holster.

"That's what I thought," Andre said. "You are not bringing that weapon in my vehicle."

"I might need it, if things get sticky."

"We're going to get a guy who robbed a

bank fifty years ago. How old is he now? Seventy-five?"

I counted in my head. "He was thirteen in the camps, in 1944, so he's seventy-eight," I said.

"I can handle a seventy-eight-year-old man. I don't need you backing me up," Andre said.

"Anybody who can hold a gun is capable of being dangerous," I told him.

"I know. That's why I don't want you standing behind me with a firearm," he said. "Go back inside and put that up."

I didn't move.

"I'm not taking you anywhere as long as you have that," Andre said.

"I don't like you," I said.

"Then why did you call me?"

I unfolded the walker and wrestled it back up the three stairs. When I got up to our unit, I found Rose inside, watching television.

"Why are you wearing your coat?" she asked. "It's a hundred degrees out."

I balled up the jacket and threw it on the floor.

"Is that your gun you've got?" She looked worried now.

"I'm just putting it away." I fumbled my old shoe box down off the shelf in the closet and wrapped the gun back in its cheese-cloth.

"Why did you have it out in the first place?"

"It doesn't matter."

"It matters that you're walking around with your gun strapped on. I don't want you to get hurt again."

"I've got this under control."

"What is it you've got under control? Is this about Mr. Connor? Vivienne Wyatt found me during mah-jongg and gave me quite an earful."

"I've settled up with Connor. Everything is fine." I put the box back on the shelf and threw the holster in the back of the closet. I started to pick up the jacket, but I didn't really need it, so I left it for Rose to deal with. Bending over was pretty difficult; that was why I'd quit wearing shoes with laces.

"She made me promise to get rid of your hatchet. I think she'd just about lose her mind if she knew you had a gun in here. You shouldn't be wearing that around."

"I know. That's why I am putting it away."

"June twenty-first was last week," Rose said. "It's been seven years. I thought it was better if I didn't mention it, since you've been so preoccupied with your rehab. But maybe we should have done something.

Maybe we should have talked about it. Maybe we should have gone to the cemetery."

"Funny you should mention that," I said.

"Why is that funny?"

"It isn't. Never mind."

"It's not weak to mourn, Buck. I know you have feelings."

"I never said I didn't. But I don't see any point in talking about them."

"I've been married to you sixty-four years, and he was our son. It's been hard for me as well to leave the house behind. I shouldn't have to feel like I am alone with this."

"You're not alone," I said. "I will be back by dinnertime. Everything is fine."

And then I grabbed the walker and pushed it out the door.

9
2009

"You got to understand, I ain't upset with you over Jennings," Andre said. "He was always good to me, but when it came down to a situation where it was you or him, I appreciate that survival has got to trump other concerns in that kind of scenario. I take issue, though, with your underlying philosophy of police work."

I squirmed in my seat and fiddled with the belt. I didn't like being a passenger in somebody else's car. "How do you mean?" I said.

"You got this kind of moralistic Old Testament view of justice; smiting down the evildoers and shit. You can't look at crime that way. Crime is, like, a social phenomenon. You have to get past this idea of punishment and look at how to remedy the root causes. Otherwise, you're just blaming the desperate for being born into adverse circumstances."

"I've met plenty of thieves, but I ain't never met a man who stole because he was hungry," I said. "People steal because they want drugs, or because it's easier than work, or because they lack the moral and intellectual capacity to understand that it's wrong to hold people up at gunpoint."

"Even so, we're still talking about a social problem. I read about this study that finds a very strong correlation between toxic lead exposure and crime. When little kids are exposed to lead, it disrupts their brain development. Lead causes lower IQs and it damages the capacity for empathy and self-discipline."

"Sounds like a bunch of hogwash to me."

"You can look at the statistics. The proliferation of lead-burning automobiles predicts the urban crime wave of 1970s, and the widespread adoption of unleaded gasoline predicts the decline of crime through the 1990s."

I let out a contemptuous belch, and Andre turned up the air conditioner to blow it into the backseat.

"That's how you and I are different," I said. "You look at crime as a computer program. As a collection of statistics. It's easy to take a compassionate view of criminals when you treat them as a group of the disenfranchised and the downtrodden. You have to sympathize with them in the aggregate, because on an individual basis, these motherfuckers are goddamn intolerable. And statistics turn the suffering of the victims into an abstraction. Crime, to me, was always personal; a thing people do to each other."

He turned his head away from the road and looked at me, like he was appraising a side of beef. "How did your son die, anyway?" he asked.

The stretch of I-240 we were cruising down was called the Avron B. Fogelman Expressway. They had Jewish highways now.

"What kind of question is that?" I said.

"I don't know. Just curious, I guess. Is it some kind of a secret?"

"No. I just don't like talking about it."

"I mean, why not? Was it, like, cancer? Was it a car accident? Was it — something else?"

"There was a thing about it in the *Commercial Appeal.* Go be a policeman and pull it up on the microfiche if you want to know what happened. Just don't bother me with it."

"Okay, first of all, don't get all snippy with me, old man. And second, I don't think a microfiche is a thing that exists anymore."

"What does it matter to you, how he

87

died?" I asked. "Is there something you want to understand about me that you think will somehow be illuminated if you know that?"

"I mean, maybe. I don't know. I was just making conversation."

"He was my son, and he's dead, and I buried him. Talking about it just drags him back up, so I have to bury him again. What's the use?"

"I don't know. Maybe talking and dealing with it is how you get past it."

"There's no getting past it. Better to just leave it alone."

"Suit yourself, Buck. Ain't my problem."

"You're right. It isn't."

We rode in silence the rest of the way to the small Jewish cemetery, out on South Parkway in a blighted part of Midtown Memphis. A hundred and twenty years ago, all the Jews had lived in this area, but over time, the neighborhood turned black, and then most of the blacks moved away and the area turned industrial, and then the industry went away and it turned desolate. The cemetery's neighbor was now an abandoned factory. Across the street was a freight yard filled with shipping containers.

The railroad tracks were just fifty yards from my son's grave, and the rumble of trains frequently interrupted funeral services. To the east was some kind of weird quarry; a deep scar cut in the landscape with stagnant, standing water in the bottom of it. The cemetery was small; a couple of green acres amidst the dust and ruin, maintained by the membership fees of an aging and shrinking synagogue congregation.

The people who had lived here had gone. The shipping containers were on their way somewhere over the horizon, and so were the freight trains.

For me, though, this place that everything else passed through was a destination. An ending point. Everything around here was transient except me. I came here to get here; to this tiny patch of earth that held my dead. This place, to me, meant permanence. It wouldn't be so very long before I'd come here for the last time, and I wouldn't leave.

We parked in the lot and walked through a gap in the hedge around the cemetery grounds. There was an awning up over a fresh grave, which meant there'd been a funeral recently, but we found the place empty and silent, except for a stray dog chasing a squirrel among the headstones and Elijah, who was looking at graves with his lawyer in the oldest section.

I never really wanted to come here; I had avoided it the previous week on the anniversary of my son's death. I'd avoided even mentioning the anniversary to Rose, because I was afraid that conversation would end with a trip to this place.

And now I had come to the cemetery without hesitation to arrest a man I hadn't even thought about in decades, before that morning. I lit a cigarette and decided to take the opportunity to refuse to have a moment of self-realization.

"At least this doesn't seem to be an ambush," I said.

"Were you expecting an ambush?" Andre asked.

"I didn't really know what to expect."

"I'm glad you pulled me into this."

By the entrance to the graveyard, there was a plastic barrel full of gravel and a small water fountain. I picked up a couple of small stones. "So that is the legendary Elijah?" Andre asked, pointing at the trim, gray-haired figure at the other side of the cemetery.

"Yes," I said.

"He don't look much like a thief."

"Good thieves never do." I stopped on the path. "Hang on a second."

I took a left turn onto the grass, pushing

the walker in front of me. Andre followed. Brian's monument was big and new, made of black limestone. There were empty spaces next to it: for his wife on one side, and for Rose and me on the other. I knocked on the stone with my fist, and set a piece of gravel on top of it.

"What are the little rocks for?" Andre asked.

"It's what Jews leave when we visit cemeteries, because we're too cheap to pay for flowers," I said. I didn't know what significance the rocks had; somebody must have told me once, but I didn't remember anymore.

My mother was buried next to the plots where Rose and I were supposed to go. I left a rock on her gravestone as well.

"Esther 'Bird' Schatz," Andre said. "Your people do like their nicknames."

"I don't talk about the kinds of names your people like," I said.

"Not where we can hear you, anyway," Andre said. He squatted down, to read the inscription on the headstone. "She died in 1998? She must have been ancient."

"A hundred and four."

"I don't see your dad here. Is he still alive or something?"

"He's in one of the older sections. He died

in 1927. I was six."

"So, I guess not all the Schatzes live as long as you and your mom."

"My father was murdered," I said.

Andre waited for me to elaborate on that, and when I didn't, he said: "I'm sorry."

My dad's funeral was one of my earliest memories. Back then, the cemetery was mostly empty; only a couple of small sections filled with graves, and several more that were just empty, rolling lawns. Beyond that, the part of the property where my son would one day be buried hadn't yet been developed; it was just trees and undergrowth.

Not many people came to my father's funeral, and I didn't know most of them. I can't recall their faces, but I remember how stricken Grandmother Schatz looked.

"Your father believed in something that was inconvenient to some ruthless, powerful men," my mother told me. "One day, you might believe in something. I hope you'll remember that the things you believe in won't keep you safe."

People were trying to talk to her, but she ignored them and led me off, away from the fresh earth we'd piled onto my father and down a row of graves.

"You've learned something about the

world today, Baruch," she said.

"I did?"

"The world isn't a nice place. The world isn't a friendly place. The world isn't a fair place. Your father is dead because he believed in a world governed by fairness and justice. He believed in a world that doesn't exist." She led me down to a corner of the cemetery where graves were smaller, to where there was only a space of a couple of feet between the headstones and the footstones.

"Look at that," she said, pointing at a monument no more than eighteen inches high, made of poured concrete in the shape of a lamb. There were several more just like it, farther down the row.

"Do you understand what you are looking at?"

"These are graves for little children," I said.

My mother nodded. "Believing the world is nice doesn't make it true. Believing the world is nice doesn't make you safe. People will hurt you for any number of stupid reasons. People will hurt you for no reason at all."

"No, they won't," I said. "I'll hurt them first."

Eighty years later, in almost the same

place, what I said to Andre Price was: "There's nothing you can do about it." I stuck my hands in my pockets. Elijah and his lawyer were now examining those tiny monuments in the old section. The years and the weather had worn the little lambs into unidentifiable lumps.

"Let's go arrest a bank robber."

Something I Don't Want to Forget:

My mother was always a thin woman. Thin arms; slim waist; pale, pinched lips; narrow eyes, like a gunslinger's. She wore her hair in a bun so tight that it pulled the skin of her face, which exaggerated the natural severity of her features. She might have been a pretty woman, if she'd allowed herself to be a little softer. But she had no use for softness or prettiness, and after my father got himself killed, she didn't have much use for men, or the things men believed in.

When I was eight years old, somebody grabbed her from behind and dragged her into an alleyway. I was in second grade, and when class let out, she wasn't there to walk me home. I remember waiting almost two hours in the office of the Jewish day school before a police officer arrived to get me.

He told me something bad had happened, and I climbed into his squad car — an old tin lizzie with police markings — and took a ride to the precinct house. My father's death was still fresh in my mind; the funeral service in the hot, crowded little cemetery chapel and the smell of turned earth. I was terrified. The cop sat me on a hard wooden bench and told me not to move. I waited for a long time, watching as officers hauled in the bad guys for booking.

Most of the crooks seemed resigned and docile, and allowed themselves to be led to the holding cell. One man struggled, and multiple officers ran to subdue him with clubs and fists. When they were finished, there was blood on the man's head, and his body hung limp as two police dragged him away.

Eventually, the cop who had picked me up from school came back, and he told me I could see my mother, but that I mustn't be scared or cry.

Then he took me into a small office, and she was sitting there, waiting for me. Her face was swollen and purple-black around her left eye. Her clothes were covered in blood; thick red-brown stains.

I didn't say anything. I didn't know whether to run into her arms or run away.

She just smiled at me. A couple of her teeth were broken, and her mouth was all bloody.

"You should see the other guy," she said.

She took me home, and cleaned herself up, and fixed my supper and put me to bed. She never told me what happened, and I knew better than to ask. But I was curious, and I was always a bit of a snoop. So, when I joined the police force, eighteen years later, I went to the records morgue to find the report on my mother's attack.

Here is the earliest thing I can remember about Bird Schatz: I was maybe four or five years old. She took me to a big department store downtown to buy clothes for Rosh Hashanah. We rode a bus together, and she told me that I must hold her hand all the time, or somebody might steal me away and chop me up into little pieces. She bought me an oxford shirt and a pair of slacks in the boys' department, and then she sat me on a chair in the ladies' section, and had the salesgirl watch me while she tried on clothes. She chose a plain white cotton blouse and an ankle-length skirt made of stiff blue fabric.

Her new skirt fit fine off-the-rack, but as soon as she got home, she took out the sewing kit.

"What are you doing?" I asked her.

"I'm hiding razor blades in my clothes," she said. And then she showed me how she buried the sharp edge inside the reinforced fabric of the skirt's waistband, and how she secured it with enough threads to hold it in place, but not so many that she couldn't easily tear it loose if she needed it.

"Why are you doing that?"

"In case somebody tries to rape me," she said.

If you're wondering how my mother did her laundry, the answer is: by hand, and very carefully.

It turned out she was still sewing razor blades into her clothes a few years later, when she had an occasion to use them.

I've since seen lots of wounds inflicted by women on male assailants; usually scratches on forearms and bruises on faces from open-hand slaps. Since I was a homicide detective, the fact that I ever had a reason to pay attention to those wounds suggests things did not turn out well for these women. I also happen to know that in police-sponsored women's self-defense classes, we advise striking or kicking at an assailant's genitals. My mother didn't scratch at her attacker's face, and she didn't kick him in the balls. She went at the bastard like a wildcat; she lunged for his vitals, and she burrowed into him.

With her razor blades and her fingernails, she tore through an inch and a half of belly fat and a wall of abdominal muscle, and she unspooled his guts all over the pavement.

"You should see the other guy," is what she told me. She wasn't kidding. They had to clean the son of a bitch up with a mop.

After I read that file, I took a calculated risk to my personal safety and I asked her about it.

"I remember his breath against my neck when he grabbed me. He said, 'I've got something to show you.'" Even years later, she flinched a little at the memory. "In the end, it was me who found something to show him, just before he died. I showed him his pancreas."

My mother kept sewing razors into her clothes until her sixty-fourth birthday, in 1956, when Rose bought her an electric washing machine, and I bought her a handgun to keep in her pocketbook.

10
1965

People on television were talking about the strike downtown.

"Ungrateful, is what they are," said a man the station identified as Mr. Alvin Kluge, of Kluge Shipping and Freight. I squinted at the set and tried to guess how big his neck was. The television screen was a small convex bubble sticking out of a heavy wooden cabinet. The black-and-white image was fuzzy and ghostlike, but I figured the man's collar size was eighteen inches, at least; a throat too big to get both hands around.

If you were dealing with a customer who had that kind of bulk, and you wanted to choke him out, you had to get behind him and jam a police baton up under his chin, and then press a knee against his back, and pull the baton with both hands, hard enough to close the windpipe. You could bring down a man the size of a small bull that way in twenty seconds, usually without causing much lasting injury.

If you didn't care whether you injured him or not, there were lots of other ways to bring a man down, no matter how big he was.

"Ungrateful? The lack of perspective is appalling!" Everything Brian said these days sounded like one of the new rabbi's sermons. "They take and take and take, and then they expect gratitude from the people they exploit."

"You didn't use to talk like that," I said.

"I didn't use to be aware of the rampant injustice in the world, because I was a small child, and my parents are complacent."

"You hear that, Rose!" I shouted over the television. "We're complacent."

"No, we aren't!" she yelled back. "We're Ashkenazi."

"We give them work. We give them a living. And this is how they thank us," said Kluge on the TV. His jowls were either quivering with indignation, or else Brian needed to get up and futz with the rabbit ears again.

"You pay them a third less than you'd pay a white man to do the same work," Brian said.

"How is it any business of yours what a Negro gets paid?" I asked.

"Twenty years ago, when the Germans were marching the Jews into the ovens, the people of Europe were asking each other the same question. How is it any business of ours that Jews are getting shipped off to death camps?"

"Oh, stop being so sanctimonious."

"Hey, Mom!" Brian yelled. "Dad says I am sanctimonious."

"No, you aren't!" she yelled back. "You're adorable."

The man on the screen was still talking: ". . . Shiftless, lazy, unreliable, disloyal. Have to watch them like hawks to make sure they don't steal."

"He's the victim now." Brian balled up a section of my newspaper and threw it at the television. "This fat, rich vampire thinks he's the victim."

"I just don't see why it's our problem. I have enough to worry about without opening a vein for the colored. You have to worry about your bar mitzvah."

"It's our problem because, twenty years after Auschwitz, it's happening again," he said. "Or it's been happening all along, and it's still happening."

"And what are you and the rabbi going to do about it?"

"We can stand up, goddamnit," Brian said.

"Watch your mouth," I said.

"Watch your mouth!" yelled Rose.

On television, a black man, identified as labor organizer Longfellow Molloy: "Send us your prayers, 'cause we need God's help. If you have anything to give, we don't want to ask for any money except a fair wage for a day's work, but we've got several churches running food drives to help the strikers, and canned goods are deeply appreciated. These men ain't been paid in weeks, and their children are hungry. And anyone who wants to come down and march with us in front of Kluge Freight is surely welcome. Because they can't treat people like this. It's not right."

Brian continued: "We can stand in solidarity with the men striking for their human rights at Kluge Freight, and with the people who are sitting in at the lunch counters, and with the people who won't go to the back of the bus."

"Nobody cares where you sit on a bus," I said. "You don't even ride the bus. Your mother drives you everywhere. If you were on a bus full of Negroes, you'd be scared out of your mind."

"I'm not scared of Negroes. I'm scared of a society that can mistreat a whole group of people based on arbitrary characteristics.

The rabbi says there are seven times as many blacks in America as Jews. Anything that can be done to them can be done to us much more easily."

"He's right about that," I said. "We are vulnerable. And that's why we should stay out of what's not our business, lest our insertion of our big, Semitic noses into their feud reminds the goyim and the *schvartzes* that they all love Jesus, and they think we killed him."

"All that is necessary for evil to flourish is for good men to do nothing."

He might have been right. He seemed right enough that I felt bad about discouraging him. But I always liked doing nothing, when given the opportunity, and I thought doing nothing was generally a prudent course of action. Evil was probably going to flourish anyway.

I did nothing, immediately, about my meeting with Elijah. Maybe I should have reported it to my superiors, but Brian was right: The Department had been doing wrong by the coloreds, and I wasn't sure wrongs wouldn't befall Jews if I let people know that a gang of Jewish robbers was trying to corrupt Jewish police officers, thereby forming a Jewish conspiracy. Neither the Memphis Police as an institution, nor the various people who comprised it could be trusted to handle information like that in a sane way.

I'd overheard plenty of nasty comments around other cops: stuff about cheap Jews and Jews controlling government and Jewish bankers. None of them were especially ashamed to say these things when I was within earshot.

Memphis law enforcement had what you might call a checkered history on race. In 1919, Mayor Frank Monteverde was elected with the support of the black community after promising to integrate the police department. So he hired three black detectives.

These men were charged exclusively with arresting black criminals, because it would be unfair to subject white men to arrest by Negro officers. But when they raided a gambling den frequented by black patrons, the white crime boss who owned the operation took umbrage at having his place searched by Negroes, and sent a mob to lynch the detectives.

The blacks escaped, but one of them discharged his weapon and injured a white man during the altercation. As a result, all the blacks were fired from the force and the Memphis Police remained entirely white until 1948.

During that period — from around the time I was born until just before the war — a man named Clifford Davis was Memphis's Commissioner of Public Safety, and he was some kind of big to-do in the Ku Klux Klan; a wizard or a dragon or a fairy or something. During his tenure in office, the police force was about two-thirds Klansmen. By the mid-'60s, things had gotten more progressive, but only slightly. The reason Davis gave up running the police was that he got elected to the United States House of Representatives. And then, he got reelected another twelve times.

There were still very few black officers on the force, and only four Jews, but an awful lot of the boys Davis hired were still around, and some of them were wearing fancy epaulets and answering to intimidating titles. A Jew was something less than white to these people, but it was close enough to get by, as long as they were focusing their bigotry on other preoccupations. So, I was loath to call attention to my heritage.

It was entirely conceivable that, if they found out what Elijah was doing, they'd put the handful of Jewish cops on the Memphis police force on an open-ended unpaid leave, and then the department might carry out some kind of campaign of intimidation against the Jewish community.

I didn't take a bullet in France to get treated like my grandparents were treated in the old country or, worse, to get treated like a Negro, so I had to take care of this problem on my own, quietly. I'd run Elijah out of town, and if he wouldn't run, I'd bury him someplace out of the way. No reason to give the redneck brass cause to go on a Jew hunt in the department.

11
1965

"Let me tell you something about Memphis, Detective," said Longfellow Molloy, the labor agitator. "Memphis don't make nothin'. Memphis don't grow nothin'. Memphis exists but for one purpose: Memphis moves things. The rail lines and the highway and the river all come together in this place. Memphis is one of the five biggest inland ports in the history of Western civilization. Fifteen million tons of cargo come through here, ship to shore, and shore to ship. Loaded and unloaded, from the bellies of barges into the trailers of trucks. Onto train cars. And do you know how fifteen million tons of cargo gets loaded and unloaded in this town every year?"

I knew he'd only asked the question so he could answer it himself, so I sat quiet and let him blow off steam.

"Black hands," he said. "Black hands do all that lifting. Memphis earns its bread from moving things, and black folks do all the moving. Fifteen million tons, ship to shore, and shore to ship. We carry it. Those men marching outside the offices of Kluge Shipping bear this city on their backs seven days a week for a dollar seventy-five an hour. We're trying to organize and ask for the square deal every hardworking American deserves. And you come up here and you treat us like criminals. You come into my office, where I do the Lord's work, and you treat me like a low-life thug. Sir, I will not have it."

Paul Schulman had given me two leads on Elijah: that the target was somehow related to striking freight workers, and that Ari Plotkin had a piece of the job. Plotkin was simpler to get at; I could just pick him up and kick the shit out of him until he spilled whatever he knew. But if I did, Elijah would know about it immediately, and my best lead would be burned. So I'd decided to sniff around the strike first. And since I didn't really know who else to talk to, I decided to pay a visit to the angry black man I'd seen on the TV. Not exactly brilliant deductive work on my part, I'll admit, but I never said I was Sherlock Holmes.

Molloy described himself an "activist" or an "organizer," but he was more of an instigator. He'd come to Memphis a few months earlier and rented a small office across the street from the downtown skyscraper that housed the headquarters of Kluge Shipping and Freight. Kluge was one of dozens of companies that handled river cargo, and it was a medium-sized outfit at best, but it was notable for paying poorly, and its laborers were almost all black, so it was an ideal target for a civil rights rabble-rouser. The forklift operators and longshoremen were receptive to his talk about wage inequalities and dignity, and he was starting to cause pain in many rich, white asses.

Over the course of the last couple of months, Molloy had gotten more than half the company's colored workers organized. Six weeks previous, 120 men had walked out of the company's facility on Governor's Island. Since then, they'd been marching around in front of Kluge's downtown office, waving signs, hassling businessmen, and frightening secretaries.

"A group of black workers try to affiliate themselves with a white labor union, and they are rebuffed, even though all who work with their hands ought to be brothers," Molloy said. "And when those workers try to organize and peacefully demonstrate for a decent wage, they get themselves surrounded by fifty cops armed with clubs and guns and fire hoses and vicious dogs."

"There ain't no dogs over there."

"Maybe there ain't no dogs yet, but sooner or later, they always bring the dogs."

We sat there looking at each other, while I thought about the time some drunk SS guards threw a Jewish kid from Detroit named Marc Grossman into a toilet shed, and then shoved a couple of German shepherds that they'd starved for a few days in behind him. The Krauts watched the proceedings with their noses pressed against a greasy window, and the next day, they made us clean up the mess.

"Fifty cops, Detective," Molloy said. "No more than half the strikers are picketing on any given day, and we gotta keep a few protesters out on Governor's Island so the scabs have to cross a picket line to get onto the job site. The rest of the men have to take on day labor a couple times a week to keep their roofs, or they have to see to their children when they send their wives out to clean white folks' houses. Fifty cops to subdue sixty freight workers, plus a few dozen concerned citizens who show up to support our cause. And then they send you up here to hassle me. You don't scare me, Detective. I think it's you people who are scared. You and your cronies see what's going on outside, and you know that ain't just a few disgruntled longshoremen protesting a freight company. You know it's the start of something. Things cannot keep being the way they've been."

There was a little philosophical question I always liked to think about when schmucks were yammering at me: Did the man's character shape his worldview, or did his worldview shape his character?

I wasn't smart enough to figure whether the chicken came before the egg, but either way it worked out, a man's view of society revealed something about his own tendencies. I, for example, believed the world was hard and dangerous, so I was hard and dangerous myself. Similarly, conspiracy theorists and paranoids, the folks who suspected everyone of plotting against them, were often treacherous.

"I don't need to listen to this," I said to him.

"And I don't need police coming up into my office. But I don't seem to have much choice in the matter. If you're going to arrest me, let's spare the foreplay." He presented his wrists to me.

"I just want to ask some questions. If you want me out of here, you need to settle down and give me some answers."

He paused for a second and really looked at me. "Maybe I should call my lawyer."

Guilty men — the pro-level scumbags — liked to lawyer up real fast, but the self-righteous types did as well. Sanctimonious pricks were very concerned about their rights. I wasn't sure yet which kind of ass-hole I was dealing with. I decided not to make any assumptions; I didn't really care what Longfellow Molloy was up to. If he was scamming his people, it wasn't my job to stop him. I was after a slippery Jewish bank robber.

The problem was that I knew approximately bubkes about what Elijah was plan-ning; my only real clue was that it had something to do with the strike. So Molloy was going to have to tell me something.

"I've got a tip that there's a robbery going down that has something to do with the strike," I said. "I ain't accusing you of anything. Your people may be the victims. Your office may be the target. If I am going to stop this thing, I will need you to co-operate."

Molloy had clean fingernails, and he kept his hair neat; slicked down close to his skull. He had a way of letting his gaze drift down to the floor as he spoke, and then he would notice himself doing that, and look up deliberately to stare daggers at me.

In a white man, I'd have seen this as a sign of dishonesty or, at least, of a fundamentally strange nature. But maybe a Negro looked at the floor because he'd been born into a world that expected him to keep his eyes down, and Molloy looked up when he did because he wanted to live in a world that was different.

He was also wearing a three-piece suit. A lot of cops I knew didn't like to see a colored boy in a business suit; and they'd have taken one look at this one and bet that he was up to no good. But I suspected that if I put Molloy up against a wall and turned his pockets out, I'd find no label in his jacket, and only a cheap kind of lining.

There were colored ladies working out of their homes; out of tenements and row houses, sewing clothes to make ends meet, and some of them did very fine work. A white man with similar skills could take home five or six times what any of those ladies earned. Molloy had probably paid only a small fraction of what a comparable garment would cost me at Oak Hall or Goldsmith's. I'd have had half a mind to try to buy such a suit myself, but the blacks tended not to be forthcoming with referrals for some reason.

"And yet, somehow, with these supposed criminals out there, you're interrogating me. Ain't that the way it goes?"

"It's nothing personal. You just might be able to tell me some things I need to know."

He sat down behind his desk and held out his hands, palms up. "Well, then ask."

"Have you collected any kind of union dues from the strikers?"

"Ain't you read the newspaper? The union won't take us. Can't make any headway with the leaders of the Local; they're bigots. The whole lot of them. Been to Washington to visit the national organization. There's resistance, they tell me, which is a diplomatic way of saying they don't want our kind."

"You didn't collect money from those men, anyway?"

"Those men don't have any money. These men are poor; much poorer than they ought to be, hard as they work. That's why they're out there marching."

"Have you got a large sum of cash on the premises? Is there a safe here?"

"What do you think I am? Do you think I am fleecing these people? Are you accusing me of running some kind of scam?"

"I'm not accusing you of anything. I know

there's a gang out there planning a robbery that is somehow related to the striking workers."

"That's got nothing to do with me. I have nothing here worth stealing. I've got this one-room office, and I'm about to fall behind on the rent. I sleep on the floor, most nights, unless one of the strikers or a member of the clergy offers me a hot meal and a bed someplace."

Sitting on a filing cabinet behind Molloy's desk was a dirty glass with a toothbrush in it. Maybe a better detective would have spotted that sooner, and drawn appropriate conclusions.

"If that's the truth, maybe I came to the wrong place, and I suppose I'm sorry if I caused you distress," I said. I wondered what my son and his rabbi would think of this conversation, and I felt, right then, the way I'd felt after Brian saw me beat down Paul Schulman.

"If you looking for someplace with a lot of money, maybe you should go to a bank."

I had to admit, that wasn't a bad idea.

Something I Don't Want to Forget:

On television, the man my grandson wanted to elect president was trying to talk himself out of a tight corner:

"The remarks that have caused this recent firestorm weren't simply controversial. They weren't simply a religious leader's effort to speak out against perceived injustice. Instead, they expressed a profoundly distorted view of this country — a view that sees white racism as endemic, and that elevates what is wrong with America above all that we know is right with America; a view that sees the conflicts in the Middle East as rooted primarily in the actions of stalwart allies like Israel, instead of emanating from the perverse and hateful ideologies of radical Islam."

"He'll have to work a lot harder than that, if he wants to convince any Jews that he's a supporter of Israel," I said. "How many years did he go to Jeremiah Wright's church? It's practically the same as following Farrakhan."

I was in a bad mood, because I didn't realize how much worse things were going to get for me. It was March 2008, and I was still nearly a year away from getting shot in the back and losing my house, my independence, and my dignity.

I stuck my cigarette in my mouth so I could write part of what Obama had said in my notebook, and then I wrote "Jeremiah Wright = Anti-Semite" underneath it, so I'd remember the context.

"Are you copying down what he's saying?" Rose asked.

"I want to remember it, for when Brian calls later, to talk about this."

"William," Rose said.

"What?"

"Our grandson's name is William."

"Wasn't that what I said?"

"He says we've got to vote for this guy," Rose said.

"Who says?"

"William. Our grandson, William."

"Oh. What does he know?"

"He knows a lot. He reads the *New York Times*. I'm still hoping Hillary gets the nomination."

"Never going to happen," I said. "It's this guy, or else it's John McCain."

"Who told you that?"

"I don't remember."

"It was probably William."

"Yeah, it probably was."

"I wanted to live to see a woman president. Now I guess I won't get to."

"The efforts of women throughout thousands of years of human history, all building up to the coronation of Hillary Clinton, and then this guy has to spoil it," I said.

"You can be really obnoxious sometimes."

On television, Obama said: "Did I ever hear him make remarks that could be considered controversial while I sat in church? Yes. Did I strongly disagree with many of his political views? Absolutely — just as I'm sure many of you have heard remarks from your pastors, priests, or rabbis with which you strongly disagreed."

"You have to give him that one," Rose said.

"Wright baptized Obama's children."

"Abramsky davened with Brian at his bar mitzvah, and you hated Abramsky."

"Not the same thing."

"It's almost exactly the same thing."

"I can no more disown him than I can disown the black community," Obama said. "I can no more disown him than I can my white grandmother — a woman who helped raise me, a woman who sacrificed again and again for me, a woman who loves me as much as she loves anything in this world, but a woman who once confessed her fear of black men who passed by her on the street, and who on more than one occasion has uttered racial or ethnic stereotypes that made me cringe."

"You'd probably like his white grand-mother," Rose said.

"John McCain is a war hero."

"William says McCain isn't up to the task of fixing the economy."

"The country never would have got into this mess in the first place, if only somebody had consulted William."

"William says McCain would make Phil Gramm Secretary of the Treasury."

"Is that a bad thing?"

"William seems to think it would be."

"I liked things better when Brian was still with us, and William never remembered to call."

"I also liked things better when Brian was still with us."

"Yeah."

On television, my grandson's president was starting to get more emphatic, punctu-ating his sentences with aggressive gestures: "Legalized discrimination — where blacks were prevented, often through violence, from owning property, or loans were not granted to African American business own-ers, or black homeowners could not access FHA mortgages, or blacks were excluded from unions, or the police force, or fire departments — meant that black families could not amass any meaningful wealth to bequeath to future generations."

Rose was sobbing now, softly into her sleeve.

"Is this bothering you? We don't have to watch it. We can see what's on the animal channel."

"No, it's not this. It's just . . ."

"For all those who scratched and clawed their way to get a piece of the American Dream, there were many who didn't make it," Obama said. "Those who were ultimately defeated, in one way or another, by discrimination. That legacy of defeat was passed on to future generations — those young men and increasingly young women who we see standing on street corners or languishing in our prisons, without hope or prospects for the future. Even for those blacks who did make it, questions of race and racism continue to define their worldview in fundamental ways."

"I understand," I said. I stubbed the cigarette into the ashtray and set the notebook down so I could light another. "We don't need to talk about it."

"It's good to talk about it," Rose said. "I mean, it hurts, but I think it's good."

"Wounds don't heal over if you pick at them all the time."

Obama was reaching a crescendo: "In fact, a similar anger exists within segments of the white community. Most working- and middle-class white Americans don't feel that they have been particularly privileged by their race. Their experience is the immigrant experience — as far as they're concerned, no one's handed them anything, they've built it from scratch. They are anxious about their futures, and feel their dreams slipping away; in an era of stagnant wages and global competition, opportunity comes to be seen as a zero-sum game, in which your dreams come at my expense."

"I think I like him," Rose said.

"I don't trust him. He doesn't look like a president to me."

"Neither does Hillary, I bet."

"What kind of name is that, anyway? Ba- rack?"

"Baruch."

"What?"

"You said 'Barack' and I said 'Baruch.' "

"Yeah, I heard you. What do you want?"

"Never mind."

I tapped my cigarette against the side of the ashtray. "Oh, I get it now."

"Barack. Baruch. Barack. Baruch." She laughed.

"Just because you're right doesn't mean

that you're right," I said. "Let's see what kind of animal program is on. I bet there's one of the ones you like, with the penguins."

"In the end, then, what is called for is nothing more, and nothing less, than what all the world's great religions demand — that we do unto others as we would have them do unto us. Let us be our brother's keeper, Scripture tells us. Let us be our sister's keeper. Let us find that common stake we all have in one another."

I reached for the clicker.

12
1965

There were many banks in Memphis, but the one closest to the Kluge offices seemed like the one most likely to have some connection to the strike. So, that's where I went.

Sherlock Holmes said that when you eliminate the impossible, whatever remains, however improbable, must be the truth. In my experience, it's better to just start with the obvious, and hope you don't have to take things any further.

The downtown branch of the Cotton Planters Union Bank was a block and a half away from Longfellow Molloy's window, and maybe two hundred yards from the picketers outside the Kluge offices. It was also one of the biggest and wealthiest banks in the city; with a retail bank occupying the ground floor of the skyscraper, and its offices for administrative staff and management occupying five stories above that.

The bank manager, a genial fellow named

Charles Greenfield, was a member of my synagogue. He congratulated me on my son's upcoming bar mitzvah, but politely refused to tell me anything about the bank's business.

"Can I offer you a drink, Detective?"

"Sure," I said. "Scotch, rocks. The oldest one you've got."

He had the kind of office you get when you want everyone to know what a big *macher* you are. It occupied a corner of the building and had two walls of glass, with views of the river.

He had the place done up like some sort of expensive cigar club. Leather chairs. Leather sofa. Heavy wood desk. Deep rug. And, of course, the fully stocked bar, which I was happy to take advantage of.

He pursed his lips. "The offer was a formality; I assumed you'd decline."

"Why would I turn down free Scotch?"

"I thought cops weren't supposed to drink on the job."

"We're not," I said. "But we're also not supposed to put a blue light on the dash to get out of traffic or beat people up for getting mouthy, and I do both of those things on a near-daily basis, so I figure there's no reason to get all fastidious about a glass of whisky."

His face cycled through several subtle variations of an affected expression of disinterest as he tried to decide whether I was threatening him. He settled on a blank frown that wasn't quite blank enough. Rather than looking bored, he looked like somebody trying to look bored, and that meant I'd shook him up a little bit.

His assistant, standing next to him, didn't look like he needed to be shaken much at all. He was ready to explode like a bottle of soda pop.

Greenfield strode across the room to the bar and filled a glass with ice from a silver bucket. Somebody's job was to keep this guy's ice fresh all day. He poured the whisky himself, though, so as not to seem fussy.

Greenfield had big hands and broad shoulders underneath the fine wool and chalk stripes of his suit. His family had connections that got him into the navy during the war, which had seemed a little softer gig than dodging mortars in the Argonne. But sailors had seen some ugliness in the Pacific, and Greenfield looked like he knew how to handle himself.

"You'll have to drink fast, because this is likely to be a short conversation," he said, pushing the Scotch into my hand. "If you're going to question me about the bank's clients, we've really got nothing to talk about until you show me a subpoena."

"I'm not investigating your clients," I said. "I'm trying to prevent a robbery. You know you're less than two blocks away from a mob of agitated colored protesters."

He laughed at me. "Those protesters are surrounded by dozens of police already. I feel pretty secure here."

I eyeballed the assistant. "He doesn't look secure."

"Nobody cares what he thinks," Greenfield said. "That's why he's got his job, and I've got my job."

The assistant looked to be about ten years older than Greenfield; a smaller man with dishwater-blond hair turning gray around the temples, and thin wrists. He had a prominent nose, close-set beady eyes, a short upper lip, and a weak chin. This was the kind of man who had to learn to tolerate being passed over from below. He did not bother responding to Greenfield's insult. Perhaps he was resigned to the fact that nobody would ever take his side.

"Now, I appreciate your concerns, Buck, but I really don't think there's anything to this, and I've got business to attend to, so if you could finish your drink and find your way out, I'd be mighty appreciative."

"I'll get out of your hair if you want me to, but I've got a very solid tip that there's a robbery being cased nearby, so if you've got any reason to believe you're the target, you had better tell me what you know, or I won't be able to help you."

Greenfield settled behind the imperial expanse of his desk. "I'll take it under advisement."

The assistant started coughing.

"You want to say something?" I asked him.

"Charles, if you're not going to tell him, I will," said the little man.

Greenfield shrugged. "It's on you, then. I'm going to state my objection to this and hear you acknowledge it, though, because I will have to report this breach of confidentiality to Nashville, and I'll be telling them you volunteered information to the police over my objection."

"I understand your objection, I've worked twenty years for this bank," the assistant said. "I'm going to speak my conscience. I don't think this is a violation of client confidentiality, anyway. It's the bank's money I'm concerned about, not any client's."

I took a sip of my whisky, lit a cigarette with a wooden match, and draped my arm over the back of Greenfield's sofa. "What's your name, friend?"

"I'm Riley Cartwright. I'm a senior loan officer and an assistant manager of this branch."

"Well, Mr. Cartwright, I'm here to help," I said. "Tell me about your problem."

"We've got over a hundred and fifty thousand dollars in our vault right now, and I am absolutely terrified of a robbery," he said.

"That's because you're old and you're stupid and your worldview is obsolete," Greenfield said. "There's no place safer to put money than in a modern bank vault."

"Why have you got so much money on the premises?" I asked.

"We get an armored truck down from Nashville with cash every week," Cartwright said. "Usually, Kluge issues paychecks on Fridays and the boys come in and cash them. Negroes ain't prone to keeping their money on deposit."

"Kluge doesn't really pay them enough to save much, anyway," I said.

Greenfield showed his irritation by squeezing the bridge of his nose with a thumb and forefinger. "You're not one of those, are you?"

"I'm not one of anything," I said. There was a heavy crystal ashtray sitting on the substantial hardwood coffee table in front of me. I ignored it and flicked ash onto the rug.

"I hope you aren't," Greenfield said. "Those Negroes are nothing but malingerers, marching around on the sidewalk and insisting the white man owes them something. If they want to get paid more, they should learn a skill, instead of acting all entitled."

I paused and did some math. The cash in the vault below us exceeded the lifetime take-home pay for a Memphis police detective over the course of a twenty-five-year career. The workers at Kluge would cripple themselves hauling freight long before they ever earned half that much.

Bank robbery is a dumb crime. Almost nobody gets away with it; there is too much security and there are always too many witnesses. But I sort of understood why somebody might try.

A hundred and fifty thousand dollars. Just sitting there. Hard to even comprehend.

"There are only a hundred and twenty strikers. Five weeks' pay for the lot of them is less than fifty thousand," I said. "Why have you got triple that?"

Cartwright started counting on his fingers. "Kluge has workers who didn't walk off the job, and they've brought on some scabs to try to keep their shipments moving. But none of those people want to cash checks in view of the strikers. They're going out of their way to do their business at other branches, away from the picketers."

Greenfield got up and poured himself another drink. "Probably afraid of walking out of here with a pocket full of cash and getting robbed by the marchers. I can't say I blame them."

Cartwright continued: "Our other business has fallen off as well; people are avoiding this whole area, either out of support for the strike or because they're scared of the Negroes. But we've been getting a truck full of money every week, even though nobody is coming to withdraw. It's just piling up in the vault."

"Which is, like I said, a perfect place for it," Greenfield said. "This isn't the 1930s. Robbers can't just walk into a modern bank with a gun and take what's in the vault."

"If you don't need the cash, why does the truck bring more every week?" I asked.

"There's really no protocol for canceling our armored truck delivery," Greenfield said. "Cartwright doesn't understand that we have contractual obligations to the armored truck company to pay them for the routes, and they have agreements with the unions representing their drivers and guards to give them the work. Anyway, at the end of the quarter, we will balance our books, and send any excess cash back to Nashville, as we do four times a year. Until then, it is perfectly safe in our vault. The circumstance requires no deviation from routine procedures. We can't disrupt our business every time some Negroes get upset or some criminal comes sniffing around."

"I've been arguing that we should return the extra cash at once, instead of waiting for the end of the quarter," Cartwright said.

Greenfield leaned back imperiously in his deep leather chair. "But that's not the procedure."

Cartwright slapped a hand to his forehead. "Getting robbed isn't the procedure, either. That mess in the street out there may just seem like a small dispute between a company and its workers, but the whole city is a powder keg, and that might be the spark that ignites it. The police know it; that's why they're swarming over the strikers. The Negroes are looking for any excuse to riot, and when they do, Memphis will burn. And we are sitting at ground zero on top of a big pile of money."

"If the whole city burns, our vault will be

sitting unscathed and gleaming in the ashes. And if somebody comes in here to rob the bank, all they can do is take the cash in the tellers' cages; twelve hundred dollars, at most," Greenfield said. "Our vault is brand-new and quite secure, and no facility like it has ever been successfully robbed. Each teller has an alarm button beneath his counter. Our loan officers also have buttons attached to their desks, and I have one here in my office. There's no way to take over the entire bank in time to stop somebody from pushing one of those buttons, and once the button is pushed, this vault is basically impregnable."

"No vault is impregnable. That's hubris, Charles."

"Have you heard of a thief called Elijah?" I asked. "Because I believe he's in town."

"I'd be interested to hear exactly what you know, and how you know it, since Mr. Cartwright has been kind enough to inform you of confidential information about our bank," Greenfield said.

I flicked ash onto his rug again. "While the investigation is ongoing, I have to protect the identities of my active informants," I said.

"Glad to know we can expect reciprocity from the police department when we provide helpful information." Greenfield gave Cartwright a look that reminded me of the way a semi-truck might look at a squirrel lying prone in the highway. "I have heard of Elijah. He's very good at finding banks that have neglected their security measures. Expert thieves will always avoid a modern vault like ours. They go after softer targets."

"A softer target isn't filled with a hundred and fifty thousand dollars in cash," I said.

"Fort Knox is packed to the rafters with gold bricks worth millions, but Elijah hasn't broken in there, has he? As soon as anyone in the bank presses an alarm button, the police are notified by telephone and the vault automatically closes and locks. When the vault is sealed by the alarm, it starts a three-hour timer, during which the door cannot be opened. My key won't work. There is no combination. It's just sealed for three hours. It's made of tempered steel, and the door is eighteen inches thick. If you're experienced with an industrial blow-torch, you could possibly get through it an hour before it unlocks, but by that time, the police will have the place surrounded."

"What if somebody cuts your telephone wires?" I asked.

"Triggers the alarm automatically," Green-field said. "We live in an age of scientific marvels."

"Even so, why don't you just return the money, like Mr. Cartwright suggests?"

"Because the established procedure is to rebalance our cash reserve when we do our quarterly accounting."

"You're like a robot, following your protocol," Cartwright said.

Greenfield sipped his drink. "Yes, I am."

I flicked my spent cigarette into the crystal ashtray and lit another one. "Why?"

"If there is a robbery, my conduct will be subject to review, both by my superiors and our insurers. If I have deviated from protocol by ordering an unusual armored truck, and that truck gets robbed, I will lose my job and the insurer may deny coverage. It's a lot easier to rob an armored truck than a bank vault, you know. Truck robberies are about twenty times more common than vault robberies."

"Tell me about how a bank receives an armored truck," I said.

"That's not something we are willing to disclose," Greenfield said.

"They pull up to the loading dock in the alley behind the bank," Cartwright said.

"So the door in the alley leads straight to the vault?"

"The loading door is constructed from

reinforced steel and mounted in a reinforced doorframe which is affixed in a reinforced wall. It has a sturdy bar lock on the back of it. There's a security cage in the hallway, leading from the loading door. Tampering with the cage triggers the alarm and locks everything down," said Greenfield. He seemed to be considering whether it might be possible to lock Cartwright in the vault. "During business hours, we keep two armed guards stationed in front of the vault, so they'd hear anyone messing with the loading door, and they'd have plenty of time to hit an alarm before someone breached the security cage. No one is ever allowed to be alone with the vault while it's open, not even me. If one of the guards needs to piss, somebody else has to come and stand in his place while he's in the john. I know, in the movies, every security apparatus has some Achilles' heel, but in reality, most bank vaults aren't built with vulnerabilities. We've foreseen every contingency, and planned for all of them."

"But the truck is vulnerable?"

Greenfield shook his head. "Not particularly. It's an armored truck. They're like tanks. They're designed to withstand robbery attempts, and crewed by experienced and heavily armed guards. But a bank vault will always be a more secure place to put cash than any place that isn't a bank vault."

I considered the fact that I knew Elijah was in town and planning something only because he'd made sure I knew it. If he'd wanted to find himself a corrupt cop to deal with, it seems like he'd have gone looking for somebody with a reputation for dirty dealings. He had to have known I'd probably turn down his invitation.

It could be that Greenfield was right, and the vault was safe. Maybe Elijah was hoping I'd flush the cash out of the vault and into the open, so he could steal it in transit. But maybe he'd found some vulnerability in Greenfield's security protocol. If I did nothing, he was essentially free to execute any plan he might have to take down the vault, but if I tried to move the cash, I was possibly helping him get the money into an armored truck that he could rob much more easily.

"Is there anything else I can help you with?" Greenfield asked.

"I guess not," I said.

"Well, then, congratulations, again, on your *simcha*. Give your son my best wishes, and get the hell out of my office."

13
2009

"I want to make sure we all understand that my client is cooperating," said the lawyer.

His name was Meyer Lefkowitz, and as soon as I met him, I could tell he was a piece of shit. Actually, I knew he was a piece of shit before I met him, because I'd seen his television commercials. In one of them, a cartoon spaceship crash-landed in Memphis, and Lefkowitz helped the alien pilot get a settlement from its insurance company.

My grandson had told me that an effective criminal defense lawyer is someone who can be trusted by the courts to negotiate on behalf of people who cannot, themselves, be trusted.

That made sense; criminal lawyers don't usually get their clients off, because their clients are almost always guilty. They don't spend time going to lots of trials, like the lawyers on television. What they do is make deals. Even in my day, the penalty a criminal would get for a jury conviction was much heavier than a decent plea bargain, and as the court dockets have gotten more crowded, the plea deals have gotten sweeter and the punishment for going to trial has become progressively more brutal.

A good criminal defense lawyer, therefore, is somebody who maintains a close relationship with the prosecutor's office, and can use that established relationship and a reputation for trustworthiness and reasonableness to get the best deals for his clients. In other words, you probably want a lawyer who looks like an accountant or a librarian.

Lefkowitz was fortyish, with thinning hair that he had built up into a sort of Astroturf pompadour through the liberal application of some kind of greasy-looking industrial polymer. He wore a pinstripe suit with wide lapels; the fabric looked expensive, but it was badly tailored and poorly cared for. He had a heavy gold watch with diamonds on the bezel, and he wore rings on six of his fingers. He looked like a gangster from a James Cagney movie.

All this meant that he was probably bad at his job. When a ninety-year-old man with a Members Only jacket thinks your style is dated, you need to pull your goddamn head out of your ass. Lefkowitz was so buffoonish and so thoroughly bedecked in signifiers of corruption that it was unimaginable that any opposing counsel might seriously negotiate with him.

"His cooperation is duly noted," said Andre Price. He had Elijah handcuffed and leaning against the back of his police car, and he was examining the contents of the thief's pockets.

"You will return my client's effects to him, until they can be inventoried at booking and a receipt can be provided," Lefkowitz said.

"I ain't trying to steal from this old man," Andre said. "I just want to make sure he doesn't have anything he can lockpick his handcuffs with, or use as a weapon. Detective Schatz says your client is real slippery."

"My client will make a statement when you can offer him immunity and protection," said Lefkowitz.

Andre smiled and shook his head. Elijah had been carrying a wallet, a matchbook, a key to a motel room, and one of those glass Internet phones. Andre opened the wallet.

"No identification?"

"I don't carry any," Elijah said.

"Who are you?" Andre asked.

"I am a ghost. I am a dead man."

"I thought your client was cooperating," Andre said to Lefkowitz.

The lawyer's shoes were brown and his belt was black. I never trust a man whose belt doesn't match his shoes. "My client will make a statement when you can offer him immunity and protection," he said again.

"You're not being very cooperative, either," Andre said. He picked up the phone and poked at the screen with his finger. Nothing happened.

"It's not turned on," Elijah said.

Andre found a button on the side of the device and pressed it. The screen lit up with the words ENTER PASSCODE and a numeric keypad.

"What is the code to unlock this?" Andre asked.

"If I go around telling people my security code, it won't be secure, will it?" Elijah said.

"I can't believe this shit," Andre said. "I've got to spend my whole damn afternoon fucking around with Statler and Waldorf." He stuck the wallet and the phone back into Elijah's pants pocket, put his hand on the back of the thief's head, and pushed him down into the backseat of the unmarked Crown Vic.

"You will take my client to one of the smaller precincts for booking. I don't want you walking him past all the people at 201 Poplar," Lefkowitz said.

"Fine," Andre agreed.

"This is an important request. My client believes he is in very real danger."

"I said I'd do it."

"I will follow you, and I will meet with my client as soon as he's booked. You will not question him except in my presence."

"Wouldn't think of it," Andre said, and he shut the door behind Elijah.

I stubbed out the cigarette I'd been smoking and folded up my walker. I'd left it in the backseat on the way over here, so it was easy to grab. But Elijah was sitting there now, so the walker had to go in the trunk, which meant I had to walk around the side of the Crown Vic without it, to the front passenger door, trying not to lean against it to steady my weak legs.

As I did this, Andre made no move to help.

14
2009

For a man in a perp cage with his hands shackled behind his back, taking a ride to the East Precinct house to get booked for serious crimes, Elijah was looking awfully pleased with himself, and I didn't like it. Andre didn't seem to like it, either.

"Dude, they call it witness protection for a reason. If you ain't a witness, you don't get protected. So if you want me to do you any favors, you better be ready to admit to some bad behavior, and you better be ready to rat out all your friends."

"I will do what I must to get what I need. A man like me doesn't have much use for friends," Elijah said. "The world, in my experience, contains two kinds of people: the kind I can use, and the kind who are useless."

"I see two kinds of people in this car," Andre said. "We got the motherfucker in the front seat with the badge, and the motherfucker in the backseat wearing handcuffs."

I wondered what sort of motherfucker I was.

"Funny you should mention the hand-cuffs," Elijah said. He arched his back so he could shift the weight of his body onto his wrists, and then he slid out of the bracelets. He waggled the cuffs triumphantly at Andre.

"Did you leave him with a lockpick?" I asked.

"Hell no," said Andre. "I frisked him. I don't know how the hell he just did that."

"There are two kinds of people," Elijah said. "The kind who are content to be shackled, and the kind who will yank their own thumbs from their sockets to escape from bondage."

"That's a neat trick. Looked like it hurt," Andre said. "And now you can put the cuffs right back on, because I ain't letting you out of that cage until you are properly restrained. Unless you want me to hit you with the Taser."

"Can I Tase him?" I asked.

"Maybe. If you behave yourself," Andre said. Then he leaned on his horn. "Hurry it up! Sunday-driving motherfucker."

A panel van in front of us was going very slowly. Andre changed lanes to get around the slowpoke, but the van sped back up, cut in front of us, and slowed down again.

"What is up with this guy?"

I started to get nervous, but I was always nervous. Paranoia is the first symptom of dementia in the elderly. It was almost like white noise to me.

"Maybe you should pull him over and give him a ticket," I said.

"I am a detective. I ain't a traffic cop."

"I always used to keep a pad of tickets in my glove box, in case I wanted to hassle somebody," I said.

"There are a hundred things wrong with doing that," Andre said. "I bet you used to pull over black folks for driving in the wrong neighborhoods. Also, we issue traffic tickets with computers these days."

"Of course you do," I said.

In the backseat, Elijah wove his fingers together and then violently twisted his hands in a way that jammed his thumbs back into place with an audible popping noise.

I looked in the side-view mirror at the lawyer, who was following us to the police station. Lefkowitz's ride was as tacky as his suit. He was driving a big Cadillac Escalade truck, which my grandson once accurately described as the preferred vehicle of people who are trying too hard.

It used to be, when a man wanted to put some money into a car, he got himself something with a twelve-cylinder engine, a performance transmission, a heavy-duty suspension, and racing tires. Now an expensive car was wrapped in chrome, upholstered with leather, and inlaid with hardwood: a precious, ornamental thing unable to get you to the corner grocery store without burning through half a tank of gas at four dollars per gallon.

Andre's cheap, government-issue Crown Vic could run rings around Lefkowitz in his sixty-thousand-dollar Escalade. That truck was a rolling monument to softness, inefficiency, and overconsumption; the perfect symbol for the age of epidemic obesity.

Bill O'Reilly was just talking about this recently: People used to want to be Steve McQueen, but now the kids were all trying to be like a rapper called Pee Diddler. This used to be a nation of men, and now it's a country full of strip malls and ugly cars and cell phones with no buttons. It was easy for me to think sometimes that there was no place in the world anymore for men like me. But that wasn't true. Valhalla was a place, and there was also a place for me out on South Parkway, next to my son.

I wondered how Lefkowitz could afford

all the stuff he had. Crime paid, to be sure, but defending Memphis thugs and settling traffic accidents wouldn't generate enough cash to keep a man in Cadillacs and diamonds. I figured he was leveraged up to his eyeballs. I bet his gold watch had somebody else's name engraved inside the band, and he'd bought the Escalade at a steep discount, coming off the end of someone else's two-year lease.

Behind us, a beat-up-looking Ford F-150 truck cut Lefkowitz off and pulled right up to our back bumper. Traffic was pretty light for people to be so aggressive, but Memphis has always been known for its discourteous drivers. Andre didn't seem to have noticed the truck; he was still bitching about the guy in the panel van, and about having to play straight man to Mel Brooks and Carl Reiner.

In front of us, the Sunday-driving van crossed an intersection and then stopped short for no reason. Andre had to slam his brakes to keep from rear-ending it.

"The fuck is with this guy?" Andre said. "I wish I did have the damn ticket pad." He shifted into reverse, but there was no room to back up, because the truck was sitting right up against our back bumper. We were stuck in the middle of the intersection, and these guys had boxed us in.

"Oh shit," I said, and I hurriedly pulled on my seat belt.

Andre didn't quite seem to realize what was happening, until he heard the sound of a revving engine. He barely had time to brace before a big-ass Chevy Suburban slammed into the driver's side of the police car, and an air bag exploded in my face.

15
2009

The crash and the air bag jangled my head for a good twenty seconds, and when I reoriented myself, three men had already jumped out of the back of the panel van in front of us and were dragging Elijah from the backseat of the police car.

They were all wearing panty hose on their heads to obscure their features, but I could see they were black guys; and several of them were pretty big.

I looked in the side-view mirror. Behind us, two more pantyhose men were getting out of the Ford truck that had boxed us in. Behind the truck, Lefkowitz threw his Escalade into reverse, backed up a few feet, then U-turned into traffic and peeled out in the opposite direction. A few seconds later, I heard his tires squeal as he lost control of the Caddy, and then the sound of shattering glass and crunching metal. What an asshole.

"You fucked up now," one of the thugs was saying to Elijah. He was the smallest of the five men, but he had a commanding sort of posture, and gold on his fingers and around his neck. "You have no idea the kind of trouble you're in."

"Ought to do him right here," said a second. "Send a message to anyone else who thinks they can steal from us."

"You won't, though, will you?" Elijah said. "You need what I took. You're desperate."

"We can make you tell us where it is. When we start hurting you, you'll tell us everything.

"I've been hurt before, by better men than you."

"We'll see about that." One of the captors was binding Elijah's wrists and ankles with plastic handcuffs, and another was pulling a hood over his head.

I jostled Andre. He turned his head and looked at me. The pupils of his eyes were different sizes. The Crown Victoria police cruiser is a sturdy vehicle, but not many cars can fully protect you when you get T-boned at an intersection by a big truck. He had probably suffered a head injury, and there was a lot of blood on his clothes.

There was a lot of blood on my clothes, too. My cheeks stung where the air bag had hit me, and my nose was throbbing. I put a hand to my face, and it came away wet and slick. This was not a good thing, so I tried not to think about it.

"Pull it together, kid," I said to Andre. "It's time for you to be a hero."

"Think you all smart with your Members Only jacket. You look like Bob Dole," he said, and his head lolled to one side.

Outside, the panty hose men had Elijah trussed up like a pig. They threw him into the back of the van, and he landed with a heavy thud. For elderly patients, a fall-incident strongly correlates with death inside of twelve months, even where the injury appears superficial. Especially when a bunch of angry black guys with panty hose on their faces are kidnapping you.

"What about those other two?" one of the guys from the Ford truck asked the leader.

"I don't need them. Y'all deal with them."

The Suburban was backing up from the wreck, to make a U-turn. I could see its front fender was hanging loose, and the headlights and front grille were all smashed up, but the engine sounded okay. I hoped that meant he hadn't hit us too hard, and Andre might not be too badly injured. The three kidnappers climbed into the panel van behind Elijah, and when the door shut, they peeled out. Only the two from the Ford truck were left, and they were arguing about which one of them was going to kill us.

"He told you to do it, so you got to do it," said the larger of the two. He was easily a couple of inches past six feet and he must have weighed 250. I could see his hair was braided into cornrows underneath his panty hose mask.

"I ain't even got a gun," said the second. "I didn't sign on for this shit." He was smaller; maybe five-seven, and skinny.

"I've got a gun. You can use my gun."

"It's your gun. You want it used, you can use it."

"But he told you to deal with it."

Andre was still semiconscious and babbling. I reached across his waist and unfastened his seat belt. Then I gingerly tried to roll him to one side. Just my luck he'd made me put away my .357 before we left Valhalla. Just my luck he was left-handed, and I had to try to reach over him to find his holster.

At least the thugs weren't paying attention to me. They probably thought we were pretty messed up from the wreck. We must have looked pretty messed up. The little one was saying: "Look at that car. That is a cop car."

"Ain't a cop car. Cop cars have the word 'Police' written on them in big letters. That car has got no lights. Got no sirens."

"Is so a cop car. Did you see the cage in the backseat? Did you see the radio antenna on the back of it? That is a cop car, and so those dudes are cops. Do you want to be killing cops?"

"I want to be doing what I'm told to do." The big one pulled a plastic-looking handgun out of the low-slung waistband of his baggy jeans and tried to push it into the smaller one's hands.

The little one didn't want to take it. "I say we just leave. We got the guy we came here for. Didn't agree to killing cops."

"He said you have to do it."

"And if I do it, the next time you get picked up for possession with intent or some dumb shit, you'll rat me out to get yourself a plea deal, and then I'll get a lethal injection for killing cops. I ain't never killed nobody. You want it done, you can do it. If Carlo wants it done, he can do it. I was promised two hundred dollars to back y'all up today. I ain't killing no cops for two hundred dollars."

"Fuck you," said the big one. "I ain't no snitch."

"I ain't saying you're a snitch. I just don't

want to find out if you're a snitch."

I found the snap on Andre's belt holster, and got his police-issue .38 loose. It was cool metal, painted matte black. Light-weight, with functional squared-off edges. It was a gun with very little personality, but it would do the job. I flicked the safety catch and checked to make sure there was a round in the chamber. I lifted the door latch, but the door was a little sticky, probably because the car's frame had warped in the crash. I pushed my shoulder against it.

"I can't believe I got to do this," the big panty-head was saying. "He told you to do it. You a pussy-ass motherfucker, you know that?" He tried again to force his friend to take the gun.

With my weight behind it, the door sprung open, but when it did, I pitched sideways and off balance. Even though I didn't have much of an aim, I managed to shoot the little guy. Firing the .357 felt like wielding Zeus's thunderbolt. By comparison, shoot-ing the little .38 felt like changing the channel on the television, but it made a big noise, and the bullet blew the kid's kneecap apart. He fell down and started screaming. The cheap plastic gun clattered to the ground, and while the big guy chased after it, I managed to slide out of the car and climb to my feet, supporting my weight by clinging to the open door.

By the time the big kid came up with his weapon, I had steadied myself, and I had the .38 trained on him.

"Why don't you drop that?" I said.

He did not immediately comply. He wasn't quite pointing the gun at me, but he had his finger inside the trigger guard.

"Just be cool, old man," he said. His hands were shaking a little bit.

"I am cool," I said, and I shot him three times.

The first bullet hit him right above his left eyebrow, and pulped the part of him that dreamed and the part of him that knew how to speak. The second bullet went in just below his bottom lip, shattered all the teeth in his jaw, shredded his tongue, and lodged itself in his brain stem. The third one hit him in the shoulder while he was falling to the ground. I think he was probably already dead by then.

"You killed Clarence!" the little guy screamed. "Oh, God!"

"I warned him," I said. "I don't warn anyone twice."

The plastic handgun was on the ground, a couple of feet from where the little guy was writhing on the pavement and clutching at his leg. I needed to get hold of it, before he started thinking straight and tried to grab it, but my walker was still in the trunk, where I couldn't get it. I took a few wobbly steps forward, but that turned out to be as far as I could get. I let my legs give out in the most controlled way I could. It was a little more like kneeling than falling, but not much. At least I didn't hurt myself much worse than I was already hurt. I crawled the rest of the way to the loose gun on my hands and knees, like a baby. Once I had it, I felt safer, and I managed to pull myself into a sitting position on the pavement before the paramedics arrived.

16
2009

The woman in the EMT uniform took a tentative step toward me. She looked afraid.

"I'll need you to put those down so I can help you," she said. She was a young, light-skinned black girl with her hair pulled back from her face. She wasn't wearing much makeup, but she didn't seem to need it.

I looked up at her. "What? I'm okay. Somebody needs to help Andre." I started to point, and was surprised to find that my hands were full of guns. I tried to remember how I'd lit the cigarette I was smoking with my hands full of guns, and could not. I handed the guns to the girl.

"These aren't mine," I said.

"Okay." She didn't quite know how to respond to that, but the police had arrived, and one of them came over and took the guns away from her.

"I'm going to need to examine you," she said. "You're covered in blood."

"I am?" I looked down at my shirt. It was soaked in dark red down the front. "Shit. Is all of that from me?"

"Looks that way."

"Well, you should see the other guy."

Two paramedics were trying to immobilize the kid I'd shot in the leg, but he was flailing around and clawing at himself and screaming. The medical examiner was zipping the dead one into a rubber bag. A grim-looking emergency team was strapping Andre to a gurney.

"Are you shot?" the girl asked me.

"I don't think so," I said. I had a couple of seeping abrasions, and I guess my nose had been gushing, though I had been too dazed to even realize it.

I took the cigarette out of my mouth. It was covered in blood. I laughed at it. "Hey, this thing looks like a used tampon."

The girl was moving her finger back and forth in front of my face.

"Can you follow my finger with your eyes?" she asked. I tried to. "Can you remember what happened to you?"

The chain of events that had brought me to this point was admittedly a little blurred. "The goddamn air bag punched me in the face. My doctor has me on a blood thinner called Plavix. Keeps me from having a stroke, but it makes me bruise up like a rotten peach. Sometimes I rip myself open jostling against the nightstand, or I cut myself shaving, and we have to go into the emergency room."

"I think you're in shock," she was saying.

I'd had a couple of nosebleeds that were bad enough to require trips to the emergency room, just from dry weather. The air bag had hit me really hard.

"Just tell Rose I am all right. No need to worry her over this. If you need anything, ask my son."

Now I was lying on my back, somehow, and being carried toward an ambulance. I wasn't sure how that had happened. They ratcheted the gurney partway upright, either because I was in shock, or so the blood from my nose would not run down my throat.

"They got Elijah," I said. "He told me they were coming for him, and I didn't believe him, and now Andre is hurt, and they got him."

"This mask is to make it easier for you to breathe." She put it over my face, and I felt the cool flow of air against my damaged nose.

"It was that scumbag Lefkowitz. He must have told them where we were. I know we weren't followed to the cemetery. We have

159

to get Lefkowitz. He'll know where they took Elijah. There's still time to get him back alive, I think, if we're lucky."

She jabbed a needle into my arm, and then I started to feel sleepy. I was semiconscious at best when they wheeled me out of the ambulance and into the hospital, and while a doctor in surgical scrubs was shouting for units of O neg, I got bored and dozed off.

Something I Don't Want to Forget:

A journalist with a lot of blackheads on his nose had a lot of thoughts about cops: "If I had to choose one convention out of our police thrillers and action-adventures that aggravates me, it would be that the heroes never shoot first," he said. "They've got to let the bad guys open fire before they can retaliate."

The interviewer nodded emphatically. "And when they do retaliate, they kill everybody."

"See, that's something we've heard for six years in response to 9/11. We didn't start it, but we're going to finish it. As long as we don't strike the first blow, we're entitled to unlimited and disproportionate retaliation."

I snorted at the television. When I was growing up, we were taught that you don't poke a sleeping bear with a stick.

"Of course, if they were going for verisimilitude, there are plenty of situations in which it makes sense for a policeman or a soldier to open fire before an aggressor does," the journalist added.

"Absolutely," said the host. "If they let the bad guys shoot first every time, eventually one of the bad guys won't miss."

"I think the real-world bad guys have better aim than the bad guys in most of the movies and television shows we see."

"And, of course, you spent some time with real cops while writing your true-crime thriller *Last Watch,* which is soon to be a major motion picture. How do real cops differ from the cops we see in movies and on television?"

"I think the thing most people don't understand is that any interaction a police officer has with members of the public is fraught. When these guys leave for work in the morning, they don't know if they'll make it home in one piece. Any time you interact with a police officer, you are dealing with an armed man who knows he is not safe. There are three hundred million firearms in civilian hands. When an officer makes a traffic stop, he doesn't know whether the driver has a handgun in his glove compartment. When a cop responds to a domestic disturbance, he doesn't know whether the door is going to be answered by a man holding a shotgun. Every year, a hundred law enforcement officers in this country are killed by suspects."

"That doesn't seem like a lot."

"It's more than enough to keep that danger on every officer's mind. And that number would be a lot higher if police weren't trained to shoot first when confronted by a suspect they have reason to believe is armed. These are men with families. You can't expect them to give pushers and psychopaths a fair chance to kill them before they retaliate with force. Police shoot and kill about five hundred suspects a year in the United States. Subsequent investigations find the vast majority of those shootings are justified."

"Investigations by the police agencies that employ the shooters."

"Well, yes."

17
1965

I was parked on the street in front of the bank building, slouched low in my Dodge and listening to football on the radio. I had a bag of hamburger sandwiches on my passenger seat, and I was sipping on a warm, flat Coke.

Staking out the bank wasn't a great plan, and I knew it. There was no way I could keep eyes on both the front door and the side door where the armored trucks made their drops, and I couldn't really sit out in front of the place for long enough to stop whatever Elijah had going on. I just didn't have any better ideas.

I had bought myself some time to work on this by telling my captain that I was looking into Longfellow Molloy; there were plenty of folks on the police force who would have loved to see that smart-talking Negro locked in a jail cell. But I wasn't planning to give them anything on him, so my excuse wouldn't justify days or weeks spent chasing Elijah. I was going to have to do something, soon.

I had several unappealing options: The first was to take a risk, and encourage Greenfield to move the money as soon as possible. I could monitor the loading of the cash onto the armored truck myself, and even escort the package back to Nashville. If I was lucky, and Elijah was putting together a hit on the vault, I might be able to get the money out before he learned of the transfer. But if I was wrong, and he was prepared to hit the truck, I'd be playing right into his hands, and there would probably be a gunfight, and I would probably die.

My second option was to go after the one remaining lead Paul Schulman had given me. He'd told me Ari Plotkin was involved in Elijah's scheme. Plotkin was a more refined breed of hood than Schulman, and unlikely to snitch as easily as his low-rent colleague, but I was prepared to hurt him worse, if it meant finding out how to stop the robbery. Unfortunately, if I took Plotkin down, Elijah would find out pretty quickly. He'd know I knew which bank he was robbing, and he'd assume I'd know whatever Plotkin might be able to tell me. He could modify his plans to account for this, and I'd be back where I started.

My third option was to inform the department of what I'd learned. My delay in reporting my meeting with Elijah and my information about his target would, at best, be seen as an exercise of poor professional judgment on my part. More likely, it would be seen as evidence of a racial defect of some sort.

This could easily stymie my career advancement for years. Or it might get me fired. Or maybe I'd just start getting put in dangerous situations without proper support, until an unforeseeable tragedy occurred. Any of these outcomes was unacceptable; the less the police department learned about Elijah and his web of Jewish corruption, the better.

Which led to the fourth option, the one my pride didn't want to let me consider: I could let Elijah get away with it. Since there was no official investigation, I was free to just walk away from my pursuit. I was a policeman; it wasn't my job to stop crimes before they happened, only to clean up the mess afterward. Charles Greenfield was entirely nonchalant about the possibility of his bank being robbed, and I didn't see any reason why I should care about it more than he did.

Elijah wasn't stealing from people who were struggling to pay their bills. He wasn't stealing from hungry children. He wasn't stealing from the Negroes marching in front of Kluge Freight. He was stealing the fully insured contents of a bank vault. It wasn't a victimless crime, exactly, but the victim lacked a face, and lacked a capacity to suffer. There was nothing in that vault I cared about protecting.

But I had to protect myself. If Elijah got caught, my foreknowledge of his activities might be revealed. Even if he didn't get caught, his accomplices might. No law enforcement had ever gotten close to catching Elijah, but the people he worked with weren't always as good, and weren't always as lucky. Their next job might not be quite so well planned, or they might do something stupid with their money. Whatever the story, his people ended up in custody sometimes, and, when they did, they ended up talking. This was the only reason anyone knew Elijah existed at all. If his people talked this time, they might say my name.

How many of his crew knew about my meeting with him? His five thick henchmen. The bartender. How many others might have heard about it? What if there were other Jewish cops involved in the scheme who knew he'd met with me?

If I let the robbery happen, I could never be sure my complicity in it would stay secret. If I were a regular white policeman, I could have just reported the contact to the brass and been in the clear, but I was a Jew inside a sick institution, and I had no easy answers.

If the law was so debased and its guardians were so perverted, maybe Brian was right, and I should find myself a new line of work. Maybe Elijah was right, and I should just acclimate myself to a dirty lifestyle. What moral imperative prevented me from helping myself to the contents of that bank vault, at the expense of a faceless victim-entity that was incapable of suffering? Maybe justice was a meaningless concept in a world where the police lined up in force to protect Alvin Kluge and his money from the Negroes he exploited.

Maybe I should have just done whatever Elijah wanted. If I were on the inside of his scheme, I could tie off his loose ends afterward at my leisure.

While I was considering these options and watching the front entrance of the bank, Elijah opened the passenger-side door of my car and slid into the seat.

"Hello, Baruch," he said.

I damn near jumped out of my skin. How was it even possible to open a car door without making noise? I reached inside my jacket, but Elijah laid a hand on my arm, to keep me from drawing my gun.

"Let's not be uncivil," he said. I heard a tap on the back window, and I looked behind me. Elijah had a beefy henchman positioned on each side of the car. If I shot him, they'd shoot me.

"Don't worry, Baruch," he said with a little chirp-laugh. "I'm not here to kill you. If I killed you, I would probably attract the attention of the police, who seem, thus far, to be blissfully unaware of my activities. I wonder why you haven't told them anything."

"Maybe I have," I said. "Maybe the net is closing around you, and you can't even see it."

He chirped again. "I think not, Baruch. There are fifty cops down in front of Kluge, ready to crush those poor Negroes, and yet there is only you guarding this bank."

"They're not all that far away."

"But they're far enough, and they won't be paying attention," he said. I realized that he'd probably already found another cop to be his inside man on the police force. If that was the case, he knew with certainty that I hadn't informed the department of his presence in Memphis.

He seemed completely unconcerned about revealing such information in my presence, but I wasn't overly optimistic that he was likely to let any particularly useful details slip about how he planned to take down the vault. Arrogance, in my experience, frequently carries with it a dose of hubris, but sometimes arrogance is justified, and this seemed like one of those cases. I had a reputation as a pretty smart cop, but it helped that the guys I went after were generally pretty stupid. Elijah was not stupid, and he wasn't likely to spoil a carefully devised plan by mouthing off to me.

"I wanted to congratulate you on your son Brian's upcoming bar mitzvah," he said. He handed me a sealed envelope with the words "For Brian" written on it in a looping script. When I took it from him, I touched the paper only at the edges, so I could dust the thing, later, for fingerprints. I wouldn't find any; that would have been too easy.

"I will kill you if you go near my family," I said.

He ignored the threat: "When I was your son's age, I did not get to study with a rabbi.

I did not get a party to celebrate my emergence into manhood. I was living in the ghetto, in a cramped, moldy flat occupied by three other families as well as my parents and my sister. I thought it was the worst place in the world, but that was only because I lacked imagination.

"Hitler was unencumbered by such deficiencies; his mind was a whirling phantasmagoria of barbarity, and from that font sprang Auschwitz. And, to tell the truth, he imagined worse than Auschwitz."

"A whirling phantasmagoria? Are you shitting me?" I said.

He stopped, and frowned at me for twenty or thirty seconds. I used the pause to consider whether it was redundant to modify "phantasmagoria" with "of barbarity." I wasn't sure, but I figured Elijah had probably looked it up at some point. His story seemed rehearsed; a thing he'd told many times before. There was a chilly edge to his voice that made me wonder if any of the people he'd told this to were still alive.

He started talking again: "Auschwitz, you see, was merely a slave-labor camp where a lot of people happened to be killed, and where four industrial crematoria happened to be running all day and all night, incinerating corpses and fogging the sky with oily black smoke. You hear about Auschwitz because there are people who were in Auschwitz that survived; people who can tell their stories.

"You'll never meet anyone who was sent to Treblinka. A million people went to Treblinka, but all of them are dead. Treblinka was not a prison camp, like Auschwitz. Treblinka was a factory. Treblinka was a slaughterhouse.

"So, when the SS soldiers came to the filthy ghetto apartment block where we'd been sent after my father's home and his shop were confiscated, and they waved guns in our faces and cleared everyone out, and when they marched us to the railway station and they packed us so tightly into a shipping car that we could not sit, we were lucky, because the train was only going to Auschwitz.

"I was lucky when I got off the train, smeared with feces and urine that wasn't all my own. I was lucky when the guards sent me and my father to the right, rather than to the left, where they sent my sister and my mother. I was lucky when my mother refused to be separated from us, and wept and begged, and they shot her in the face while she held my sister in her arms. I was lucky because they only killed my mother, and did not kill me as well.

"I was lucky, because I was in Auschwitz, and people survived Auschwitz. My father was lucky, too, but he didn't appreciate the good fortune that HaShem had bestowed upon him. After he saw what they did to my mother, my father could not eat. He could not raise his voice to praise the Lord's name. He probably would have died on a pile of mildewed straw if the guards hadn't dragged him out of the barracks each morning for roll call. On the day he could no longer stand on the parade ground, they beat him to death. If we want HaShem's blessings, the rabbis say, we must meet Him halfway. My father could not take advantage of the opportunity that God gave him by sending us to Auschwitz.

"Of course, most of the rabbis got sent to Treblinka, so perhaps they weren't as wise as they thought."

Here, he chirped cheerily.

"Why are you telling me this?" I asked.

"I want you to know," he said. "I want you to understand the hypocrisy implicit in your position. I want you to understand how ludicrous and self-defeating it is for a Jew to serve as an agent of coercion on behalf of the Christian state, and I want you to try to comprehend the inescapable logic of my

173

way of doing things."

"Well, I ain't going anywhere, I guess, as long as you've got those guns pointed at me," I said. "So, go ahead and convince me."

He smiled, and I flinched a little. Those Auschwitz teeth of his were tough to look at.

"After my father died, I knew that I had to get out of that place, so I waited and I listened. I was assigned to a labor detail of twenty prisoners supervised by two SS guards. Each day, we went to an evacuated Polish village near the edge of the camp, and we stripped salvageable materials from the buildings, which were scheduled for demolition. One of the guards was a corrupt and greedy man. He stole from the salvage, and he ferreted away anything of value he found abandoned in the houses.

"One day, I approached and spoke to him as he smoked a cigarette outside the house, out of earshot of his partner. It was dangerous to do this; speaking to a guard could get you shot. But I knew how to pique this man's interest.

"I told him that my father had been a wealthy shopkeeper before the Nuremberg Laws nationalized Jewish property. I told him that, when we learned we were to be sent to the ghetto, my father had hidden away his wealth; cash and jewelry. He'd hoped we could recover it after the war. I told the guard I was the only person left alive who knew where this treasure was hidden, and I promised it to him, if he could get me out of the camp.

"He thought about it for a few minutes, and then he went inside the house and bashed the other guard's skull in with the butt of his rifle, and he shot all the other Jews on the detail. Then he grabbed me by the arm, and pulled me into the woods, and told me to wait there.

"I imagine he told his superiors that the Jews had attacked his partner and he had killed them in retribution. But how he justified his butchery was not my business. All I know is that, according to official records, I was killed that day, in that ruined Polish village, and buried in a mass grave. People survived Auschwitz, but I am not one of them. I am numbered among the dead.

"I waited in the woods until nightfall, when I heard someone calling from the road. I crept to the edge of the forest, keeping to the shadows, and I saw a young woman in a little cart pulled by an old mule. I went to her, and she hid me under a pile of old rags, and drove me back to her shabby farmhouse. She said she was the guard's lover, and he had told her to spirit me away, so that they could get my treasure. I didn't wait for him to return, however. I found a knife and stabbed her to death, and I stole everything of value from her house. I had to stick the knife into her fifteen times before she stopped struggling. My resolve never wavered.

"I lived out the war on the run, and I survived by taking whatever I needed. I never called it stealing. I don't believe stealing is a thing that exists. The Nuremberg Laws that nationalized my family's assets also endowed me, from a very young age, with a deep skepticism toward the concept of property rights. It's not as if the ostensibly rightful owners of this country's wealth have come by it honestly, any more than the beneficiaries of the Nuremburg confiscations earned theirs. Men strip the hills of timber and then blast deep scars in the earth to find coal, with the state's full blessing, and yet I am a criminal for occasionally helping myself to a few stacks of paper. Kluge builds himself a limestone mansion with the proceeds of Negro misery, and you're camping out in your car to stop me from stealing the payroll he's refusing to disperse to his workers. As far as I am concerned, people are entitled to keep what they have only for as long as they are able to stop me from taking it from them."

"Maybe I don't see it that way," I said. "Maybe I think actions need to have consequences."

"What will you do? Lock me up? Kill me? I have already been locked up. I have already been killed. These things happened and will happen again, not because I am a criminal, but because I am a Jew. So why should I not be a criminal as well? Why should I spare anyone's property?"

The smart thing to do would have been to humor him, and see if I could draw him out a little and get him to reveal something about his plans, but finesse had never been my specialty, and I was sick of listening to the asshole.

"Because I am a feral dog," I told him. "And I don't like you shitting where I eat."

He chirped. "I feel sorry for you, Baruch. You are a grumpy sentinel crouching here, eating your cheap, greasy food and holding your futile, lonely vigil. But what is going to happen is going to happen, and you can't do anything about it."

"We'll see," I said.

"Yes, I suppose we shall," he said, and he slid noiselessly out of the car. I had an idea that I should make an exception to my general policy about fair play, and just shoot the son of a bitch in the back, so I kicked my door open and climbed to my feet, drawing my gun as I stood. But somehow, Elijah and his men had already vanished.

I picked up the envelope he'd given me, still holding it by the edges, and opened it by slitting the side with my pocketknife. It contained a store-bought birthday card for a child ON YOUR SPECIAL DAY. Tucked inside the card, I found three one-hundred-dollar bills; he'd thrown away as much money as I was paid for two weeks of hard work, just to taunt me.

Technically, I should have turned the card and the bills over to the department, as evidence. Maybe a specialist could have done a better job of checking it for fingerprints, and found something useful on it. Or maybe the serial numbers on the bills might have connected Elijah to some robbery.

But I was already too deep into my one-man vigilante mission, or my cover-up operation, or whatever it was. I pocketed the bills. There was really nothing else I could do.

Maybe Elijah was trying to push me down a slippery slope. Or maybe I was already sliding. Maybe I'd been sliding for a long time.

18
1965

I never thought of myself as an emotional man, but I was furious at Elijah. He'd put my family and my livelihood at risk, and he was contemptuous toward my values; toward the life I'd built and the stuff I stood for.

The thing that made me angriest was the fact that he was probably right. I was ensconced within and dependent upon a system I couldn't trust. I worked side by side with men whom I didn't like, and who didn't like me, and I might be forced, on any given day, to rely on these men in a situation that involved mortal peril.

But what the hell was I supposed to do? Join Elijah and his herd of Jewish buffalo? I had a family to take care of, and a synagogue membership and a mother. I wasn't a rootless, vengeful ghost.

Elijah knew I'd figured out that he was robbing the Cotton Planters bank, so getting Greenfield to move the money was now too dangerous a gamble to consider. But since Elijah knew that I knew, I felt like I wouldn't be tipping too many cards by pursuing Ari Plotkin, the local hood Paul Schulman had told me was involved in the scheme.

Plotkin was a world-class sanctimonious shitball. He had a picturesque little ranch-style house within walking distance of the synagogue. He davened three times a day, and his wife wore a wig and kept a strictly kosher kitchen, to the point where he'd bought her separate dishwashers for their meat and milk dishes. And he paid for his proper Jewish lifestyle with theft and fraud.

Burglary had once been a specialty of his, though he seemed to be doing less of that as he got older. He was a go-to man for anyone looking to fence stolen goods. He had a small-time bookmaking operation mostly serving the betting needs of the Jewish community, and he'd been involved in selling fraudulent stocks to widows and pensioners.

He wasn't above sticking somebody up at gunpoint, if there was enough money in it, but he'd only been caught doing that once. He beat the rap by shaving off his beard, which made it difficult for an eyewitness to identify him. If he'd rated highly enough to attract Elijah's attention, I suspected he was also into some dirty and lucrative business I didn't know about. His house was nicer than mine.

Plotkin figured his activities were okay by God, as long as he didn't steal from Jews. But it wasn't God who was going to be judging him on this particular night.

It was a Friday, which was the Jewish Sabbath, so I knew Plotkin was likely to be at home. I found him sitting on his front porch, reading — seriously — the Talmud. When he saw me climb out of my car, he hurried into the house.

I walked up to the door and pounded on it with my fist.

"Let me in, Ari," I said. "There are things I need to discuss with you."

"I know my rights," he yelled through the door. "I don't have to talk to you. No police can come into my house without a warrant."

"Have you ever seen one of those programs on television, where the policeman tells the criminal that there's an easy way and a hard way to resolve a situation? Because this is one of those."

"I think we should resolve this the way that involves you talking to my lawyer."

"I think we're going to resolve it the way

182

that involves you talking to my foot," I said, and I kicked the knob a couple of times, until the lock splintered out of the door-frame.

As the door swung open, Plotkin rushed at me brandishing what looked like a silver candlestick, but I already had my .357 drawn. I shot him in the leg, and he fell to the floor at my feet.

"For future reference, the easy way would have hurt less," I said.

I stepped over him and walked farther into the house, to make sure no other threats were lying in wait for me. The kitchen branched off the narrow entry parlor, and that was where I found Plotkin's wife cowering behind the linoleum counter and clutching their daughter, who looked to be about five or six. Both the woman and the girl started screaming when they saw me with my gun.

"Get out of here," I said.

"Go away!" Plotkin's wife shouted. "I will call the police."

"I am the police," I said, and I showed her my shield. "Get out of the house. Your kid doesn't need to see this."

"Where am I supposed to go?"

"Do I look like a goddamn travel agent? Just leave."

She fled through the broken front door, wailing and covering her eyes as she passed her bleeding husband.

I checked the other rooms of the house, to verify the place was clear, and then I returned to the front entryway, where Plotkin was flopping around in a slowly expanding pool of blood.

In my tour of the house, I had noticed that his heavy, hardwood dining room table was set for Shabbos dinner. I went and grabbed hold of the white linen tablecloth, and yanked it, sending china plates and crystal glasses smashing to the floor. The tablecloth looked like it might be some kind of heirloom. I tore it into ragged strips as I returned to the wounded scumbag by the front door.

"No sense in letting you bleed to death before you tell me what you're up to," I said as I tied pieces of tablecloth around his injured leg in a makeshift tourniquet.

"That belonged to my grandmother."

"I guess I could have used my shirt to bandage your wound," I said. "But it cost me five dollars, and I didn't want to get Plotkin all over it."

"You are detestable."

"They say you can get Plotkin out with some club soda and a little bit of salt, but I don't want to ruin a five-dollar shirt finding out if that's actually true."

"I hate you so, so much."

"I don't like you, either, Ari, but if you talk quickly, I'll try to get you to a hospital in time for the docs to save your leg," I said.

"I don't have to talk to police, I know my rights."

"You're a clever one, aren't you? The Constitution grants you a right against self-incrimination. Go ahead and sit there and be silent. However, that tourniquet is cutting off blood flow to your leg. If you take the tourniquet off, your blood will just pour out. The exit hole in the back of your thigh is the size of an apple. You are all fucked up, my friend. If you don't get treatment quickly, your leg will probably have to be amputated above the knee. And if you don't get to a hospital in the next couple of hours, they won't have to bother with an amputation, because you will bleed out, even with the tourniquet. So you can exercise your rights as an American for as long as you like, but if you don't tell me what I need to know soon, you are going to die."

"Murder," he said. "This is murder."

"I came here to question a known offender," I said. "Sometimes unfortunate things happen when known offenders get belligerent. You tried to hit me with a damn candlestick. My son has this mystery-solving board game, and half the time, the murder in that game is done with a candlestick. If we'd been in a conservatory when you came at me with that thing, I might have shit in my pants. Shooting you was really the only reasonable course of action."

"You pig," he said. "You jackbooted gestapo thug."

"You can spend as much time as you want insulting me," I said. "I ain't the one leaking all over the floor. But if you'd ever like to walk again, you should hurry up and tell me what Elijah is doing."

"You can't torture me into confessing to you. I'd rather bleed to death out of spite."

I showed him my gun.

"I don't think that's true," I said. Then I spun the cylinder, theatrically pulled back the hammer with my thumb, and pressed it against his forehead. "You're either going to tell me a story, or I will find other ways to amuse myself. It's not really a good idea to insult a jackbooted gestapo thug."

"How can you behave as you do, and still call yourself a Jew?" Fat tears were rolling down his cheeks.

"I could ask you the same question, you self-righteous, thieving hypocrite."

"I don't commit brutality against my own people."

"You ain't my people, Plotkin. I am nothing like you."

"And for that, I thank HaShem."

With a fairly elegant and practiced maneuver, I managed to light a cigarette without holstering the .357. "You want one of these?" I asked.

"I wish you wouldn't smoke in my house. My child sleeps here. You are putting my child at risk."

"Well, I wish there wasn't a Jewish bank robber organizing a Jewish gang in my city. If this scheme of yours goes pear-shaped, all of us are likely to be treated the way you and your friends deserve to be treated. Folks around here tend to discriminate indiscriminately. Seems to me, I ain't the only one here who is bad for the Jews. Seems to me you're the one putting my child at risk. So you might as well take this cigarette, because everything comes down to this, Ari: You might think you have God on your side, but you've got Smith and Wesson in your face. I am goddamn furious right now, and I will be perfectly happy to kill you over this. Do you believe me when I say I'll kill you?"

He looked up at me, and his eyes were brimming with tears. "I do believe it."

"Good for you. So, you understand the stakes: Either you're fixin' to talk, or you're fixin' to die."

He took the cigarette, and he talked.

19
1965

"When the *schvartzes* start burning things down, that's when we go into the bank," Plotkin said.

"Who are you working with?" I asked.

He gave me three familiar names; young Jewish men getting started on the wrong path. Kids in those days all wanted to be Meyer Lansky.

"How do you know the colored will riot?"

He grimaced. "Because they're *schvartzes*. Because it's inevitable."

That was information the department didn't have; we were still trying to forestall racial violence by meeting the Kluge demonstration with a show of force. I wondered if we were intimidating them or inciting them.

"You're going to break into the vault?" I asked.

"We're going to take everything."

"How?"

"We're going through the front door with guns."

"What about the alarm system?"

"That's the beauty of the plan. Nobody will answer the alarms; not for a while, anyway. The police response will be very slow. There will be robberies happening all over the city, and the streets will be mobbed with rioters. We'll be gone before any help arrives, and we will wear masks on our faces. When it's over, the *schvartzes* will take the blame."

Whoever had put Plotkin up to this had evidently not briefed him on any of the elaborate security measures Charles Greenfield had described to me. This was not the elegant plan I'd expected. "Elijah told you this?" I asked.

"His man." Plotkin described one of the slablike goons. "I've never seen Elijah."

"What's his role in the scheme?"

"Elijah's guy told us about the bank, explained how we can use the riots for cover, and pretty much worked out the whole plan for us. After the job's done, he's helping us to get away clean. His cut is a third of the take."

"How much do you expect to get out of the bank?"

"He said we could get ten thousand.

Maybe as much as fifteen." This was about five times as much as Greenfield said a robber could plausibly get from robbing the tellers' cages at his bank.

This Plotkin plot was half-assed. If these guys went through the front door, all they'd manage to do was set the alarm off, and then get themselves caught or maybe killed. There was no way this was the thing Elijah was planning. He must have been setting these kids up. But to what purpose? The alarm would lock down the vault, making it inaccessible to Elijah. Did he want the vault locked, for some reason?

This would require some thought.

In the meantime, there was work to do. I called in the paramedics to come save my perp's leg, and then I called for some patrol units to back me up when I went to fetch the coconspirators Plotkin had named. They were all at home, on account of the Sabbath, and they all went downtown quietly.

I stuck the three men in separate interrogation rooms and asked each of them a bunch of questions. At the end of the night, they all signed statements, confessing that they'd planned to rob the bank, but omitting any mention of Elijah.

I wasn't thrilled to have a gang of Jews locked up in Memphis for conspiracy to commit robbery, but their thwarted attempt at two-bit thuggery would be forgotten much faster than a successful $150,000 heist committed by a famous Jewish thief with a gang of Jewish accomplices and the assistance of corrupt Jewish police.

Just in case you think me hardhearted: I put in a phone call to the District Attorney for Ari and his crew, told him that those boys had cooperated fully, and suggested a lenient deal wouldn't be unreasonable. Given that they hadn't even got close to pulling off a robbery before they got caught, I figured it wouldn't take a whole lot of prison time to convince them to dedicate their future efforts to noncriminal enterprises.

The three accomplices each got four years of state time, and were eligible for parole after eighteen months. Plotkin was sentenced to seven years and served three, since he was the ringleader, and also, he assaulted me. He walked with a limp for the rest of his life.

While he was doing his time, though, his *frum* little wife had to go and get herself a job. After that, she was never as pliant or servile around the house as she had been before. His kid had some problems as well, and wound up pregnant by a goyish boyfriend when she was fifteen.

I think Plotkin may have blamed me for this misfortune, but if he'd gone in the front door of that bank, he'd have got himself twenty-five to life up at the federal farm, or else just got killed, and he wouldn't have even been able to give his daughter away at her shotgun wedding.

He made his choices, and they were his to live with. If you choose to be a scumbag, there are consequences. I feel like he should have been appreciative of my leniency. Asshole tried to hit me with a candlestick.

20
1965

Brian came home from services the next morning and told me that the rabbi had asked to speak with me. I didn't really have much to say to the rabbi, but after the Schulman incident, it seemed like I needed to extend the kid an olive branch, so, when the Sabbath ended at sunset, I drove to the shul to meet with the man.

Abramsky had been in Memphis for the better part of a year, but his office looked like a place somebody was still moving into. One wall of the room was covered with built-in bookshelves, and he'd filled half of them up, but cardboard boxes stuffed with books were still piled on the floor.

"Thank you for coming to speak with me today, Detective Schatz. I'll be with you in just a moment," he said. He was standing at the far side of a heavy wooden antique desk nearly as big as Charles Greenfield's, but dinged and worn where the bank manager's had been polished and sleek.

The chair behind the desk was inaccessible; walled off by banker's boxes full of papers, and the desk was mostly covered with stacks of mimeographs and notepads and manila folders overfilled with loose pages. The place was so stuffed with junk that the corner of the desk he was standing in front of was really the only patch of usable workspace left in the office.

With the index finger of his right hand, Abramsky kept track of his place on the page of a massive leather-bound Talmud. The book was huge; two feet by eighteen inches, if I had to guess the size of it, and the Hebrew print was so tiny that Abramsky had to squint to read it. The pages were tissue-thin, but the book was still about five inches thick, and, needless to say, it was all in Hebrew.

As he read, Abramsky scrawled right-to-left in cursive Hebrew script on a yellow legal pad with his left hand. His lips were moving as well, and I wondered if he was silently speaking the words he was reading, the words he was writing, or something else entirely.

I had no way of knowing what the hell he was reading or writing or saying, though, because, while I can sound out Hebrew words phonetically, I don't speak the language, and can't read it with any comprehension. So I busied myself by looking over his bookshelves.

He had all the expected siddurs and Tanakhs and the various Torah commentaries; huge books like the one he was reading, with gilt edges to the pages and gold-inlay on the covers.

I was surprised, however, to find a whole shelf of paperback detective novels: Raymond Chandler and Dashiell Hammett and Ross Macdonald and a collected volume of the works of Conan Doyle. And the spines looked cracked, so he'd probably really read them. Farther down the wall of bookshelves, I spotted what seemed to be the stuff he'd read in preparation for moving to the South: Faulkner and Twain and *To Kill a Mockingbird.*

He also had fifty copies of a book about Jewish views on death and mourning. I figured he must give a lot of those away to need so many; the synagogue had been around since the 1870s, and it was an aging congregation even in 1965. The hallway outside his office was covered with big, heavy memorial tablets. Each tablet had four columns, and each column had a hundred little plaques slotted into it. Each plaque was inscribed with the name of a deceased member of the congregation. Next to each name was a little light, like a white Christmas tree bulb. The lights had to be illuminated to commemorate *yahrtzeit;* the anniversary of each person's death. There were no switches for the bulbs; the only way to light them was to tighten them in their sockets, and the only way to shut them off was to unplug the whole rig, or unscrew the hot little bulbs individually, by hand. Somebody had to go up and down that hallway every week, tightening and loosening, so we'd know whose turn it was to be remembered.

I wondered if Abramsky had to deal with the bulbs himself, but I decided he probably didn't. That was the kind of thing the synagogue would hire a Negro to do.

Regardless, that hallway full of memorials and that shelf full of books about grieving suggested that this man's job was so depressing that it was probably a relief for him to teach bar mitzvah lessons to hyperactive twelve-year-olds. I'd much rather deal with a grisly, guts-out crime scene or even a stinking, bloated river-floater than spend an afternoon sitting in a hospital and praying with a person who was losing a fight against something terminal.

Abramsky completed whatever he was doing with his big, fancy book and deposited his notepad on top of a pile of similar notepads that were also covered in his sweat-smudged Hebrew script.

There were two old-looking leather chairs opposite the desk, which weren't totally covered in paper. He slid into one of them, and I cleared the mess off the other so I could sit as well. "Sorry about that," he said. "If I don't write down the thoughts and observations I have when I am studying, I will forget them later on. I'm sure you know how that is."

"Not really," I said, tapping the side of my head with my finger. "I mostly just keep everything up here."

"Then you're very fortunate, in that regard. Thank you for coming to see me today. I wanted to talk to you about your son." As he spoke, he leaned forward. He was a soft man, a thing with rounded corners, but he vibrated with weird energy. His hands were always moving; slashing the air to punctuate his speech or crawling across his body as he listened.

"Is Brian on pace to be ready for the big event?" I asked. Although we didn't adhere strictly to many of the traditions, we still attended the Orthodox synagogue, because my whole family was buried in the affiliated cemetery. So, at his bar mitzvah, my son would have to daven an entire Torah service in front of the assembled congregation. I didn't even want to think about what my mother would say if the kid screwed it up.

"Yes. He's doing very well. I think he is just memorizing his *haftarah,* and I'd prefer to see him read the Hebrew, but I'm confident he'll make you very proud, regardless."

"So, what's the problem?"

"Brian continues to be troubled by what he witnessed in front of the synagogue earlier this week. I have to say I'm troubled about it, also."

I clenched my fists. Things had been tense at home for weeks because of the ideas this prick had been putting into the kid's head. "I didn't give Paul Schulman and Ari Plotkin anything they didn't have coming to them."

"Plotkin? What happened to Plotkin?"

"I went over to his house last night, and I shot him."

It took Abramsky a moment to process this. "Is he — ?"

"In the hospital," I said. "And under arrest for conspiracy to rob a bank, and for assaulting a police officer. He won't be attending synagogue anytime soon."

Dismay registered on his face for a couple of seconds, but he tamped it down and blanked his expression. "I'm not unaware that some members of this congregation don't lead lives as morally upright as I might hope they would. But I don't consider it my place to judge them."

"No," I said. "It's my place to judge them. It's your place to chant with them in Hebrew so that they feel like they're right with God when they go out and steal food from the mouths of widows and orphans."

"And why is that such a personal affront to you, Baruch?"

"When your father's corpse turns up in a ditch on the side of the highway, you develop a little bit of a soft spot for the widows and the orphans."

He sort of shuddered when I said this, and I realized that it was new information to him. I really needed to stop blurting out whatever was on my mind. "Do you want to talk about that?" he asked.

"Hell no," I said. "Don't be ridiculous."

"Then let's talk about Brian: I don't feel it's appropriate for a rabbi to drive a wedge between a father and a son, so I found myself in the unenviable position of having to defend your conduct, Baruch. And that's why I felt I had to speak to you. Because I think somebody needs to speak with you."

"I'm here, ain't I? If you want to talk, go ahead."

"As you may be aware, the Torah portion for Brian's bar mitzvah is *parshah Vayera,* in which HaShem smites the corrupt cities of Sodom and Gomorrah."

"Sure, I know the story," I said. "They were sex fiends, and God killed them all."

"Well, Christian interpretations focus on the sexual aspects of the Sodomites' depravity, but there's more to it. The commentaries explain how the people of these cities were miserly and cruel. They wallowed in decadence while beggars starved in their streets. They were vicious to outsiders, using and exploiting and killing them for sport. And they were blasphemers as well; the passage about the Sodomites' lust for 'strange flesh' refers not to homosexual behavior, as is commonly believed, but to their unholy desire to rape God's angels."

"Bar mitzvah study has gotten weirder since I was a kid," I said.

"The Torah has been the same for five thousand years."

"I guess we just skipped over the parts about 'strange flesh,' then."

"Perhaps, but all of the Torah is sacred, and when you take pieces of it out of context, you lose sight of the thing as a whole."

"So, what's your point?"

"For their barbarity and brutality, HaShem determined that the people of Sodom and Gomorrah needed to burn. But Abraham pled for clemency, and HaShem agreed that if ten righteous men dwelt in Sodom, then He would spare the cities. So He sent his angels down to search, and the angels stayed in the home of Abraham's nephew Lot. But the people of Sodom learned of Lot's guests, and mobbed the house demanding that Lot turn over the angels. HaShem was appalled, and so the city was condemned. HaShem told Lot to take his family and flee, warning them to 'look not behind you' as they escaped the burning city. But Lot's wife disobeyed HaShem and she looked back, and when she did, she was turned into a pillar of salt. Some say that, by looking back, she revealed that she longed for the carnality and decadence of Sodom, and thus deserved to be purged along with the city. But many scholars believe that, when she beheld the glory and terror of HaShem's wrath, the sheer awe of it unmade her. When Brian and I discussed this, he said he believes Memphis has become like Sodom."

"He's not wrong," I said. "There's too much bad history, and too much bad blood here. We've heaped too many indignities upon the colored, and we've been doing it for far too long. The whole place could go up in flames any day now. And when it does, we'll deserve it as much as the Sodomites did."

"Brian told me he worries that you are like Lot's wife; that you've adopted the deviant values of a bigoted society and a repressive and brutal police force."

"He doesn't know what he's talking about. If I'm repressive and brutal, it's to keep the world off his back, and to shield him from some hard truths."

He leaned forward and put his hand on my arm. I flinched. I don't like it when people touch me. "I know this, and that is what I told him. I told him that you are not like Lot's wife. I told him that you are like HaShem's angels, prepared to bring justice to the deserving, but also looking for hope and redemption in a fallen city. It is right that a boy should honor his father, and so I felt obligated, as his teacher, to defend you to him. But I did not like having to say that, because I don't believe it was the truth."

I shook his hand off my arm and pulled my pack of Lucky Strikes out of my pocket.

I tapped it a couple of times against my palm and then shook a cigarette out.

"I'd prefer if you didn't smoke in here," Abramsky said. "The ventilation isn't great, and smells tend to linger."

I'd noticed the office was redolent of musty books and stale farts, but I'd been too polite to comment on it.

"Your preference is duly noted," I said, and I lit up anyway. "Say what you need to say, and then I'll get out of here before I stink the place up too much. And while you're talking, you can get me an ashtray."

"I haven't got an ashtray."

"That's fine. I can use an empty Coke can, or a glass with a little water in the bottom. Or, I guess I don't really need anything, if you don't want to get up. It ain't my carpet."

He got up, and dug a beige coffee mug out from under a pile of papers on his desk. He held it out to me, and I flicked my ash into it.

"Now, I don't believe you think of yourself as being like the angel," he said. "I think you see yourself as HaShem. But you are not HaShem. Only HaShem is HaShem. And I want you to keep in mind what happened to Lot's wife when she looked upon His wrath. I want you to keep in mind the harm that terrible justice can do, not only to those whom it is inflicted upon, but also to everyone in the general vicinity. Because, though Brian will become a man in the eyes of the Jewish people when he reads from the Torah at his bar mitzvah, you and I both know his childhood ended when he saw his father beat Paul Schulman to the ground in front of the synagogue. That's what you've got to live with, when you dispense wrath."

I gestured with the cigarette, and he offered me the coffee cup. I stubbed the butt out in the bottom of it.

"Did Brian believe what you told him about me?" I asked.

"I don't think so," he said. "He's smart. Smart people are hard to lie to."

I nodded. This was true. The kid knew his old man was no angel. "Thanks anyway, for your discretion," I said.

"And I'd urge you, in the future, to exercise yours," he said.

I had to laugh at that, but I don't think Abramsky understood why.

21
1965

The first thing I did Monday morning was pay a visit to the offices of Charles Greenfield. He kept me waiting until about half past ten, just because he could. His office had north-facing windows, and the sunlight piercing through the canopy of clouds that day, at that time, hit the room at the perfect angle to make Greenfield and his various accoutrements look kind of glorious. He sat on his deep leather throne, with the window behind him, and from my vantage point across the gleaming expanse of his desk, he appeared to be encircled by a luminous halo.

"I've arrested a gang of robbers who had plans to take down your bank," I said.

He didn't seem impressed. "If the problem is resolved, I don't see why you should waste any more of my time or yours by coming here to discuss it." As he said this, he gave me the kind of smirk that let me know he realized he'd wasted much more of my time than I had of his.

"The men I arrested intended to enter your bank through the front door and rob the tellers with guns. I believe they were unwitting dupes in a more elaborate scheme to rob your vault, and I am concerned that scheme has not been scuttled by the arrest of these conspirators. Your money may still be at risk."

He stroked his chin. "The instant those men entered with guns, a teller or a loan officer would trigger the alarms and the vault would have sealed. If that is the plan, it's not a very good one."

I lit a cigarette. "You told me last week that the alarm causes the vault to lock down until the end of a three-hour timer, and that even you cannot open the vault after the alarm is triggered."

"That's correct."

"It occurs to me that Elijah's plan to rob you involves, and even depends on you triggering the alarm and locking yourself out of the vault."

"I'm not sure I follow your logic."

Here, I leaned forward. "Are you familiar with 'The Adventure of the Red-Headed League'? It's a Sherlock Holmes story. A robber devised a plot to dig a tunnel into a bank vault from the basement of an adjoining building. If a thief cracked into your vault from above or below, or broke in through a wall, he could easily clean the place out in three hours. All he'd need to do is contrive an event to cause your staff to trigger the alarm, which would lock you out. The thief would be long gone before you could even get the door open and discover the theft."

"And what do you propose that I should do about this?" Greenfield asked. He had a kind of feral look in his eyes.

I'd seen a nature documentary about how solitary polar bears in the wild roam hundreds of miles looking for prey. When two of the males encountered each other, if they were attracted by the scent of a female in heat or a whale carcass rotting on the beach, they would fight viciously, sometimes leaving one of them seriously injured.

In this place, Charles Greenfield was the big bear, and his dominance went unquestioned. The men he kept around him, like his assistant, Riley Cartwright, were cringing, subservient types. Any outsiders who visited would likely be subdued by his size or his fine suit or his expensive furniture. This was a man who was used to being the master, and deeply resented people who tried to tell him what to do.

"I'm glad you asked, because I'm going to tell you what to do," I said. I didn't give a shit about his suit or his title or his office, and I wanted to make sure he knew it. The rotten whale-stink of this place was attracting new attention, and he was going to have to embrace that reality. In the last five days, I'd put two men into the hospital, which gave me a pretty good claim to being the biggest, meanest bear. "I think you should hire extra security, and station a guard inside the vault as well as on the doors. I think you should hire an engineer to check your foundation and the ceiling above, and make sure that no attempts have been made to breach the vault through any of those surfaces. I'd also urge you to reconsider moving the bulk of your excess cash someplace else, and to hire extra guards to escort the money to its destination."

Greenfield laughed. "Mr. Schatz, this is a bank. Do you know what a bank is?"

"I'm familiar with the general concept," I said.

"A bank is a place where people like me go to work every day next to a room filled with money. Do you know who would like to steal from a room filled with money?" He cocked his head curiously, but I just inhaled from my cigarette. This was clearly going to be the part where he got territorial and sprayed his polar bear piss all over everything. He let the silence start to feel uncomfortable, before he said: "Everyone, Detective. Everyone would steal from a bank if they thought they could. So, when you come in here and tell me that you think somebody wants to steal from me, you're not telling me something I am not already aware of. The reason banks are able to function when everyone would like to steal from them is that we make it very difficult to steal a lot of money from a bank. Nobody is tunneling into my vault. My vault is constructed from eighteen-inch walls of tempered steel sunk into a concrete foundation, and booby-trapped with a lot of alarm triggers. Do you know what kind of a tool you need to break through a two-foot-thick wall of concrete?"

"A sledgehammer?"

"A jackhammer, probably. There's only one way, really, to tunnel through concrete, and that's the noisy way. I'm sure we'd have noticed. I don't think any Sherlock Holmes shenanigans are taking place in my bank."

"Greenfield, I'm not trying to insult you, but I think there is real and credible information suggesting that a sophisticated criminal plans to steal the cash in your vault. I am advising you to take precautions."

"And what I have explained to you, Detective, repeatedly and at length, is that I have already taken every precaution reasonable. We have multiple layers of security. We have planned for every contingency. And, having done so, we are free to dedicate our time to doing our jobs and conducting our business, business which you are currently distracting me from."

"I appreciate that you are confident in your security," I said. "But this is an unusual threat that I believe requires an unusual response."

Greenfield did the thing where he squeezed his nose again. "You said you believe the men you arrested for plotting to rob my tellers were suckers Elijah was using as a distraction from his real plot, right?"

"Yes."

"Consider the possibility that they were being used not to distract you from a robbery on my vault, but a robbery on something else entirely unrelated to this bank."

"I've thought about that. But the bank is the most likely target I am aware of, and if he's out to steal something else, I have no idea what it might be. I've been unable to identify any other targets related to the

Kluge strike that are valuable enough to attract his attention."

"That isn't my problem."

"Unless I'm right, and he's after your vault."

"Well, then, you've informed me of the risk. I shall take your suggestions under advisement. So you've done everything you can. Now, if you'll excuse me, I must devote my attention to less fanciful matters."

"Prick."

"Excuse me?"

"Nothing. I didn't say anything. Thank you very much for your time."

I left because I couldn't think of anything else to say. I still didn't intend to let Elijah rob the bank, but if he somehow pulled it off, I figured it couldn't happen to a nicer guy than Charles Greenfield.

22
1965

I left Greenfield's office through its heavy wood double doors, passed the desks of his two busy secretaries, and then I was standing in front of the elevator bank; he had taken a whole wing of the office suite for himself, and then knocked most of the walls out to make one big sunny cathedral in which to worship himself. Must have been nice.

I pushed the button to take me down to the bank's grand lobby on the ground floor; a vast, shimmering cavern full of pink limestone columns running from the pink limestone floor to the arched, vaulted pink-limestone ceiling.

As I exited the elevator, the brass tellers' cages were to my left, and, to my right was a reception area for clients awaiting appointments with loan officers and other upstairs officials.

And of course, that's where Elijah was;

sitting in a leather chair, drinking coffee and reading a newspaper.

I glanced around the lobby; nothing seemed out of the ordinary. A few people were conducting business with the tellers, but the place was mostly empty. As Greenfield had told me, the nearby strike had scared away most of the bank's business.

I didn't hear any alarms, and I didn't see any of Elijah's beefy henchmen, and I didn't see any Jewish criminals waving guns at the tellers. But that didn't mean the robbery wasn't happening right in front of me.

I went and sat in the chair next to Elijah's.

"What are you doing here?" I asked.

He showed me his Auschwitz smile. "Would you believe me if I told you I was applying for a small business loan?"

The nerve of this guy.

"You're under arrest," I said. "We're gonna stand up, and we're going to walk out of here. If you attempt to resist, I will subdue you with force."

He sucked his lips around the broken stubs of his teeth. "Not sure that's a good idea," he said. "You don't know what's waiting for you outside."

The only public entrance to the bank was a single set of revolving glass doors. I'd never seen Elijah without his oversized accomplices before, and it stood to reason that if they weren't in here, they might be out there. There was a good chance I hadn't just coincidentally run into Elijah in the lobby of the bank he was planning to rob. If he had set this encounter up, he doubtless had his exit planned, and he had the advantage.

"I'd be walking face-first into a buzz saw," I said.

"I actually didn't arrange for there to be a buzz saw, but you'd definitely be riddled with bullets on the sidewalk." He was chirping now, and I didn't appreciate it.

This was a chess game, and my adversary had the next several moves planned out. What could I do?

I considered the loading door. I could potentially bundle him out that way and sneak past his crew.

"I derive a great deal of amusement from the way your face looks when you're thinking really hard," Elijah said. "Right now, you're wondering whether you can take me out through the loading door."

To do that I'd have to walk him right past the vault. I'd have to open the security cage in the hallway beyond. Could that be done without disabling the alarm? I'd have to un-bar the side door, and I didn't know that the alley beyond was clear. If his crew were waiting there, that might be their way inside. With the security cage unlocked, they could walk right into the vault.

There was clearly some reason he was here; clearly some reason he was stringing me along. Maybe that was it. Maybe that was the plan for the robbery. I wasn't willing to be their dupe.

"I don't think you're going to try to take me out that way," he said. "So there are two doors and you can't take me out of either of them. And do you really, in your heart of hearts, want to arrest me, Baruch?"

He folded his newspaper and took a sip from his coffee cup.

I didn't want to arrest him. I wanted to kill him, or run him out of town. I did not want him to sit down in an interrogation room and start talking. He stood by and watched while his mother was shot in the head. He stood by and waited, while his father was beaten to death. He set in motion the chain of events that caused a Nazi guard to shoot twenty Jews on his work detail. And he didn't seem too torn up about any of it. Some people truck their baggage around, and others travel light. This man was ruthless and self-interested; the sort who could burn every bridge he'd ever

216

crossed and never look back.

How many jobs had he pulled? Ten? Fifteen? There could be a corrupt Jewish cop involved in every single one of those schemes. If he was willing to expose them all, some ambitious twerp in the U.S. Attorney's office would probably give him immunity from prosecution for his crimes. Catching a bank robber was a modest professional accomplishment for a law enforcement official, but exposing a web of police corruption was the kind of thing that made people's careers, as long as it wasn't a web of Jewish corruption, and the people doing the exposing weren't Jewish.

"You've got no involvement in my schemes, and yet, if they were revealed — if I talked — you'd be destroyed. Inequitable, isn't it, Baruch?"

"Goddamnit."

"If your police department functioned the way it ought to, you could call for backup, and a dozen officers would arrive within minutes to overwhelm any support I might have waiting outside. But you can't call anyone, because you're afraid to let your friends know what I'm up to."

"I could kill you right here," I said.

He chirped again. "Can you? Your institutions have certainly tolerated your thuggish excesses in the past. But the violence they allow you to commit against addicts and deviants and the underclass tends to re-inforce and support the prevailing social order. Shooting an unarmed, well-dressed white man in a bank disrupts that order. It's bad for business, Baruch, and they won't let you be bad for business. When we met, I said you reminded me of a dog, and you are, indeed, a useful working animal. But all dogs meet the same fate when they take to biting people."

He was probably right

"You are all alone, Baruch, and you can't stop me. You are going to let me walk out of here."

But there was a hitch in his voice; the tini-est hint of uncertainty. It was enough to make me reevaluate the entire situation.

I took a long, hard look at Elijah. I saw a weasely little crook, scared and small and hiding behind his fifty-cent words and his fake European charm. He thought every-thing belonged to him. He thought he could waltz into my city, help himself to $150,000, and leave me to clean up the mess.

But he didn't understand what he was dealing with. I wasn't the dutiful servant of a corrupt agency, like my son thought I was. And Abramsky was right that I wasn't the angel, looking for somebody to redeem. I certainly wasn't the bumbling peon Greenfield seemed to believe I was.

I was a towering column of smoke rising above the desert. I was molten brimstone raining on the wicked. I was darkness blotting the sun and I was blood in the water. I was frogs and locusts and savage beasts. I was a razor blade sewn into a hemline.

I looked at the revolving door, and then I looked around the lobby, and I knew what I was going to do.

Elijah was smiling at me, and I smiled right back at him.

Everything that had seemed so complex was suddenly clear. He was a problem, and I was a solution. He was a nail, and I was a hammer. This was a man I could break six different ways, using only my hands.

"I must have really messed things up for you, arresting Plotkin and those boys," I said. "You weren't even here looking for me, were you? If you were expecting to see me, you never would have come without your buddies to back you up. You wouldn't set up a confrontation here, inside the bank you're planning to rob. Somebody might remember your face, if they saw us arguing. I have caught you casing the bank, trying to put a new plan together."

"Don't be ridiculous," he said. "Plotkin doesn't matter." But the quaver in his voice was now more pronounced. He was afraid of me, and he was right to be afraid.

"I don't think there's anybody waiting outside. I think I could throw handcuffs on you and march you right out that door, and nobody would stop me."

"You won't take that risk," he said. "And you don't want to arrest me."

He wasn't smiling anymore. I still was.

"You're right, I don't want to arrest you, so I am going to let you go, free and clear," I said. "But first, you and I are going to go to the men's room for a minute."

I stood up and punched him in the stomach, hard enough to knock the wind out of him. The door to the men's toilet was on the same wall as the elevator, about six paces directly behind where Elijah was sitting. I grabbed him by the arm and dragged him through it. He was too stunned to resist, and nobody seemed to notice.

Even the bathrooms in Charles Greenfield's bank were fancy. The walls and floor were paneled with slabs of pink limestone, like the lobby outside. The fixtures all looked new and clean, and the mirrors above the sink were framed in brass. The line of urinals inside was unoccupied, and the toilet stalls were all empty. This was expected, since I hadn't seen anyone enter or leave the men's room the entire time I had been sitting in the lobby.

I slammed Elijah against the stone wall, hard enough to bounce his forehead off it, which kept him dazed long enough for me to produce from underneath my jacket the wrath of God, wrapped in soft leather and mounted on a coil of stiff spring. I whacked his knee with the blackjack, hard enough that it made a noise like shattering ceramic. Before he collapsed, I grabbed him by the lapels of his tailored suit jacket and clapped a hand against his mouth to keep him from screaming.

"Like I told you, I'll let you walk out of here," I said. "But you're gonna walk real slow, and every step you take is going to hurt like a son of a bitch. You won't be making any quick getaways on foot for a while, and you won't be sneaking up on people, either."

I pressed his right hand against the wall of the bathroom, splayed out his long pianist's fingers, and then bounced the lead weight off it so hard that the blow left a spiderweb pattern of hairline cracks in the stone panel underneath.

"I hope you weren't intending to break

open any safes with that hand," I said. "It won't be much good for delicate tasks. At least, not anytime soon."

Then I clubbed him in the gut as hard as I could; the lead weight hit him right above the navel, and the follow-through carried the blow up to his sternum. He vomited all over the floor. When I let go of him, Elijah collapsed into the puddle of his own sick and started writhing around, so I flailed at his legs with the blackjack and hit his back and his chest a couple of times for good measure.

Then I hung the club from my belt, stepped over the damp, stinking pile that had once been a proud, smug man, and washed my hands at the sink.

"I told you not to pull any jobs in my town, and you didn't listen, and now look at what has happened to you," I said. "Was this part of your plan?"

He sort of gurgled.

"It seems I've finally found a way to get you to stop talking," I said. "You probably feel like you're about to die, but you're not. A truncheon is considered one of the more humane ways to subdue a perpetrator. The damage it does is mostly to soft tissue. It hurts, but it heals. Except for the hand. If I were you, I'd have the hand looked at."

He grunted something unintelligible.

"I can't understand what you're saying, but I assume you're thanking me for my restraint," I said. "I certainly could have hurt you a lot worse. I didn't, because I want you fit to travel. So, when you manage to pick yourself up off the floor, do the prudent thing and put some distance between yourself and Memphis. You may think this was a beating I just gave you, but really, it was a warning. Take heed, because I don't warn anyone twice. The next time I see you, I am going to kill you."

I shook my hands dry, lit a cigarette, and dropped the burning match on the floor next to Elijah. Then I stepped over him again and walked out of the bathroom and across the lobby. The echoes of my leather soles against the pink limestone floor sounded to me like cannon fire.

"You can't smoke in here, sir," said a guard who hadn't noticed me dragging a man into the toilet, but immediately spotted my cigarette.

"Yes, I can," I said. "Watch me."

And since I was on my way out the revolving front door anyway, that's what he did.

Outside, I saw no signs of the beefy henchmen. I pulled my handgun out of its shoulder holster and edged around the side of the building to check the alley by the loading door, but there was nobody there, either.

I had to give Elijah credit; he'd almost bluffed me. But almost only counts for horseshoes and hand grenades.

Something I Don't Want to Forget:

I'd developed a habit of watching a talk program about movies before my nap on Wednesday afternoons. It was less shouty than Fox News, and if I turned on the animal shows, I'd sit and watch them until dinnertime without falling asleep. The show occasionally featured actors and directors, but most of the guests were critics and academics. I hadn't seen most of the movies they talked about; I hadn't been to a theater in a couple of decades. Since these people weren't natural TV talkers, they spoke softly and looked weird, and I appreciated these characteristics.

The host was my favorite person on television. He was an exceptionally florid man with a Silly Putty face, and he looked like he hadn't bought any new clothes since he was thirty pounds lighter, so his head splooged up out of his too-tight shirt collar like toothpaste coming out of a tube. When he got excited, he wobbled back and forth, and I believed, if I watched the show long enough, I'd eventually get to see him tip over.

"So, we've seen a rise in the popularity of gritty sorts of characters and antiheroes," he said. "Why do you think that is?"

The guest was a critic from the Internet; a

mousy-haired pinheaded woman with squinty eyes and a broad wet mouth that seemed like it was much too big for her scrunched-up little face.

"Antiheroes are nothing new. Many of the figures of the Classical and Norse mythological traditions had significant flaws that modern audiences would consider antiheroic. Milton published *Paradise Lost,* starring a sympathetic Satan, in 1667. And of course, Nabokov wrote *Lolita* from the perspective of the odious Humbert Humbert, and *The Godfather* cleaned up at the Academy Awards in 1972. These are all antecedents to the sort of characters you see on contemporary programs like *Breaking Bad* or *The Sopranos.*"

I liked watching her. When she was busy concentrating on whatever the hell it was she was saying, it seemed like she forgot to swallow, so as she talked at length, her mouth was slowly filling with saliva. This had potential to develop into something interesting.

"The traditional heroic figure represents the establishment," she continued. "He's the new marshal bringing the law to an unincorporated Western town, or the superhero foiling some villain's plot for world domination, or the tough cop stamping out

crime in his city. He stands for the perpetu-
ation of the status quo and the continuity of
the existing power structure, often against
antagonists who are not unambiguously evil,
but rather, harbor contrary values to those
of the prevailing society, or who envision a
different kind of social hierarchy."

The host had grown progressively wob-
blier as she spoke, and he finally piped up
to interject: "And you think heroes like that
are out of fashion these days?"

This gave the Internet woman a chance to
swallow, which disappointed me terribly. I
was rooting for the dam to burst.

She said: "I think, in times like this, the
status quo becomes less persuasive. In the
early 1970s, the country was at the end of
more than a decade of civil rights strife, the
war in Vietnam was in full swing, and the
presidency was mired in scandal. The audience, at that time, was prepared to embrace
Vito Corleone, who responded to an ossi-
fied and exclusionary power structure and
widespread anti-immigrant bigotry by building an empire outside the boundaries of the
law.

"The same thing is happening again today.
The status quo and the establishment seem
less noble after eight years of the Bush
administration and seven years of endless

war and the Wall Street crash and the banking- and auto-industry bailouts, I think. We feel powerless against greater social forces, and so we're prepared to root for a somebody like a put-upon science teacher who reinvents himself as a drug lord."

"And what happens to our more traditional heroes in the meantime?" the host asked.

She sucked back the rolling wad of spit before it spilled over her bottom lip, and swallowed again. I cursed at the screen.

"They become dirtier. James Bond is the perpetrator of secret government assassinations. Batman is a white millionaire who goes out at night in a rubber sex-suit to beat up the urban underclass. That Western sheriff, bringing the law to some border town, is just taming the place so the railroad tycoons or the mining barons can take it from the frontiersmen and prospectors who staked it out first, and that supercop is starting to look like the boot of the elites on everyone else's neck."

I gave up on the program, and changed the channel. She wasn't going to drool all over herself, and she wasn't going to convince me to accept her moral equivalencies.

The film critics and professors on television often say that every bad guy thinks he's the good guy. That's maybe the case in comic books and dime-store novels, but the truth is that a good two-thirds of your violent criminals are too stupid to think at all.

They're not really moral agents choosing to do wrong; they're simply acting on impulses, motivated by their basest desires for drugs and sex. They're unable to appreciate the consequences of their actions, either for themselves or for the people they hurt. They're nothing but vicious animals. That's not a racial thing, either; it's true of the whites just as much as the colored.

Most of the rest are what psychologists might call sociopaths; the ones who are smart enough to know better, but broken enough not to care.

Really, it's only a tiny minority among your criminal types who bother to try to rationalize or justify their behavior, or to ground their crimes in any sort of principle. You don't meet many like Elijah over the course of a police career.

But equivocations like Elijah's are always too shabby to stand up to scrutiny, and men like him are not really much different from other thieves and murderers; when you strip away the bullshit, all they're doing is hurting other people for selfish reasons.

And I don't know much about heroes and antiheroes, but if you haven't been hurt by some thug or psycho or outlaw philosopher recently, it's probably because somebody like me got to them before they got to you.

23
2009

My mind slid into semiconsciousness from out of a whirling phantasmagoria of nightmares. The first thing I became aware of was rhythmic beeping, with incomprehensible static noise behind it. The beeping filled me with deep instinctive panic, and it took me more than a moment to recognize the sound as belonging to hospital machines; to a cardiac monitor.

I tried to look around, but all I could see was darkness. I realized this was because my eyes were closed. I tried to open them, but could not summon the strength. I couldn't move my arms, either, but I could feel the cool, oppressive weight of a bedsheet on my bare legs, so I figured my inability to move was a drug thing rather than a spinal thing.

Now the noise behind the beeping was congealing into voices, and I slowly began to understand the words.

". . . sent her home to have a shower and some rest. She was here all night."

"Don't know how she's put up with him for so long."

"Can't believe he was in another shoot-out. Does anyone know what it was about?"

"The policeman he was riding with is worse off, I hear."

"You really didn't need to fly in."

"Why isn't he awake yet?" I recognized my son's voice. I was glad he was there. It seemed like I hadn't talked to him in a long time. Why was that?

"They had him under sedation. They were worried about a brain bleed, but the MRI came back clean. Apparently, he was just in shock, and he broke his nose. They had to transfuse him, which knocked out his blood thinners, so they're worried about clots. Otherwise, he should be okay."

I was sedated. That was why my limbs felt so heavy; why it felt like wading through dense mud just to force my brain to think.

"Well, I wanted to be down here, regardless. I'm always expecting that phone call about him."

"But you're missing work at your new job."

"I'm a summer associate at a New York law firm; they understand the concept of a family emergency, and I think they'll be able to live without me for a day or two. The clients won't even let them staff me on the real matters, so my assignments are mostly make-work, anyway. Today, I'm missing a three-hour lunch, a partner giving a group lecture about negotiation tactics, and an open-bar cocktail event."

"But what happens if they don't offer you a full-time job?"

"That's a pretty fucking inappropriate question, Mom."

Okay, this wasn't my son; it was my grandson, William, who was now wearing thousand-dollar suits to his office in a Manhattan skyscraper, but still let everybody call him Tequila Schatz. I wanted to tell him to watch his goddamn language, but I couldn't quite force my jaw to move. My tongue felt dry and sticky and heavy in my mouth.

"It just keeps me up at night thinking about you in that city, and the decisions you make," my daughter-in-law said. "There always seems to be something important you're not taking care of."

"Look, I don't really want to have this conversation right now."

"You never want to have this conversation."

Where was Brian? Oh, God.

When I'm awake, I can push my rage and fear and grief down into someplace where I don't have to think about it, but when I dream, it comes back up on me like bad Mexican food.

Every time I wake up, I briefly linger between there and here, and then I push through the curtain, and the weight of everything I've lost comes crashing down on me, and I shatter. I thought maybe I wouldn't have dreamed under sedation, with my brain and my heart slowed down and pickled in chemicals. But I must have. Coming out of it, with my mind spinning in druggy half-speed, the whole awful process took longer, like slowly peeling a sticky bandage off a crusty wound.

It's no wonder so many folks stop remembering things as they get older, when memory serves no purpose except to make old pain fresh again. It's no wonder people stop getting out of bed. What's out there in the world, except for scrambled eggs and disappointment?

On the other hand, I really wanted some scrambled eggs; I hadn't eaten for quite some time. I also wanted a cigarette.

I tried to figure out how long I'd been unconscious. There was an oxygen tube running to my nose, but I didn't have a feeding tube down my throat, so I'd been out for hours, rather than days, which meant there might still be some slim hope of getting Elijah back before his kidnappers murdered him.

If William had gotten a standby ticket on the first plane out of New York, he could have been in my hospital room six hours after the accident. But it had probably been longer. Rose might not have called my daughter-in-law, Fran, right away, and Fran might not have immediately called William. He might not have been able to get a direct flight.

If they'd sent Rose home to shower and change, that probably meant she'd been here overnight, which probably meant that Elijah had been in the hands of his kidnappers for between sixteen and twenty hours. The fact that I was able to maintain this train of thought, at least, was a good sign. The drugs were wearing off.

My daughter-in-law said: "I get so mad at him when I think about what he's put her through. I sometimes worry about what will happen if she dies before he does."

"He's at that place. Won't they take care of him?"

"Assisted living is for people who can

mostly take care of themselves. I don't think he can, anymore, and in a year or so, as the Alzheimer's progresses, he's just going to get worse."

"It's not Alzheimer's. He says he might have mild cognitive something-or-other."

"You've spent a fair amount of time with him recently. What do you think?"

"I've noticed he's starting to sort of go downhill. He seems angry for no reason sometimes. And a little confused, I guess."

"She seems tired."

"She's been sitting up in the hospital all night."

"No. She seems tired all the time. She seems like she's tired of everything."

I couldn't do much more than twitch my hands, and my eyelids were still stuck together. But my arms and legs were starting to get that pins-and-needles feel, instead of just being numb.

"Valhalla won't be able to deal with his temper, without her to calm him down. Do you think they'll make sure he eats and watch while he takes his pills, and all the things she does? He'll need full-time nursing care, and I don't think he'd be able to tolerate having those people around all the time."

"When you say 'those people,' do you

mean — ?"

"You know what I mean."

"Water, goddamnit," I said.

"Oh, shit. He's awake."

24
2009

I was propped up in my adjustable hospital bed, sucking on ice chips, and I was feeling very anxious, because Elijah was probably off being murdered someplace. Since I didn't like Elijah, this shouldn't have bothered me so much, but I felt personally offended by his murder because the man had been kidnapped despite my firm objection into Clarence's face.

I had a plaster splint stuck on my busted schnoz. It pinched a little, and made a whistling noise every time I inhaled, and there was an itch underneath it that was driving me nuts.

My grandson was sitting in a chair next to my hospital bed looking at me like he was staring into a coffin, which wasn't improving my mood much. He was dressed in a suit and tie, which meant he'd come here straight from the airport. He looked masculine, and almost intimidating dressed like that. It set me on edge. I still thought of him as a child.

When he was little, I used to make William shake hands with me, and then I'd crush his little paw in mine, rolling the knuckles between my fingers. I couldn't do that anymore. His forearms were like steel bands.

He said he worked out five days a week, for seventy-five minutes at a time, and saw a trainer three times a month. I'd seen him exercise when he was home from school, and he did his routine at the Jewish Community Center gym. His workouts were not like my trips to see Cloudy-ah; he ran against resistance on the elliptical trainer for an hour at a time, and came off the machine so drenched in sweat, he looked like he'd just been baptized.

Despite his efforts, there were still twenty or thirty pounds of excess chub hanging on his squat frame; when I hugged him, his chest felt solid, but I could have grabbed on to handfuls of him. The boy liked to eat.

Sometimes he'd call up, just to tell his grandmother and me about some weird New York restaurant he was at. He'd go to a Japanese place and eat sushi. He liked a Vietnamese oxtail soup called "fug." He'd try the beef bull-googly bippity-boppity at a

Korean barbecue restaurant that made him cook his own meat, or he'd have chicken tickers Marsala with sag veneers and Narnia bread at an Indian place.

Stranger still: He called once to tell us that he was eating at a restaurant where the food was "influenced by the flavors and textures of traditional Moroccan street cuisine."

"Do you need to get some kind of vaccination before you go eat at a joint like that?" I'd asked.

"Very funny."

"Is it expensive?"

"No, it's really quite reasonable. Small plates cost twelve to fourteen dollars. Entrées are mostly between twenty-six and thirty-four. Sangria is only thirty bucks a pitcher."

"The Moroccans must be doing really well these days."

After twenty hours unconscious, I wouldn't have minded some Moroccan street cuisine, though, and I might have paid thirty bucks for sangria if they'd let me drink it straight from the pitcher. I hated goddamn ice chips. I figured the nurse was probably right that I wouldn't be able to keep anything down if I swallowed it too quickly, but I was thirsty, and the ice wasn't helping. I hate hospitals.

"What's happening with Elijah?" I asked. "Have they found him yet?"

"I don't know who Elijah is," my grandson said. I could tell immediately that he didn't believe there was any Elijah. "You were riding in a car with your friend Andre Price, the police detective. Do you remember Andre?"

"Yes, I remember Andre," I said. "How is he doing?"

"Not well, but he's alive. They've got him in a medically induced coma. He had a serious head injury, and there's some swelling that they're trying to bring down."

"We had a man called Elijah in the backseat of the car. He's a bank robber responsible for crimes that have been unsolved for fifty years. He was turning himself in. The men who hit us kidnapped him when they fled the scene."

"Nobody has mentioned anything like that. The police told us they believe Price was the target of the attack, because of a drug murder he's been investigating. I think you might be a little confused."

The police didn't even know about Elijah. That was the problem with being an invisible ghost: When you went missing, nobody looked for you. Odds were that he was already dead. I told him, if he was killed, I would "rain vengeance" on his enemies. I didn't want to have to go and do that.

"I guess I need to talk to the police," I said.

He nodded. "They want to talk to you. We've been telling them that you need to rest."

"I think I've rested long enough."

My grandson left the room, and came in ninety seconds later with a tall black guy who had a detective's shield clipped to his belt.

"I'm Rutledge," he said. "Narcotics." He was maybe forty-five and his hair was turning gray at the temples. He had the demeanor of somebody important. "I've heard a lot about you, and based on what I saw today, I guess a lot of it is true."

He turned toward Tequila and crossed his arms in a way that said he wanted to speak to me in private. Tequila nodded to show he recognized the gesture, and then he sat down in the chair next to my bed, to show he didn't give a shit. Apparently, he'd progressed to the point in his big-city lawyer education where he no longer felt intimidated by figures of authority. I was very proud of him. Everyone should be fortunate enough to live to see their grandchildren become stuck-up and entitled.

When it was clear Tequila wasn't going anywhere, Rutledge, Narcotics, scratched his chin for a minute, and then decided he could say what he wanted to say in front of my grandson. "I want to assure you that we are going to get these guys," he said. "Things have been bad the past couple of years. The city is hard up, and we've had fewer bodies and less overtime to throw at some of these problems. I'm not going to pretend we haven't lost ground. But this attack on a police detective in broad daylight, in the middle of the street, has really woken us up. Price was one of our best, and you've got a lot of fans in the department. I think the boys see you as kind of a mascot."

"You have no idea how gratifying it is for me to hear that," I said. It wasn't good that he was talking about Andre in the past tense. What had happened to him was kind of my fault.

Rutledge continued: "People are angry about this, and fired up. The coffers are open, and, with the full backing of the City of Memphis and Shelby County, we are rolling everything we can behind the largest drug interdiction operation I've seen in twenty years on the force. Our federal friends are pitching in as well. The U.S. Attorney is pursuing charges against street pushers that he would never have bothered with before, and guys who would have kept their mouths shut and served state time are lining up to snitch when the FBI threatens them with federal mandatory minimum drug sentences. It's shock and awe out there in the streets, Buck."

I nodded. All those men and unlimited overtime, and a spirit of cooperation with the federal government, and nobody was looking for Elijah.

"Who were the kids I shot?" I asked.

"Clarence O'Donnell, age twenty-two. According to the report, paramedics attempted resuscitation, but I doubt they tried very hard, considering his brains were splattered all over the street. Pronounced dead at the scene, obviously. He just got out of prison a couple of months ago; he was caught trafficking teenage prostitutes, and pled guilty to assault and false imprisonment. He did eighteen months for it, against a three-year sentence. I've got a daughter, Mr. Schatz, so I've got to say: If I were you, I wouldn't feel too bad about shooting Mr. O'Donnell."

"I've never felt bad about shooting anyone," I said.

He laughed. "You wouldn't, would you? The second one is Jacquarius Madison, age twenty. Couple of minor juvenile offenses. Served probation. Graduated high school. He was a student at Tennessee Tech until last fall. Guess he got mixed up with some of the wrong people."

"Has he said anything yet?" I asked.

"Shortly after we arrested him, a slick-looking sharkskin lawyer showed up and said he was Madison's counsel. Madison talked to him for five minutes, and then sent the guy away and asked for a court-appointed attorney."

"Why would he do that?" I asked.

"I know this one," Tequila said. I think he might have actually raised his hand and jumped up out of his seat a little. "The first lawyer was mobbed up; sent by the outfit that attacked the car. Madison didn't want that lawyer, because he plans to cut a deal that involves informing on those guys."

"That would be my guess as well," said Rutledge. "But after he talked to the court-appointed guy, Madison refused to talk to us again. Something the lawyer said must have scared him."

Had the people who took Elijah managed to bribe or intimidate the court-appointed lawyer? How could they have gotten to him so quickly? How could they have even found out what lawyer had taken on the case? Were these people omniscient? I needed to find out what I was up against.

"I want to talk to Madison," I said.

"I don't think that's a good idea," Tequila said. "A judge wouldn't think it was very appropriate for you to talk to him, especially without his lawyer present. It could be used to throw his statement out later."

I reached over and grasped his wrist as hard as I could. "I want to apologize to the kid, for blowing his leg apart," I said.

"I thought you never felt bad about shooting people," Rutledge said.

I shrugged. "Jesus. That's horrible. I'm pretty sure I never said that. That doesn't sound like something I'd say at all."

Rutledge, Narcotics, looked over to Tequila for some sort of backup or confirmation. Tequila sat there silently, and gave him nothing.

"Madison is still here in the hospital," Rutledge said. "He's scheduled for another surgery tomorrow, to try to put his knee back together. But I'm not sure what purpose it would serve for you to speak with him."

"I was a cop for thirty years," I told him. "I understand why you're worried, but I am not going to compromise your investigation. I just want to talk to the kid for a couple of minutes."

"Even if I refuse, you're going to go looking for him anyway, ain't you?"

"If he's still in the hospital? Damn near certainly."

"Then I guess you have my permission, since you don't need it. I know what happens to people who think they can stop you."

25
2009

Rutledge, Narcotics, gave me directions to Jacquarius Madison's hospital room, and I allowed Tequila to help me out of the bed and into a wheelchair. Then I left the two of them to babysit each other while I went to find the kid I'd shot.

Because of my age, I was admitted to the MED's geriatric intensive care unit, a sad white hallway with a bleach-on-piss smell. The staff had all the levity and good cheer one might expect from people who had watched someone die before lunch, and would watch someone else die before quitting time.

When you get to be my age, visits to the geriatric intensive care ward carry a special significance, because you have to assume that it's the place you're going to die. For an eighty-eight-year-old in failing health, there are really only two ways not to die in the geriatric intensive care ward: The first is to die so fast that the paramedics can't get you to the MED in time, and the second is to die so slowly that they ship you to hospice.

As soon as I wheeled myself off that hallway, the air somehow seemed lighter, although it still smelled like piss, because hospitals always smell like piss.

I got onto the elevator, and then couldn't remember what floor I was supposed to go to, so I picked one at random, wheeled myself down to the nearest nurse's station, and asked for help. The nurse told me she couldn't look up Madison's room number, so I decided to go back to my room to find Rutledge, and ask him to write the directions down. But when I got back onto the elevator, I couldn't remember what floor the geriatric intensive care ward was on. I was too embarrassed to ask the nurses to help me, so I pushed all the buttons, and peeked out every time the door opened until I found the right place.

When I told Rutledge I got lost, he laughed at me, and Tequila offered to take me to Madison, which I thought was a little bit condescending. I found one of my notebooks and just wrote the directions myself, because I couldn't stomach the indignity of letting my grandson wheel me down the hallway like some kind of invalid.

By the time I got to the right room, my chest was damp with sweat and my arms were tired from pushing the chair. I really didn't have time to sleep if I wanted to recover Elijah alive, but I was probably going to need a nap pretty soon.

Jacquarius Madison was not happy to see me, and he probably wasn't happy about being handcuffed to a bed, or being shot in the leg. So he was, all around, having a pretty bad day.

"Do your friends call you Jacquarius?" I asked.

"They call me Jacques."

"Like the strap?"

"You're real funny, old man," he said in a way that made it clear he didn't think I was very funny at all. "What do you want?"

"For starters, Jockstrap, it would be nice if you thanked me," I said.

"Thank you? For what? I ain't never going to walk right again, because of you."

A good orthopedic surgeon can fix a leg right up, either by fitting broken bones back together with pins, or by replacing the joint with an artificial implant. But I don't guess Jacques's line of work provided him with good health insurance. If you don't get the right kind of medical care, the ligaments can heal wrong, and the bones can fuse improperly, and you end up with a leg that won't bend.

To walk with an injury like that, you got to rotate the leg from the hip every time you take a step, or else you have to just favor the good foot and drag the bad one along. It ain't a great way to get around.

"I could have shot you in the head, like I shot your friend Clarence," I said.

"Clarence wasn't my friend. He was my cousin."

"Well, I did what I had to do, but I'm sorry for your loss."

"You don't look real sorry. But it's okay. I didn't really like him that much, anyway."

"I still could have shot you in the head."

"Well, if I'd taken the piece out his hand, I could have shot you before you ever managed to get the gun from the cop's holster."

I thought about it for a minute, trying to test that claim against my foggy recollection of the previous day's events. I decided what he was saying might have been true.

"So maybe we both ought to thank each other."

"I'm the one cuffed to a bed and all shot up. I ain't feeling real thankful. I'm feeling like I want to get some painkillers in me, and then go to sleep, so tell me what you want. I ain't in any mood for bullshit."

"I need information."

"Well, I got some information, and all I wanted to do was snitch. I was ready to sing like Beyoncé for y'all."

It was like Tequila had told me: He'd sent away his gangster-lawyer and brought in the court-appointed defense lawyer so he could sell out his coconspirators. But then he'd shut up. I asked him why.

"There wasn't a deal on the table," he said. "I told everything to the lawyer. He says the cops want information they can use to secure convictions."

"And your information won't secure any convictions?"

"Not if the guys I inform on get themselves killed before they get themselves arrested," Jacques said. "These dudes were desperate, and in serious trouble, and that was before what happened yesterday. Now every cop in the city is after them, and itchy on they trigger fingers. Ain't none of those dumb shits got good odds on making it through tomorrow alive. If I just give up the dirt on dead people I've been associated with, the lawyer says I ain't snitching; I'm giving a confession. So he told me to shut up and hope somebody important gets taken alive, so I can rat on 'em."

This all seemed sensible; prosecutors won't offer lenient deals or immunity for testimony against dead men who can't be prosecuted. If Jacques informed, and there was nobody better to use the information against, they'd use it against Jacques. The good news was that nobody more sinister than the public defender had gotten to him in the hospital and clammed him up. The bad news was that I needed to know what Elijah had gotten mixed up with, and I couldn't afford to wait to see how things shook out.

Fortunately, I had a plan. "What if I could spring you, without you needing to worry about testifying against anybody?" I said.

"How you gonna do that?"

"I'm the only witness against you, and I've got a touch of what doctors optimistically call mild dementia. Maybe I'm not sure you got out of that truck with Clarence. Maybe I don't remember you discussing whether or not you were going to shoot me. Maybe you were an innocent bystander I shot by accident while I was confused after a car crash. If you help me, I can help you."

He was clearly tempted, but he didn't trust me. "I need to talk to my lawyer about this."

"Don't be stupid, Jockstrap. You can't talk

to your lawyer about conspiring with a witness to commit perjury. Witness tampering
falls outside of a lawyer's official purview. If
you want to do this, you have got to deal
with me, and it's got to be right now."

He sort of smirked at me. "What's your
hurry?"

"Your friends took a man out of the backseat of the police car I was riding in," I said.
"I want to get that man back, alive."

"Oh yeah. That guy."

"You know that guy?"

"You gonna tell the police you shot me by
accident, and I got nothing to do with any
of it?"

"I said I'd do that. I'm a man of my word."

"All right. If you'll tell the police I didn't
do nothing, I'll tell you what I know."

I opened my notebook to a fresh page.
"Speak slowly, so I can write down what
you say, but not too slowly. I'm in a hurry."

"Why you got to write this down?"

I tapped my head with my pen. "Like I
told you, I got memory problems. Now
what do you know about the man who was
kidnapped?"

"I don't know him, like, personally. But I
know who he is. That was the man they call
the Buck."

"The Buck?"

"Yeah. The Buck."

The fuck?

Something I Don't Want to Forget:

By the way, this is why he called himself Elijah:

Every spring, Jews observe the Passover holiday, which commemorates the liberation of the enslaved Hebrews from bondage in ancient Egypt. The Passover celebration centers around a ritual meal called the seder, during which the head of the household reads the story of the Exodus from a prayer book called the Haggadah.

During the seder, we consume the unleavened matzo bread that our ancestors ate when they fled from Egypt, along with eggs to symbolize rebirth and bitter herbs to denote the unpleasantness of bondage. And at four points during the service, attendees who are of appropriate age to do so celebrate the sweetness of freedom by consuming glasses of ceremonial wine.

In ancient times, there was a dispute among rabbis over whether the Scripture instructed us to consume four or five glasses of wine during the Passover celebration. The disagreement was eventually resolved when the rabbis decided that we should go ahead and pour the fifth glass, but not drink it.

There's a related ancient tradition in which, at an appointed time during the ceremony, we open our doors and invite the prophet Elijah into the house. Traditionally, Elijah visits in order to verify that all the men present are circumcised, and therefore fit to consume the sacrificial Passover lamb, because Elijah is — and this is a real thing — the Jewish equivalent of what you might understand as the patron saint of ritual circumcision.

To give you an idea of how old these traditions are: The Passover sacrifice has not been a part of Jewish worship for about two thousand years, because a Jewish sacrifice can be conducted only in the Holy Temple, and the Romans burned down the Holy Temple along with the rest of ancient Jerusalem thirty years after the death of Christ.

Since nobody's eating holy meat anymore, there's no real reason to verify the circumcisions, so this whole component has been deemphasized in the modern service. Nobody feels particularly enthusiastic about discussing dicks at the dinner table. But, in addition to being the guy who checks everyone's penis, Elijah is also held to be the prophet who will return in the time of the Messiah to resolve all questions and disputes of Jewish law.

Disputes like the one about the fifth cup of wine.

So these days, we pour the extra cup of wine, and we open the door for Elijah, and he drinks the wine to resolve the dispute. And since the seder service runs about four and a half hours, including the meal, if we pour the wine at the beginning of the ceremony, Elijah's cup is empty by the end of it.

But, although the wine disappears without fail, nobody ever sees him come in, and nobody ever sees him drink it. Elijah is the stealth prophet; the sneakiest bastard in all of Jewish theology.

And Elijah the bank robber operated the same way. But he made money disappear, instead of wine.

L'Chiam!

26
2009

"I'm the Buck."

"No, man, the Buck is kind of like a legend. Or a myth or something. Except he's real. Crazy old Robin Hood dude, who takes down stash houses. You know what a stash house is?"

"Yeah," I said. "I was a cop once."

Elijah's bank-robbing glory days in the early 1960s were the very end of an era in which robbers could get rich knocking over banks. Your local Wells Fargo or Citi branch no longer contains what Charles Greenfield described as a "room full of money." Over the past couple of decades, retail banks have shifted from teller windows to ATM machines. You can't rob an ATM with a gun. And much less business is conducted with cash now, so banks keep far less of the stuff on hand.

If you walk into a modern bank and hand a threatening note to a teller, you probably won't walk out with much more than five thousand dollars, and it will probably have an exploding dye pack in it, and the teller will certainly trigger a silent alarm, and you will serve twenty years in federal prison.

If you want to find a room full of money these days, you have to visit one of the few businesses that still use lots of cash: a casino, a Federal Reserve bank, or a drug dealer.

A stash house is essentially a wholesale drug dealer's equivalent of a bank vault; a secret apartment or building used to store drugs, guns, or cash. Boarded-up windows; doors barred by extremely heavy locks. A place like that would be guarded at all times by at least two trusted guards, probably armed with shotguns.

Because of the almost mythic significance the man had come to occupy in my mind, I was a little bit disappointed to learn that Elijah was spending his time robbing drug dealers. It seemed painfully pedestrian and ordinary. I had imagined him stealing the English Crown Jewels or plundering the treasures of the Kremlin or something. Part of the reason I'd agreed to help the son of a bitch in the first place was because he seemed so scared that I had assumed he was into something exotic and intriguing.

But robbing stash houses made sense, in a pragmatic, unromantic sort of way. The amount of currency that might be held in such a facility was staggering. Pure heroin was worth ten times as much as gold by weight, because it was diluted to 5 percent purity for sale on the street. That meant a kilo of the uncut Afghan stuff became 200,000 hits, which could each sell for ten or fifteen dollars. And Memphis had plenty of junkies to sell it to.

The people who trafficked the pure product out of Europe and up through South America did not like to expose themselves to the dangers of frequent transactions so, instead, they dealt with distribution operations infrequently and in bulk; a suitcase full of junk in half-million-dollar bricks exchanged for a dozen fifty-pound suitcases full of strapped twenty-dollar bills.

If you could clean out a stash house right before a deal like that went down, you could easily steal two or three million dollars in cash. But if you wanted to rob it, you had to find it first; not an easy task, since the location of a stash was likely to be closely held information. And to take out a fortified position like that, you pretty much had to go in with a SWAT team.

"So Elijah robbed a drug dealer?" I said.

"Is that who was out to get him?"

"I don't know of any Elijah. The man they took out of your car was called the Buck. But, yes. He robbed a dude named Carlo Cash."

"Carlo Cash? That's his real name?"

"Probably ain't the name his mom gave him, but it's all anyone calls him."

"Who is he?"

"Okay, I only know what I heard from my cousin. But my cousin got a big mouth, so maybe I know a lot."

"You said you were afraid he'd snitch on you."

"Boy liked to talk. I don't run with Carlo's crew, but Clarence used to sling for them, and lately they been using him as muscle, 'cause he such a big motherfucker. Thought he was moving up in the world, the fat, dumb bastard. He said it was worth two hundred dollars if I backed Carlo's boys up when they went to get the Buck. I don't like getting mixed up in this shit, but I can't turn down two hundo, you feel me? I got two jobs. I stock shelves at the Walmart, and I cook fries at Wendy's. Both gigs are part-time, so I get no overtime and no insurance. I make seven and a quarter an hour, and I work sixty hours to make four hundred thirty-five dollars in a week. If somebody offers me two tax-free Benjamin Franklins for an hour's work, I can't afford not to do it."

"So tell me what you know about Carlo."

"If you need meth, blow, or pills, he can provide, but his main business is that good Taliban fire powder. He's the exclusive local distributor for some kind of Mexican cartel, so if you score in Memphis, there's better than even odds he's getting paid. That's what Carlo and his crew are about. Lots of dudes in this town own all the business on certain corners and blocks and up in certain developments, but Carlo is one of only a couple of guys who own the supply, so all those dealers have got to come to Carlo."

"Sounds like Carlo Cash is doing well for himself."

"He was, until six months ago. Now he's probably dead."

"What happened?"

"The Buck happened."

I leaned forward in my wheelchair. "Wait a second. My name is Buck. Why is Elijah called Buck?"

"He's not called Buck. He's *the* Buck. It's a name for some kind of Jewish ghost, or something."

"Dybbuk?" I asked.

"Yeah. The Buck."

According to the Jewish mystical tradition, a dybbuk was a malevolent spirit. It destroyed things and possessed people. Since Jews don't believe in Hell or the devil, a dybbuk was our equivalent of a demon. It seemed Elijah had decided to find himself a name more sinister than that of a hard-drinking, dick-inspecting ghost prophet.

"So I am assuming Dybbuk robbed a stash house and stole money from this Carlo Cash?"

"No," Jacques said. "Dybbuk robbed four of Cash's stashes."

I couldn't help laughing at the way it sounded when Jockstrap said "Cash's stashes," but he didn't seem to think it was funny at all.

"Dude stole fifteen million dollars."

"Jesus," I said. "Tell me what happened."

"Six months ago, Cash had a meet with his cartel guy. He was supposed to buy fifteen keys for six million dollars."

"Heroin?" I asked.

"If it was blow, he'd be getting seriously ripped off," Jacques said. You could buy a truckload of cocaine for the same price as a brick of heroin. "The night before the deal, one of Carlo's stash houses got robbed. Inside, the two guards was dead."

"How'd Elijah kill them?" I asked. The

thief I knew was ruthless and resourceful, but I couldn't see any way an eighty-year-old man could mount a successful assault on a fortified position defended by armed thugs. Jacques tried to shrug, but he couldn't really do it, because he was hand-cuffed to the bed.

"I don't know. Nobody called no *CSI*. The bodies went into holes someplace, and Dybbuk got away with half the money for the buy. Carlo can't raise three million dollars overnight, but his dope connection is a scary Mexican gangster, so Carlo ain't going to miss the meeting. You don't leave a man like that waiting around, and you damn sure don't want him to have to come looking for you.

"And Carlo needs the product. He's got guys on the street who depend on him. They got to get their stuff to sling, so they can get paid. If they can't depend on Carlo to provide, they will find somebody else to depend on. And Carlo has other expenses as well. There are dudes in prison who need to get paid to keep they mouths shut. And there are cops that need to be bought off. Carlo's business got overhead, you know what I'm saying?"

"So Carlo went to the meeting with only three million dollars?"

"Nothing else he could do. One of his top dudes told Clarence they were all scared shitless the Mexicans would kill everybody, but this cartel dude was, like, a suave business motherfucker. The cost of the junk is the cost of smuggling it. You know, there ain't no rich poppy farmers in Afghanistan. And once the Mexicans got it to the meeting with Carlo, the product had already been smuggled. Carlo had always been good for the money in the past, so the big Mexican gives Carlo all of the goods for the three million, but the difference had to get paid back, and with interest. So the next time, Carlo was gonna have to pay twelve million dollars: the three million he owed, three million in interest, and six million for his new shipment."

"At street prices, he'd probably get five times what he paid for that."

"Yeah, but Carlo don't get to keep most of that money. A lot of people got to get paid: dealers and lookouts and runners and muscle and middle-men. Those dudes give zero fucks that Carlo got robbed. If they don't get paid, they don't stay loyal. A lot of layers between Carlo Cash and the street, and everybody be wanting to wet they's beak. Carlo's business don't work if people don't stay loyal. So, Carlo spent the last six months selling off his legit assets, emptying his clean bank accounts, calling in every outstanding marker he got, and borrowing money from everyone who's less scary to owe money to than a Mexican drug lord. In the end, he got the twelve million, and had it squirreled in three different stash houses.

"Dude was mad paranoid. He be treating this like it was some black ops, secret agent shit. Nobody who worked for him knew the location of more than one of the stashes. He kept trying to change up his schedule to make sure he wasn't being followed and shit. But Dybbuk don't give a fuck. Dybbuk went and robbed all three stashes in the same night."

"How'd he do it?"

"No idea. If I knew how somebody could rob Carlo Cash's stash house, I'd rob that shit myself. I could do with a couple million dollars. That money was guarded by six of the baddest green beret Iraq-veteran motherfuckers Carlo Cash's money could buy. The old man killed all of them."

Elijah hadn't gotten stronger or less fragile in his seventies, so he hadn't killed those men at close range. Probably hadn't shot them, either. No way he could have got the better of all of them.

"Do you know how he killed them?" I asked.

"Like I said, I only know what Clarence told me."

"But you must have some idea of how they died. Were they shot? Were they poisoned?"

"All I know is that they dead."

So you've got two paramilitary guards armed with shotguns in an apartment full of money. The windows are boarded and barred. The door is reinforced and barred with multiple locks. It's the only way in. How does an eighty-year-old man bust in there and kill the men inside?

The best way to do it would probably be to use the sealed-up nature of the place against them, by pumping toxic gas in through an air vent or a radiator. When they smelled the gas, they might flee through the front door, at which point, the robber could possibly take them by surprise and shoot them. But if a line existed that Elijah wouldn't cross, it would probably be gassing people.

I said: "So Carlo has got to go meet with the Mexicans, and he doesn't have their money."

Jacques nodded. "Carlo is fucked. He's got to find Dybbuk and get the money back, or the Mexicans will kill him. And word is out that Carlo's in trouble, and that a lot of his guys are dead. He's looking weak to anyone wanting to take him out, and there are people who'd like to take over distribution for the Mexicans. But Carlo ain't stupid, and he finds out where Dybbuk is at."

"How'd he find out?" I asked.

"I don't know," Jacques said. "But the usual way you get information like that is to find somebody who knows, and either pay them off or fuck them up."

That was how I figured it as well. Nobody had followed us to the cemetery, and nobody followed us out, except for Elijah's lawyer. Lefkowitz must have called from his cell phone in his Escalade, and told Carlo exactly where to find us.

"So Carlo called Clarence, and Clarence called me, and we went out to get the guy who took down the stash. But I didn't know nothing about him being in the back of no cop car."

"Do you have any idea where they might have taken him?" I asked.

"They'd need to work him over, and get him to tell them where the money is."

"I understand that. But where?"

"I don't know that, man. Carlo got a lot

of places to hide shit. Hiding shit is what Carlo does."

I took a hard, careful look at the kid. Looked in his eyes; watched the corners of his mouth. Looked at his hands. I honestly couldn't tell if I thought he was lying, or if I just wanted him to be.

"All right," I said.

"Are you going to tell them you shot me by accident?"

"I said I would."

I figured a big chunk of Jacquarius Madison's story was bullshit, particularly the things he'd told me about himself. Carlo would never have brought somebody's cousin along to take part in a kidnapping plot, no matter how many men he'd lost. Drug dealers live in fear of snitches, so they don't conspire to commit major felonies with people they don't know.

But I didn't care much about that; if I could bring my vintage bank robber in alive, then Rutledge, Narcotics, could deal with Jockstrap and Carlo and the rest of them on his own.

My play at this point was to take what Jacques had told me and use it to brace Lefkowitz. Hopefully, the lawyer would spill some useful information that would lead me to Elijah.

But I was running out of time.

27
2009

I didn't have to go far to find Meyer Lefkowitz.

While fleeing the scene of Elijah's kidnapping, the lawyer plowed his Cadillac into a utility pole, which brought the car from forty miles an hour to a dead stop in seven tenths of a second. Lefkowitz himself did not decelerate quite so rapidly, and as a result, he went sailing through the windshield.

The sixty-thousand-dollar Cadillac Escalade comes equipped with special safety glass that shatters into pebbled fragments instead of jagged shards, so you can fly through it face-first and not suffer any significant injury. Unfortunately, the cash-strapped city of Memphis has not seen fit to install safety sidewalks yet, so Lefkowitz got good and mangled when he hit the pavement.

He was admitted to the same trauma unit

where Jockstrap was being treated. He was so close, I didn't even get lost on the way to his room. I wheeled my chair through the door, and made sure it closed behind me.

Apparently, he'd got his arms in front of him before he hit the glass. One of them was immobilized in a full cast, and the other was wrapped in gauze bandages that he still seemed to be seeping blood into. Getting his arms up had protected his head, however, and while there was noticeable bruising and swelling, he seemed to have most of his face intact, except for a square bandage taped to his left cheek.

"Hello, Mr. Schatz. How are you doin'?" He smiled at me, and he still had his teeth. Must have had a real lucky landing. The worst people always have the best luck.

"I've had better days, to be honest," I said as I positioned my wheelchair next to his broken right arm.

"I am doing surprisingly well," he said, and then he laughed. Whatever he was loaded on must have been powerful stuff.

On the balance, being high on opiates tends to decrease one's capacity for deviousness and dulls the intellect. This can be beneficial to an interrogator for reasons that should be obvious.

However, there are different ways to

induce different suspects to share information. Even on drugs, Lefkowitz was probably too smart to be tricked into accidentally admitting that he'd betrayed his client to a drug dealer. He didn't strike me as the type who might be susceptible to guilt, and he had too much at stake to be cajoled into admitting something damaging.

He was still giggling. I knew it was because of the drugs, but it pissed me off, regardless.

Once you pass a certain age, you rarely see anything new, and I had seen plenty of men like Meyer Lefkowitz; this was the kind of person who believed he was insulated from punishment; the sort who viewed society and the justice system as a safety net to preserve his status and its privileges rather than a mechanism for punishing his transgressions.

These lawyers and businessmen and politicians and gangsters and playboys believed they were beyond the reach of anyone who might want to stop them from beating and raping women and children and murdering anyone whose existence they found inconvenient.

And a lot of the time they were right. Too many things that ought to have been absolute in our society were tentative and corruptible. Judges found technical reasons for excluding a suspect's confession. Key witnesses got something fishy in the mail, and suddenly recanted testimony. Evidence disappeared out of locked rooms in police stations. Jurors reached inexplicable verdicts.

Elijah lived his life in rebellion against the brutality of state action; he died in Auschwitz at the hands of a country gone mad, and was reborn as the Dybbuk the day his mother was shot in front of him.

He was never wrong about civilization as an institution; it's severely broken in all its forms. There isn't any set of rules that binds everybody. Social obligations are flexible, punishments are distributed unevenly, and the law is never more just than the men who administer it.

But even if the state isn't gassing us, our rights don't really protect us. Criminals don't care about rights, any more than the Nazis did, and the law does a poor job of protecting us from them. I learned that the day my father's bloated corpse turned up facedown in the stagnant water of a drainage ditch by the side of the highway.

I became a soldier and then a policeman, but I was never really interested in being the tool of state power that Elijah thought I was. Just like him, I was shaped by the forces that made victims of my parents.

He wanted to be an avenging ghost. I wanted to be a razor blade.

So that's what was in my head when I wheeled myself into Meyer Lefkowitz's hospital room. Also, I was thinking this: There are guys who respond to a soft touch, and then there are guys who need to be touched with a fist. Lefkowitz had a very strong interest in deceiving me, but he was also a coward, so he definitely belonged in the second category. Pain was the key to making him talk, so it was unfortunate that he was all hopped up on painkillers.

Unfortunate for him.

I was going to have to hurt him badly enough to cut through whatever it was he was on. And I was prepared to do exactly that, even though age had deprived me of many of the tools I had once relied upon. I wasn't capable of slamming a guy against a wall anymore, or of crushing a man's ribs with a blackjack. But at least, in certain circumstances, I was still capable of being dangerous.

When I taught my son to shave, I told him this: A sharp new razor blade can give you a close shave or make a clean cut, but an old, battered, nicked, and rusty one isn't good for anything but making a goddamn mess.

I lit a cigarette.

"Hey, I don't think you can smoke in here," he said.

"Who's going to stop me?" I asked. "Are you going to call someone up and tell them I'm smoking?"

"I think they've got explosive oxygen in here."

"Maybe I like to live dangerously." I flicked ash onto his hospital gown.

"I don't know. Seems to me we've had enough danger lately."

"You want me to put it out?"

"Yeah, I do."

I took a last puff. "Happy to oblige." The hospital gown he was wearing was cut in a deep V-neck to accommodate the cords attaching the electrodes on his chest to the machines that monitored his vitals. I could see the shallow pit of his clavicle at the base of his neck, and that's where I stubbed out my cigarette, pressing the burning ember hard against his delicate skin.

"You're burning me, man," he said.

"Am I?"

"Looks like."

"Oh, you're right. I smell it now," I said. "You'll have to excuse me. I'm old and I'm clumsy. I guess my hand slipped."

I brushed the cigarette butt off his chest.

The burn was already blistering ugly yellow-gray, and turning red around the edges. He didn't even seem to feel it.

I lit another cigarette. "Let's hope my hand doesn't slip again."

Lefkowitz's eyes slid out of focus for a minute, and then he sort of shook off the confusion and said: "Hey, you can't smoke in here."

"I can't?"

"No. This is a hospital." He paused. He noticed the burn mark on his chest. "Do you ever get, uh, déjà vu? Like we had this conversation already?"

"Not me," I said. "I'm eighty-eight years old. My memory ain't what it used to be."

"We definitely had this conversation already. It's really weirding me out." He tried to touch the burn on his chest with his bandaged left arm, and then he winced in pain, as the motion pulled the stitches under his bandages. The gauze turned bright red in several places. His arm must have been shredded.

Well deserved.

"Let's have a different conversation, then," I said.

"Yes. Let's." The pain was bringing him around a bit. He seemed a little more coherent.

"You called Carlo Cash from your cell phone, while you were following us to the police station. That's how he knew where to ambush us."

"No."

I took a drag off the cigarette. "You work for Carlo Cash."

"I don't."

"I know you do. You're the only one who could have given them directions to find us while we were driving. Tell me where they took Elijah."

"I didn't call Carlo Cash."

"This is your last chance to spill it, before I get unpleasant."

"Mr. Schatz, I don't know anything."

"Have it your way," I said, and I reached over with my left hand and pulled his eyelid open. With my right hand, I held my burning cigarette close enough to his naked eyeball that he could feel the heat coming off it. "I don't have much time, Lefkowitz. I want that man back alive, and if you continue to bullshit me, I am going to burn your goddamn eye out."

"Oh, please don't. Please. Please." At least this was getting him sober.

"You are mobbed up. You are a scumbag."

He started to twist and writhe, moving his head to try to get his eye out from under the cigarette.

"Be careful," I said. "I'm old. I get the shakes. My hand ain't steady."

"I settle car accidents. I don't do any business for Carlo Cash. Oh God. I don't work for them. I barely have a criminal defense practice at all, beyond fixing an occasional DUI."

I started to feel less sure of myself, and pulled the cigarette back from his eye. "Why did you agree to represent Elijah?"

"Because he came into my office and handed me twenty thousand dollars in cash. I told him he needed to find someone better qualified, and he said he was in a hurry."

"Him handing you all that currency didn't make you suspicious?"

"Of course it made me suspicious. That's why he gave me so much money. So I'd keep my suspicions to myself."

"I don't believe you," I said. "You can't buy Rolexes and Cadillacs settling car accidents."

"You can if you settle a whole bunch of them. I outsource most of the work to a company in India that writes my complaints and my briefs for twenty bucks an hour. I'm on the phone all day doing nothing but negotiating settlements with insurers."

"I will find out if you're lying."

"Go check. Pull any court transcripts or judicial opinions from matters involving Carlo Cash or any of his crew. You'll find the names of the lawyers of record at the top of the first page of any of those documents. It's the same guys handling all those cases, and I handle none of them. I settle car accidents."

I took the cigarette out of his face and stuck it between my lips.

"I believe you," I said. He didn't have the balls to try to bullshit me while I jammed a burning cigarette in his eye.

But if that was the case, how the hell did Carlo Cash know what car Elijah was riding in, or where to find it?

Something I Don't Want to Forget:

"So, this guy Buck Schatz is in the news again."

I was watching a show where a tweedy rat-faced liberal host argued with a fat, sweaty conservative who always wore his neckties loose and his collars unbuttoned. This pair made any ideology seem unattractive.

"That's his name? Buck Schatz?" said Fat-and-Sweaty. "Is that some kind of joke?"

"Apparently that's the guy's actual name," said Rat Face. "This is the ninety-year-old man who keeps shooting people."

"Oh, yeah. I remember hearing about him a few months ago. He shot that killer cop guy in a hospital. What's he done now?"

"He shot two young black men. Killed one of them." I could tell Rat Face was winding up a little weasel tirade. "You know, this gets me thinking about our gun policies in America. Do we really need armed ninety-year-olds staggering around and killing people?"

Fat-and-Sweaty put his fingers to his ear-piece. "Now, these two guys he shot were participants of a brutal attack on a police officer who was badly injured. The man Schatz killed in the hospital a few months ago was responsible for four murders. And Schatz is a retired cop, so he knows how to handle and care for a weapon. I think a lot of people would point to this guy as a great example of the benefits of an armed citizenry."

Rat Face did an exaggerated television gesture of flailing disbelief. "According to news reports out of Memphis, this man Schatz suffers from senile dementia. He can't remember whether he's got a house-guest or a home intruder, and he's packing heat. This guy is armed to the teeth and he lives in a rest home! I wouldn't want to be the nurse who has to risk getting shot every time this man needs his sheets changed or his bedpan emptied."

Fat-and-Sweaty was getting indignant. "Now, a lot of people would be — a lot of people are — calling this guy a hero. I don't think it's fair to speculate about his health."

"Well, those were black men he shot this time."

"I don't see any call to bring race into this discussion."

"You don't get to decide whether to bring race into a discussion. When an old white man is shooting young blacks, race is already part of the discussion. It's incredibly problematic that you and your lunatic gun-fringe allies are hailing this demented gunman as a hero for killing one black man and crippling another."

"The police officer Mr. Schatz rescued by shooting those men was also black."

Rat Face sighed. "Your aversion to obvious facts is as shameful as it is unsurprising. This is a ninety-year-old retired Memphis cop. It's not a praiseworthy thing to have been associated with an outfit like the Memphis police during the years this man was working. The question we should ask isn't whether or not he's racist, but rather: How racist is he?"

"Well, speaking of shameful and unsurprising, did you hear what the president said today?"

"And speaking of racist . . ."

28
2009

If it wasn't Lefkowitz who gave Elijah up to Carlo Cash, then I had no idea who had done it. I'd watched Andre's mirrors all the way to the cemetery to make sure nobody followed us, and Elijah certainly would have been able to shake a tail as well.

I needed a fresh set of eyes on the problem, someone smart and helpful who might be able to look at the facts as I understood them and discern new patterns in them. Unfortunately, I didn't know anybody like that, so I had to ask my grandson.

"Electronic surveillance," he said. "You can attach a GPS tracking device to a car, and it will transmit its location to you wherever it goes."

"Like a radio transmitter?" I asked. "Wouldn't we have spotted its antenna?"

"This thing would be tiny. They could hide it in the wheel well, or under a fender. You'd never find it unless you went looking for it."

"I think I saw an episode of *CSI* where they used one of those," I said. "Used to be, if you wanted to know what somebody was up to, you had to follow him around."

"These days, if you want to know what somebody is up to, you just have to follow them on Twitter."

"What, exactly, is the Twitter?" I asked. "They talk about it on Fox News a lot."

Tequila laughed. "I think maybe we should stick to learning about the tracking devices today, and save Twitter for later."

We were waiting in my hospital room for the doctor to show up. I was back on the adjustable bed, and Tequila was sitting in a chair next to it. His mother had gone to fetch Rose from Valhalla. I was hoping to be able to check out by the time they got back, but the doctor wanted to keep me under observation until they could put me back on my blood thinner, and I couldn't have the blood thinner until the doctor was satisfied that I wasn't going to bleed to death out of my nose.

"I think we need to discuss your condescending tone later as well," I said. "But first, I guess we need to figure out how Carlo Cash planted a GED bug on either Lefkowitz's Escalade or Andre's Crown Vic."

"GPS, not GED."

"GFY. That's what I said."

Tequila flipped through the notebook I had been writing in the day before. "Why does there even need to be a bug? There's an obvious conclusion to draw from these facts, Grandpa. Lefkowitz called Cash and told him where to ambush you."

"That's what I thought as well," I said. "But I talked to Lefkowitz, and he persuaded me that he didn't do it. He's nothing but an ambulance chaser who settles car crashes."

"Maybe he lied to you."

"I don't think so. I asked him pretty hard."

"I don't understand what that means, Grandpa."

"I burned him with cigarettes."

His eyes widened, and his cheeks went pale. "Jesus. Fuck."

"Watch your goddamn language," I said.

"You burned an innocent man with cigarettes, Grandpa."

"I feel like I've told you this before, Prosecco: There ain't nobody who's innocent."

He sat there for a couple of minutes, flipping through the pages of my notebook, but not really reading them. Finally, he said: "There was only a two-hour gap between the time Elijah first walked into Lefkowitz's office and the time you met him at the cemetery. They'd have to have been tailing Elijah to know he'd retained Lefkowitz, but if they were already following Elijah, they didn't need to bug his lawyer's car to find him."

The cigarette burns would not be discussed further. This new information would go in the vault we filled with our forbidden memories; the things we didn't want to remember. There was a clock ticking on Elijah's life, and I'd done what I believed was necessary under the circumstances. But I didn't feel that great about it.

Truth is, there are a lot of things I've done that I don't feel that great about. But if you look back on whatever the wrath of God is burning down behind you, you turn into a pillar of salt.

So, you just write down the stuff you want to remember, leave out the rest of it, and keep pushing yourself forward, on a walker or in a wheelchair or with anything that can keep you moving.

"Maybe Cash had an informant of some kind in Lefkowitz's office; a secretary or a security guard or somebody who might have spotted Elijah," I said.

Tequila shook his head. "That makes no

sense. Why would a heroin dealer need to cultivate a spy in the office of a lawyer who settles car accidents? And, anyway, how would a device planted on the lawyer's Cadillac let them know they needed to attack Andre's Crown Vic?"

"I don't see how they could have bugged Andre's police car. They'd have to know that Elijah met with me that morning, and we assume he'd take care to assure he wasn't followed when he visited me at Valhalla. Then, I called Andre on the phone a few hours later. They'd have had to get a wiretap on my cell phone very soon after my first contact with Elijah to know Andre was even involved, and if they'd found some way to listen to my calls, they would still have had less than an hour to attach the device onto Andre's police car, which was parked at a police station. I can't see how they could have gotten to either of those vehicles."

"Well, if they didn't have trackers on the cars, and Lefkowitz didn't give them your location, I don't understand how they could have coordinated the ambush." He scratched his chin, closed his eyes, and rocked back and forth in his chair for a minute. "Maybe they somehow planted a tracker on Elijah himself. Maybe something he stole from them was bugged, and he was carrying it with him."

"I don't think so. Andre frisked him before he put him in the car. If Elijah had a transmitter, Andre would have found it."

I took back the notebook from my grandson and flipped through the pages.

"Here's a list of the things in Elijah's pockets," I said. "A wallet with no identification, a book of matches, a hotel key, and one of those phones with no buttons."

Tequila perked up. "A phone with no buttons? Like, an iPhone?"

"iPhone, youPhone, whoPhone?" I said.

Tequila pulled a slab of black steel and glass out of his pocket. "Was it a phone like this?" He pressed one small button on the side of the device, and the screen lit up with a picture of a numeric keypad and the words: ENTER PASSCODE.

"Yeah," I said. "It was just like that. Andre switched it on, and then he asked Elijah for the passcode, and Elijah wouldn't give it to him."

"Why would an eighty-year-old fugitive thief need an iPhone? Is he checking his e-mail while he's on the lam?"

"I don't know what he does with it," I said. "I don't know what anyone does with those things."

"Does anyone at your nursing home have a phone like that?"

"It's not a nursing home. It's an assisted-lifestyle community for older adults."

"Whatever. Does anyone your age have a phone like this?"

"Nobody I know."

He pumped his fist, like he'd just had a brilliant idea. "What if it wasn't his cell phone?"

"Then we'll have to charge him with taking somebody's phone, in addition to the eight murders and the theft of fifteen million dollars."

"It was drug money. It didn't really belong to anyone. Like, legitimately."

"You've had two years of law school," I said. "Robbing a drug dealer is still robbery. You know that."

I was reminded of something somebody once told me about the legitimacy of property rights.

"Well, the point I was making is that, if it wasn't his phone, the owner could have tracked it," Tequila was saying. "The phone has a GPS receiver in it, just like the tracking bugs you've seen on television. There's an app — a computer program — called Find My iPhone. You can open the program from your laptop, and the phone will transmit its exact location, within a couple of feet, over the Internet. These things get stolen a lot, and people activate the program, and then report the thieves' addresses to law enforcement. If the phone belonged to Cash or one of his people, they might have been able to track its location that way."

"If they could find out where Elijah was so easily, why didn't they take him sooner?"

"The phone has to be connected to the network to transmit its location. You said that it was switched off, and then Andre turned it on. Activating it made it traceable. But why would Elijah be carrying around a stolen phone that the people who were hunting him could locate?"

"I know why," I said. "I should have figured it out sooner. He's done something like this before."

29
1965

Two days after I beat up Elijah, at half past ten in the morning, I was sitting in my car outside the bank, watching the front entrance, and waiting for something to happen.

I was thinking about finding myself some cheap, greasy food when I heard shouting behind me, coming from the protest.

"What you doin', man?"

"Get on the ground!"

"Hey, we got rights!"

"On the fucking ground! All of you!"

My car was parked in a parallel space, and the front door of the Kluge office building was only about two hundred yards away, so I climbed out and started running toward the noise.

I could see officers brandishing their nightsticks, wading into the crowd of strikers, and swinging indiscriminately. Some of the Negroes had been carrying protest signs mounted on wooden posts, and they'd torn away the cardboard to make the things into bludgeons.

The loud, clear voice of Longfellow Molloy rose above the noise of the melee: "Gentlemen, we are marching to preserve our dignity. Don't let them make you act undignified."

One of the officers got hold of a bullhorn and shouted him down: "You are all under arrest. Drop your weapons and lie flat on the ground, with your hands above your heads."

Some of the protesters were trying to flee. I saw an officer chase a woman down the street and hit her in the head with a club. She fell to the ground, and he kept hitting her.

"They want to make us criminals," Molloy was shouting. "They want to make us animals. The world will see what they are doing. The world will see."

But nobody was listening to him. A tear gas canister exploded in the air over the protesters' heads, and people started coughing and clawing at their eyes. I saw four burly colored boys drag an officer to the ground, tear off his helmet, and stomp on his face. The other police saw this, too. I saw several nearby officers unholster their weapons.

"Don't shoot," I shouted at them, waving my badge above my head. "They'll riot all over the city!"

Somebody must have been in charge here, but I couldn't spot any brass. Maybe they were running the show by radio, or maybe they'd fled when the violence started.

Not all the officers opened fire, thank God. If they had, they'd have killed all the protesters and a bunch of them probably would have shot each other in the confusion. But three cops emptied their service weapons into the crowd, firing what would later be reported as eighteen shots.

A half-dozen protesters fell to the ground, killed or wounded. The rest dropped any weapons they were carrying and tried to flee. The officers were chasing down the runners, beating them with nightsticks and putting them in handcuffs.

I saw Longfellow Molloy lying in a pool of blood with one of his eyes and part of his nose missing. I thought of something Abramsky had said about the burning of Sodom: If the angels could have found ten righteous men, the city might have been spared.

Behind me, I heard a noise that sounded like a fire engine's siren. I turned around, looking for something on fire, and then realized I was hearing the alarm at the Cotton Planters Union Bank.

I hesitated. There was going to be an investigation of this debacle; somebody was at fault. If anyone ever hoped to figure out who started the violence here, we would need to immediately start taking statements from witnesses; if the protesters left, they'd be too scared to come forward to give statements, and we'd never find them again. And once the officers involved got their lies in order, there would be no hope of sorting out the truth.

But I wasn't technically even supposed to be on the scene of the protest. I didn't want my name in the reports about a racial massacre. I didn't want my photographs in any history books next to this. So I ran back toward the bank.

By now, all the office workers were trying to flee the neighborhood. The streets were jammed with cars, and people were streaming out of the revolving doors of skyscrapers on foot. It was weird to see the sidewalks so crowded; nobody in Memphis walked anywhere. It took me eight minutes to elbow my way through the crowd of panicked office workers and get to the bank. Robberies don't last eight minutes; by the time I got there, I knew Elijah and his gang were already gone.

The revolving door was locked into place, but one of the guards standing inside recognized me and let me in. The lobby was mostly empty. It seemed like Greenfield must have allowed most of his staff to go home. Only his assistant, Riley Cartwright, and five uniformed security guards were inside.

"How many were there?" I asked. "Can you describe them? Can you tell me which way they went?"

"Nothing happened," Greenfield said. "I activated the security system in order to seal the vault. It seemed like a reasonable precaution, in case riots break out."

"There was no robbery?"

He shook his head. "Everything here is fine. My security staff will stay on duty, in case any looters try to break in, but the vault is secure and inaccessible for the next three hours."

Maybe I'd actually managed to scare Elijah out of town. "Well, I guess I can be of better use elsewhere, then," I said. "Call the police if you see anything suspicious going on."

Something I Don't Want to Forget:

The Negro response to the morning's violence turned out to be more subdued than I'd feared it might be; the Kluge strike had become a focal point for the anxieties of whites working in downtown offices, but it had never really been much of a cause among black Memphians. It seemed most people had viewed the Kluge strike as a labor issue rather than a race issue.

And after six uneventful weeks of protests in front of the Kluge offices, there were no journalists around when the strike finally turned violent.

The national news media would be interested, now that our story had a body count, but without gruesome, sensationalistic images or film footage, the story wouldn't get too much play on television. Since nobody had really been paying attention to the strike outside of Memphis, only the local news people were reporting the story in the hours after the massacre.

They had to live in this town, so the Memphis journalists were treading carefully in their coverage, focusing on the labor angle rather than the racial issue. Nobody wanted to publish or broadcast the story that would set off a riot.

The strike was too small to attract much

attention from national civil rights organizations, and the freight workers tended not to be the churchgoing sort, so the black preachers in Memphis hadn't been rallying their flocks behind that particular cause. The crowd had been relatively small when the violence broke out, and most of the firsthand witnesses were arrested at the scene. Until the department started turning the protesters loose, hours after the shootings, very few people knew exactly what had gone down.

The mayor wanted the whole thing kept quiet more than he wanted somebody to blame for it, and the brass was operating under the assumption that they could sweep the whole nasty situation under the rug if they just ran a thorough and diligent investigation that reached the inevitable conclusion: The officers had conducted themselves in an exemplary manner, and that any beatings or shootings that may have been directed at the strikers were fully justified.

By the time most people who might have responded violently learned of the shootings, the streets were full of cops. By nightfall, we'd doubled our previous department record for the most arrests made in a single day, and our holding cells were full of Negroes. There weren't any riots in Memphis; at least not in 1965. The peace was kept.

Except at the Cotton Planters Union Bank. When the vault opened itself, after the three-hour alarm lockdown ended, all the money inside was gone.

30
2009

I was back on my adjustable hospital bed. The nurse had put an IV in my arm, and she'd told me they were monitoring my iron, because my bloodwork showed that I was anemic. This wasn't surprising to me. I felt exactly like I'd been in a car accident.

Rutledge, Narcotics, was sitting next to me in the hospital-issue version of a comfy chair; a cheap, flimsy-looking thing with plastic cushions. He was too tall for it, and he looked kind of uncomfortable. He was resting his right ankle on his left knee, and had his elbows splayed over the armrests. He was holding something that I had at first thought was a notepad, but which was, in fact, some kind of electronic device: either a very large Internet phone or a very small computer.

My grandson was so excited, he couldn't seem to sit down at all. He was pacing around by the foot of the bed, and I was getting annoyed just looking at him.

"I don't understand how we're supposed to find this guy based on the cell phone," Rutledge said. "We don't have the e-mail address or the password he's registered it to, so we can't trace it online."

Tequila started bouncing up and down. The only thing he liked better than knowing the answer was knowing the answer when nobody else did, so he could feel like he was the smartest kid in the class. "Telephones can be tracked by GPS," he said. "But their location can also be triangulated by the phone company, using its cell-network infrastructure. They keep records of which cell towers every phone talks to, and this data can be used to find out where a phone, and presumably the phone's owner, were located at a particular time."

Rutledge looked annoyed. "I know that," he said. "But in order to track a cell phone, you have to know the phone number. You can't just tell me that some guy has a cell phone, and then ask me to find it. Everybody has a damn cell phone."

It occurred to me that I didn't know Rutledge's first name. I flipped backwards through my notebook to see if I'd written it down, but I had not, so he probably hadn't told me.

I wondered if his name was something really black, and he was embarrassed about it. Maybe Rutledge was his first name, and not his last name. But if that was the case, then I didn't know his last name. Unless it was Narcotics. I thought about asking him, but he seemed like the sort who might get all touchy and indignant about that kind of question.

"But the type of phone is distinct, and the cell network can also detect which kind of phone it is communicating with," my grandson said. "He had an iPhone."

"So what? There are tens of thousands of iPhones in this city. Maybe hundreds of thousands. Everybody's got a damn iPhone."

"Right, but the cell providers keep logs of their towers, as well as logs of the phones, so it can look up a particular tower to see which phones were in range of it, just like they can look up a phone number and see which towers it connected to. We know the phone we're looking for was at the Jewish cemetery off South Parkway at three o'clock yesterday. That cemetery is next to a rail yard, an abandoned factory, and a big gravel pit. There's a good chance that it was the only iPhone in the vicinity of the cemetery at that time, and the phone company should be able to check the logs of the towers that cover the cemetery and find that number."

"And once they can identify the phone, they can find out where it's been since yesterday the regular way," Rutledge said. He looked impressed. "How did you even know about that?"

"I took a seminar last semester about emerging technologies and privacy issues," Tequila said. "It's a very fertile area for legal scholarship, because courts are trying to take rules created to govern analog surveillance and apply them to facts relating to new developments like cell phones and Internet activity. There are conflicting decisions among the federal circuit courts about the privacy expectations associated with some of this stuff, and eventually, the Supreme Court is going to have to weigh in and make some major decisions about whether the digital footprint is entitled to protection under the Fourth Amendment."

"I'm glad I ain't got a digital footprint," I said.

"You ought to be glad your friend Elijah has one," Tequila said.

"I guess. Do we have to get a warrant to do this?"

"No," Rutledge said. "The phone companies pull their logs for us whenever we ask."

"That's the constitutional issue; whether police should be able to obtain data like that without judicial supervision," Tequila said. "Maybe I will write a law review article about it. I'm on the staff of the *Journal of Legislation and Public Policy.*"

"Keep it in your pants," I told him.

Rutledge pressed his computer device to his ear, which I guess meant it was a cell phone.

"You're not supposed to use those things in the hospital," I said.

"Yeah?" he said. "Well, who's gonna stop me?"

31
1965

I was sitting at my desk in the offices of the Detectives' bureau at the Central Police Station. I'd left my car in front of the bank and walked back; the streets were too jammed up to drive.

The opportunity to participate in the department's campaign to suppress Negro outrage struck me as singularly unappealing, so I'd spent the hours since Longfellow Molloy's death trying to stay clear of the massacre investigation by halfheartedly following up leads in a week-old murder. I knew who had done it, but I wasn't going to be able to make a charge stick, because the asshole had gone and intimidated my two key witnesses while I was focused on the Elijah thing.

I had half a mind to go find the guy and just beat the shit out of him, but I knew that the morning's events were going to be a black eye for the department, and I was worried that the brass was about to start taking police violence more seriously. I also didn't want to draw too much attention to an investigation that I'd botched through my negligence. I sort of had an explanation for what I'd spent the last week doing, but it wouldn't hold up under intense scrutiny.

I was going to have to let this one go for now. I'd get him the next time he killed somebody.

I stuck my notes into a Redweld folder and was sliding it into my desk drawer when I heard on the radio that the Cotton Planters Union Bank had been robbed.

I picked up the phone and dialed the bank's switchboard. The operator put me through to Greenfield's extension and he picked it up himself.

"Where are you people?" he demanded. "It's been twenty minutes since I reported the theft of a hundred seventy thousand dollars, and the police still have not arrived."

On a normal day, a bank robbery would be a big deal for the Memphis Police; something every detective would need to prioritize above his regular caseload of junkies and Negroes robbing and killing each other.

But this wasn't a normal day. Today,

nobody cared about Greenfield or his stupid money.

"I thought you only had a hundred fifty thousand dollars in your vault," I said.

"We've had another armored truck delivery since then."

"You took another twenty thousand dollars into your vault after I warned you that Elijah was looking to rob you?"

"Yes. Christ, you sound like Cartwright."

"You're an ass, Greenfield," I said.

"Last time we spoke, you said I was a prick."

"You're a prick and an ass. Actually, you're that oily, wrinkled strip of flesh between a nutsack and an asshole. They call it a taint, because it ain't the one thing and it ain't the other. That's what you are."

"I appreciate your sentiment."

"I'm just telling you this for your edification."

"Are you going to continue insulting me, Detective Schatz, or are you going to do your job and capture the perpetrator of this crime?"

I clearly wasn't going to be capturing Elijah. Greenfield's state-of-the-art security system had bought the robbers three hours to escape before the crime was even discovered. Elijah was already out of the state.

And I didn't even want to see him caught, because I didn't want his Jewish conspiracy exposed. Now that he'd robbed the bank, the only way I could keep his scheme from blowing back on me was to make sure he got away clean. If this robbery ever got solved, it would happen despite my most diligent efforts.

"I think I'm just going to keep insulting you, Greenfield."

"Fuck you, Buck Schatz."

"Fuck yourself."

Now I had a problem: Ari Plotkin told me that Elijah's plan had been to rob the bank when the strike broke out in violence. Waiting outside the bank in case something happened had not seemed like a particularly effective use of my time, and I doubted that was what the robbers had been doing. Elijah must have planned his heist to coincide with the outbreak of violence at the Kluge protest, which meant he had known exactly when the violence was going to break out.

The day I'd met him, he tried to recruit me to be his inside man in the police department. But what part of his scheme required a man in the police department? It wasn't hard to make the intuitive leap: He'd paid somebody off to start a race riot in front of the Kluge building in order to distract everyone's attention from the job he was pulling at the bank. So, the Jewish heist I wanted to cover up and the police massacre that was already the subject of an intense internal department investigation were actually the same case.

I made some discreet inquiries about the bank robbery case, and learned it had fallen in the lap of the most ineffectual detective on the force, a thick, wheezy guy named Whit Pecker who was about five months away from retirement and getting a head start on being lazy and useless.

This was a lucky break for me; Greenfield wouldn't tell him about his meetings with me; the bank's insurer might deny coverage if they learned the manager had been warned about the robbery. If I was lucky, neither Elijah's name nor mine would ever even be connected with the file.

However, the men investigating the massacre were more of a danger; the three highest-ranking detectives in Memphis had all been tasked with the job of figuring out what had happened. So far, the word around the station was that they weren't having much luck. They had dozens of witnesses to take statements from, and they were getting conflicting and useless stories. The Negroes all insisted that a police officer had struck the first blow, while the cops insisted that the Negroes had begun swinging sticks and throwing bottles, and that the retaliation had been a by-the-book response.

But I had a little bit of information that the investigators didn't: I knew about Elijah's plan to corrupt a Jewish cop. There were only four Jews on the Memphis police force, and I was one of them, so while the official investigation was sorting through fifty names and fifty stories, I had a pretty short list to work with. All I had to do was ask a few friendly acquaintances a couple of discreet questions to find out that only one Jewish policeman had been on protest duty that morning.

His name was Officer Len Weisskopf. He was twenty-six years old, and now he was in trouble.

32
2009

"At three o'clock yesterday, one iPhone was switched on in the vicinity of the cemetery," Rutledge, Narcotics, said. "That phone number belongs to Charles Cameron."

"Also known as Carlo Cash?" I asked.

"Yes, sir," said Rutledge.

"I thought drug dealers only made calls on burners," said Tequila.

"Burners?" I asked.

I guessed this was drug slang by the way the detective curled his lip when he heard Tequila use the term.

"Prepaid, disposable cell phones," Rutledge said. "They do their drug business on those, but they still have regular phones, for regular stuff. Like regular people. You understand that they're people, right?"

"Yeah, of course," Tequila said.

"Just don't be thinking you all hip because you listen to Jay-Z and you seen *The Wire*,"

Rutledge said. "I've met dudes like you before."

Tequila's nostrils sort of flared. "You had that coming," I told him. I did not listen to Jay-Z, and I had not seen *The Wire,* and I would not have been surprised if Rutledge, Narcotics, had never met anyone like me before, but I decided not to say this.

"Anyway, we traced the phone to a warehouse on Riverside Boulevard."

"There are warehouses on Riverside Boulevard?" Tequila asked. "I thought that was all parks and new Downtown housing."

"You're thinking of Riverside Drive," Rutledge told him. "Riverside Boulevard is a whole different thing."

Riverside Drive and Riverside Park were part of Memphis's revitalized Downtown. The construction of a half-billion-dollar basketball arena had done a lot to improve an area of a few blocks around the Peabody Hotel.

Developers had bulldozed out the aging heart of the city and built a bunch of expensive apartment buildings and some cute little shops, a movie theater, and a lot of fancy restaurants.

A year ago, Rose and I took Tequila out for dinner down there, at a Brazilian steakhouse. I wasn't wild about the Brazilian part, but I figured they probably couldn't ruin a piece of meat too much.

For nearly thirty years, I worked in that neighborhood, at the 128 Adams Ave. police station, but Tequila had to ask his cell phone for directions, because I didn't recognize anything anymore. It cost me eight dollars to park the Buick.

You don't order a steak at a Brazilian steakhouse; you pay forty dollars for a plate, and then waiters come around carrying swords with different kinds of meat skewered on them, and you just take as much of it as you can cram down your gullet. For some reason, the waiters were called chiaroscuros.

Tequila didn't even talk to us during the meal, because he was too busy cutting and chewing and flagging down waiters to bring him more sword-meats. I watched that boy put away at least three pounds of flank steak and garlic-rubbed sirloin and Parmesan-crusted chicken drummies and bacon-wrapped filet mignon. I was almost impressed, in the same way I might almost be impressed by a freak show at a circus.

The next day, my grandson called to let me know that he'd "dropped a deuce that filled the bowl above the waterline."

"This is amazing," he said. "It's like a brand-new tropical island with rich, volcanic soil. In my toilet."

"That's great to hear," I said.

"Do you want me to text you a picture of it?"

"No. And I haven't got that kind of phone."

"I'm worried it's too big for the pipe, and it's going to clog up the works. Maybe I'd better break it apart with the toilet brush."

My works were also clogged up, which made the conversation especially annoying. I was on the third day of a course of oral laxatives, and the Brazilian meats had done nothing to get things moving; they'd only made me feel more bloated and backed up. If I didn't manage to pass something solid by breakfast the next day, I was going to have to try a suppository. If that didn't work, I'd need to see the gastroenterologist. That guy was, by a significant margin, my least-favorite doctor.

I didn't want to explain this to my grandson, so he never figured out why I was mad at him.

Anyway, the point is that, once you got past the new development spurred by the stadium construction, Memphis's post-industrial decline had largely continued unabated. A couple of miles down the riverfront from the cluster of bank skyscrapers and government buildings and Brazilian steakhouses, you ran into miles of pothole-riddled streets and disused warehouses and shipping yards.

The river had become much less important as a transportation artery, and freight that used to be hauled by hundreds of longshoremen was now moved much more quickly by a couple of cranes that were run by computers. Memphis was still a transportation city, but the shipping business was centered around the International Airport and the FedEx hub these days.

It wouldn't be hard for a drug dealer to find himself a quiet warehouse where nobody would hear him torturing people.

"Do you think Elijah is still there?" Tequila asked.

Rutledge frowned. "The last place the phone pinged the cell network was right in the middle of the river, at about two o'clock this morning."

"Like he was on a bridge?" Tequila asked.

"Like he was on a boat," I said.

Rutledge nodded at me. "And the phone hasn't transmitted since then. Most likely, it went into the water."

"With the body," Tequila said.

"That's what it looks like," Rutledge said. "I'm sorry."

"I'm not," I told him. "It wasn't Elijah's body."

"What makes you think that?" Rutledge asked.

"Because it wasn't Elijah's phone," I said.

33
1965

About twelve hours after police officers shot Longfellow Molloy, the brass decided the riots weren't going to happen, and word went out by radio that they were cutting off the overtime. I went and got a newspaper and a cup of coffee, and killed forty-five minutes. Then I went to Weisskopf's house and I knocked on the door. His wife answered.

"I know who you are. You're Baruch Schatz," she said. She clearly thought it was odd that I was knocking on her door just before midnight. She seemed to be trying to decide whether she should acknowledge this oddness, and also trying to figure out what I was doing there. She apparently could not, so she decided to just be polite: "I'm Devorah. Congratulations on your *simcha*!"

She was referring to Brian's upcoming bar mitzvah. I smiled at her, in the automatic way I smiled at people when they said something nice about my kid. "Thank you very much. I need to speak to Len."

"Do you want to come inside?"

"I'm in a bit of a hurry, so I think it would be best if I just spoke to him here, on the porch. I promise I'll only need him for a minute."

"I'll get him." She closed the door and went inside. I unhooked my blackjack from my belt; gripped the handle with a white-knuckled fist.

The door opened. Weisskopf had broad shoulders and was a few inches taller than me, but he didn't give the impression of being a powerful man. He had a face that might have been called handsome, if it wasn't just a little distorted. The nose was slightly too wide. The lips were just a bit too fleshy. The eyes were a little too small and a little too far apart. His jawline and his middle were just a little bit soft and slack from living a little bit too easy.

He was standing in the doorway, smiling at me, but not really concealing his nervousness.

"This is certainly unexpected," he said. "I don't know if we've ever really met before, but my mother knows yours, I think."

I gestured at the door, with the truncheon. "Step out onto the porch and shut that behind you."

I stuck a cigarette between my lips and lit it with a wooden match. He shut the door. He was looking a little nervous now.

"Is there something I can help you with tonight, Buck?"

I took a long drag on my smoke. "You can tell me what I'm supposed to say to my son."

"I'm not sure I understand what you're asking me."

"When I go home tonight, my son is going to be waiting for me, and he's going to want to know how I can be a part of an organization that committed the atrocity that happened this morning. He's going to ask me how I can live with myself. And I have no idea how I am going to answer that question. So, I am asking you what you think I should tell him."

"I'm not sure why you're coming to me with this," he said. "We don't even know each other that well."

"Don't you dare try to bullshit me," I said. I brandished the blackjack. "I will play your goddamn ribs like a xylophone with this thing. I will break all the teeth out of your fucking jaw."

He put his hands up, palms out. "Please don't hurt me," he said. "My wife is pregnant. We're going to have a baby."

I grabbed him by the shoulder, spun him around, and frisked him to make sure he didn't have a weapon.

"Three people are dead because of you."

"Negroes."

"Quit saying things that piss me off when I'm trying to talk myself into letting you live."

There was only one reason I didn't beat him with the blackjack until there was nothing left of his head but a smudge on the porch, and it wasn't his pregnant wife: I didn't want to have to explain why I'd done it. I didn't ever want the department to find out that Jews were responsible for the massacre. So, I was going to have to cover this up. I was going to have to put Len Weisskopf someplace where nobody would ever find him.

"How much did Elijah pay you to murder those people?" I asked.

"I didn't shoot anybody. I just hit a man with my nightstick."

"But you started it. He paid you to start it. You were his distraction while he robbed the vault."

"Maybe I was, but nobody told me about a bank robbery, and I didn't know them fellas was gonna open fire on the protesters, and I never even met Elijah. All I knew was that my job was to grab the nearest *schvartze* at exactly ten thirty in the morning and club him with my nightstick. I bet you'd have busted one of them nappy heads open if somebody offered you a bunch of money. How many people have you beat down so far this week, for free?"

I wanted to beat down one more right there, but I swallowed the lump at the back of my throat and ignored the provocation. "Who paid you? Who was your contact?"

"Ari Plotkin."

Goddamnit. Next time I needed to shoot Ari Plotkin, I'd have to remember to shoot him in the face.

"How much?"

"Thirty-five hundred."

"Eleven hundred and change for each murder on your conscience."

His brow furrowed. "And how many dead men have you got on your conscience, Buck? How many have you killed?"

"I reckon I can carry one more," I said. I raised the club, and he threw up his arms to protect his head, and took a step back.

"Oh God!"

"Where is it?" I shouted in his face, leaving flecks of spittle and cigarette ash on his cheeks.

"Where's what?"

"The money, you ass."

"It's in the house."

"Go get it."

"What? Why?"

"Because, if you don't, I am going to take this here truncheon and I'm going to beat you to death with it."

He went back inside the house. Whatever he was doing in there took long enough for me to get concerned that he was entertaining a stupid idea, so I hung the blackjack on my belt and unholstered my .357. I stepped to the side of the door, and as soon as it opened, I reached through it, grabbed a handful of his shirt, and slammed him against the wall.

I frisked him, and it turned out that he hadn't been quite dumb enough to grab his gun. He'd done as I'd told him, and retrieved a big wad of bills from someplace in the house.

"You don't get to keep this," I said. I took the money out of his hand.

"Yeah, well, it don't look like you're bagging it up for evidentiary purposes."

"Ain't none of your business what I'm going to do with it."

"So, this is a shakedown?" he asked.

"Think of it as your lucky day, Len," I

said. "I'd like nothing more than to pound you until your insides are mush. You deserve to get hurt real bad, and you deserve to go to prison."

"That's my money," he said. "That money is for my family. I earned it fair and square."

"Well, then, it's unfortunate for you that I done been endowed with what you might call a deep skepticism for the concept of property rights," I said, and I stuffed the wad of cash into my jacket pocket. "Tomorrow morning, you're going to call your sergeant and tell him you can't deal with what you saw today. You're gonna tell him you've got to quit the force."

"What am I supposed to do without my job?"

"You're gonna pack your shit up, and you're gonna leave town."

"Where am I supposed to go?"

I pressed the muzzle of the .357 against his forehead. "I'm sure you'll find someplace to settle in the broad and welcoming expanse of I-Don't-Give-A-Fuck. But you can't stay here."

"I've got a house."

"Hire somebody to sell it and have them wire you the proceeds. But you had better be out of my town before the sun sets tomorrow. If I ever see you here again, or if you even look back as you leave, I will burn you alive in the white-hot flames of God's holy fire. Do you believe me?"

"I believe you," he said.

I put my gun away. "Good," I said.

"I've got to tell you, though, that you're a goddamned hypocrite," he said. "You act all righteous at the same time you're stuffing my dirty money in your pockets. You ain't better than me. You're at least as crooked and a lot more violent. It makes me sick just to look at you."

"Then it's a good thing you won't ever have to see me again," I said. "And if you do see me, I had better not see you, because the next time I see you, you are going to die."

"You're a hypocrite."

"And you've got until sundown tomorrow to be gone from Memphis, or else your pregnant wife had best start making funeral arrangements. Have yourself a good night, you lousy piece of shit."

Something I Don't Want to Forget:
When Brian woke up, I had breakfast almost ready. I'd used the real beans to make the coffee, not the instant stuff I usually made. I'd also fixed scrambled eggs, bagels, fresh orange juice, and crispy bacon.

The fight over bacon was one of the few major arguments with Rose that I ever managed to win. Both of us were born into traditional families that kept kosher kitchens, but my mother had begun ignoring some of the more inconvenient restrictions after my father died, and by the time I was in high school, I thought nothing about eating a cheeseburger in a restaurant.

During the war, our rations generally weren't very good, and salted pork held up better than most other meats, so it was cherished when we could get hold of it. I developed a taste for the stuff.

When I got back from Europe, after what I'd seen and what I'd endured and what I'd done, I no longer had the patience to keep separate flatware for meat and dairy. When I did the shopping, I brought *treif* into the house.

Rose was offended at first, but she eventually came to understand that the rules had changed. The Jews had needed deliverance, and God hadn't shown up. The U.S. Army had to do His job for Him. I took a damn bullet doing His job for Him. So now, He didn't get to tell me what I could have for breakfast.

My concession to her was that after I filled the house with the smell of sizzling pig fat, I always made sure to cover it up with the smell of cigarettes.

My son came into the kitchen rubbing sleep out of his eyes. He was wearing flannel pajamas, and it didn't seem like it had been so long since he was wearing the ones with the little footies.

I set a plate in front of him.

"You can't buy me off this easily," he said.

"I'm not trying to buy anything," I told him. "I just wanted to fix breakfast."

There was a market that was open late, and I'd made a trip there after my talk with Len Weisskopf, mostly just to make sure Brian would be asleep by the time I got home. I didn't know what to say, and I wasn't ready to try to explain it to him.

I'd broken one of the hundred-dollar bills that Elijah had given me to pay for the groceries. Using the money felt dirty. I didn't feel particularly proud of anything that had happened over the course of the last week.

"Three men are dead, and you think you

can buy my admiration back with coffee and eggs?"

"And bacon," I said.

He nodded. "Okay. I'll have some bacon."

He ate in silence. I cooked more eggs.

Rose came into the kitchen a few minutes later. I set a plate of eggs and a toasted bagel in front of her.

"You didn't cook these in the same pan with that filth, did you?" she asked.

On our fifteenth anniversary, I tried to surprise her by bringing home a couple of live lobsters for dinner. Shellfish is forbidden to Jews, and Rose was furious. She told me to go back to the fish market and get my money back, but the lobsters had been out of the tank for too long, and the store wouldn't take them.

I wanted to cook them, even if Rose didn't want to eat any lobster meat, but she wouldn't have such unholiness in the house, and she made me throw them away. Nine dollars, right out the window.

I ended up sleeping on the couch that night, and I'd learned my lesson.

"I used a different pan," I said. "Your eggs never touched the pork."

"Good," she said. "That stuff makes me sick to my stomach."

"I know."

"Don't give Dad any guff, Mom," Brian said. "He has a busy day of shooting Negroes ahead of him."

"I didn't shoot any Negroes," I said.

"But your department did, and today, you are going to work like everything is normal."

"I'm not making excuses about what happened yesterday," I said. "Those officers probably should not have opened fire."

"Probably?" He pounded his fist on the table and nearly spilled his orange juice.

"Tensions were very high. It was a complicated situation."

"Those workers were trying to expose the barbaric practices of a company that was exploiting them, and the police treated them like a bunch of criminals. Your department allowed themselves to be used as strike-breaking thugs by that sleazy Alvin Kluge."

"Look, I know you've been listening to Abramsky a lot."

"I think for myself. But the rabbi is right about a lot of things."

"Abramsky lost family in the Holocaust," Rose said. "I can understand why he's concerned about the reach of the state and the way the police use force."

"That's an incredibly narrow viewpoint, and you know it, honey," I said. "There are other kinds of violence people need to be concerned about: Pimps and drunks beating up women. Drug dealers intimidating whole neighborhoods. Robbers gunning people down in the street. If the police can't deploy coercion and violence, we can't protect people."

Brian stuffed a whole piece of bacon into his mouth. "Those dangers seem pretty remote," he said. "Maybe the cure is worse than the disease. In order to stop a few thugs from hurting a few people, we empower a whole thug department to menace everybody."

"Have I ever told you about what happened to my father?" I asked.

"Buck, he's twelve years old," Rose said.

"So what? If he wants to be a man, he can know about these things. I was six when it happened."

For the first time all morning, Brian looked straight at me: "What happened to my grandfather?"

"We're not going to talk about this," Rose said.

I scraped the last of the eggs onto a plate for myself, and then I sat down at the table. Nobody spoke. I ate a piece of bacon and lit a cigarette.

Finally, I said: "The police force is only as good as the men who wear the uniform.

Some of those men aren't so good. But if good people won't do that job, then only bad people will do it. I have to go out there every day, and try to do the right thing. Like I said, I didn't shoot those Negroes."

"But you did beat down Mr. Schulman. I saw you do that."

"Yes, I did. And I felt like I needed to, because of the way he took off running when he saw me. I didn't know what he was up to. Maybe innocent people would have been hurt if I had ignored his suspicious behavior."

"I don't think Mr. Schulman was going to hurt anybody."

"It's good that you think the best about folks. But sometimes, people are more dangerous than they might seem."

"And sometimes violence is excessive."

"Yes, it is. Sometimes."

"Have you ever killed a man?" he asked.

Rose stopped chewing and looked at me.

I set my fork and knife on the plate and I looked him right in the eye. "You can't make an omelet without breaking an egg, every now and again."

A boy has to become a man sometime.

He stuck out his jaw and pouted at me. "Dad, I believe it's possible to prepare a full four-course country breakfast without causing a single human fatality."

I think, when he asked, he already knew. It was the sort of thing he probably was able to figure out on his own.

"Well, then, from now on, how about if you do the cooking?" I said.

34
2009

It took over an hour to get my doctor to let me leave the hospital. He insisted on putting a note in my chart that said I was checking myself out "against physician's advice." I told him to put whatever he needed to put wherever he needed to put it to get me out of there.

Fran brought Rose up to my room just as Rutledge was helping me into a wheelchair to leave. So that was a little bit of a scene, but at least William stayed behind to calm his grandmother down while I went with the detective.

There was nothing for her to be upset about. The criminals were long gone by the time Rutledge got me to the warehouse. The place was a ruin. Half the surrounding buildings looked like their roofs had caved in, and the ride got real bumpy near the end, because the asphalt was crumbling.

The police had set up crime-scene tape

around the building, and there were half a dozen squad cars with their lights flashing, parked just outside the cordon, plus several unmarked Chevys that anyone with a brain would make for police vehicles.

Usually, when you had this much police activity, onlookers would crowd around the crime scene, just beyond the tape, to see what was going on. Here, there were no civilians, which was evidence of just how desolate the area was.

A white man with thinning, sandy hair and gold wire-frame glasses came up to me as Rutledge was helping me get out of the passenger side of his car. He was dressed in plain clothes with a laminated credential around his neck.

"I just want to shake the hand of the man who shot Randall Jennings. That guy was a giant asshole," he said.

The thing hanging on his neck had a photo of him and the word FORENSICS on it. I used my decades of accrued detecting experience to draw a clever deduction:

"Are you a lab guy?" I asked.

"I am what passes for a guy in what passes for a lab in what passes for the Memphis Police Department," he said. "My friends call me Ed Clark, but my wife calls me late for dinner, and the Action News investigative team calls me twelve years behind schedule in testing all the rape kits."

This guy was kind of funny. I liked him. But I had a reputation to maintain.

"I don't like you," I said as I lit a cigarette.

He smiled. "I guess I wouldn't have things any other way."

"I brought Mr. Schatz here because he believes Charles Cameron aka Carlo Cash kidnapped a robbery suspect called Elijah out of Andre Price's car yesterday," Rutledge said. He had retrieved my walker from the trunk of his car, and he paused to unfold it and set it in front of me. "We believe Cash may have brought Elijah to this building. I'm hoping Mr. Schatz can square his understanding of the situation with the evidence you've found here."

"That sounds like something we can talk about," Clark said. The corners of his mouth turned downward. "Are y'all coming from the hospital? Is there any news about Price?"

Rutledge shook his head. "Last time I talked to the family, they said he still ain't breathing on his own. If he lives through this, he won't live well."

"God, I'm sorry to hear that. He always seemed like a real decent kid."

"He was one of us," Rutledge said. "And

now, there's hell to pay. We're taking this to where these motherfuckers live. We're burning their goddamn houses down."

"I think Elijah already beat you to it," I said. "But I like your attitude. Let's find out what's inside that warehouse."

There were three steps up to the side door of the warehouse, and no ramp. It was supposed to be illegal for a building to be inaccessible to people with handicaps, but I suspected this oversight was just one of many ways this building failed to meet code.

The stairs were too narrow to accommodate all four tips of my walker, so I couldn't steady myself by leaning on it. Rutledge had to hold my elbow as I slowly climbed, while Clark stood behind me, trying to pretend, for the sake of my dignity, that he wasn't preparing to catch me if I toppled backwards.

Inside the warehouse, the dim overhead lights had been augmented by some portable floodlights the police had brought in to help search for evidence. A large circle of floor just inside the doorway had been roped off with traffic cones and police tape. Other than that, the space looked empty. A thick layer of dust covered most of the surfaces, and looked to have been displaced from the floor only recently, when a lot of drug dealers had walked over it, and then again, when a lot of cops had walked over it.

"This is somewhat anticlimactic," I said.

"I don't know what you were expecting," said Clark.

"The last scene from *The Wild Bunch,*" I said.

"The last scene from *Reservoir Dogs,*" said Rutledge.

"Yeah. Sorry," said Clark.

"What did you find here?" I asked.

"Well, the floor was covered in dust except in the area we have roped off," Clark said. "We think that spot was scrubbed with bleach."

"How can you tell?" I asked.

"Because it smells like bleach," he told me. "This shit ain't rocket surgery. We did find traces of blood on the floor in the area that was cleaned, though. People think bleach hides blood, but people are stupid."

"So, what do you think happened?" I asked.

"I think somebody got shot there, and then somebody carted off the body and cleaned up the mess. There's no signs of dripping or blood anywhere but in that one place, so the killer probably knew how to move a corpse. Maybe they shoved him into a barrel. Maybe they had a body bag. You can pretty much roll a guy up in a plastic sheet, as long as you fold it right to keep it from leaking."

"It's likely that the stain is Elijah," Rutledge said. "They brought him here to kill him, and it looks like somebody got killed. It doesn't require a huge logical leap to presume your friend is dead."

"Doubtful," I told him. "This bloodstain is Carlo Cash. One of his accomplices shot him in the back of the head as soon as he came in here."

"What makes you so sure?" he asked.

So I told him how Elijah robbed the Cotton Planters Union Bank.

35
1965

Twenty-seven hours after Longfellow Molloy was killed by the Memphis police, Whit Pecker, the worst detective on the Memphis police force had finally connected my arrest of Ari Plotkin and his gang with the Planters Union bank robbery, so I got dragged into that investigation.

Pecker asked me in a pointed way why I hadn't bothered to tell him that I'd been investigating a plot to rob that bank. I told him that it had slipped my mind in the chaos of the previous day's events, and also that he could go fuck himself. An hour later, word came down from on high that the robbery was my case now, due to my previous involvement. As far as I was concerned, Pecker could have kept it.

I went down to the bank, where Greenfield was waiting in his magnificent office with his assistant, Riley Cartwright, a lawyer for the bank who was named Pumfrey or something, and a wraithlike insurance man called Swaine. All the seats were taken, so I had to stand, and it pissed me off.

For the benefit of his guests, Greenfield pretended to be meeting me for the first time. He called in his secretary, and she asked me if I'd like some coffee. She was very pretty in an Aryan sort of way, and Greenfield seemed delighted for any excuse to show her off to his guests.

Nobody else was drinking anything, so I assumed I was expected to politely decline her offer. I told her I'd love a cup with cream and two sugars.

"I'd heard you had arrested a sort of gang that was planning to rob us, but we never imagined anyone could have taken down our vault," he told me.

He waited with a look of dread for my response. I was only halfway done with the cigarette I was smoking, but I dropped it on his carpet and then stepped on it and ground the ember out with my heel. Then I lit another one with a wooden match, shook the match out, and threw it on the floor as well. Just to be thorough, I mashed the blackened head of the match with the toe of my shoe.

"If I had anticipated that there were any other robbers planning to hit your bank, I certainly would have come here to talk to you about it," I said.

I looked up and saw Pumpleroy and Swindle staring at me with undisguised horror. I smiled at them. Greenfield, for his part, looked somewhat relieved.

"I think it's pretty clear that the security apparatus failed, and the vault was breached somehow, when it was supposed to be locked down and sealed," Greenfield said.

"But how could that happen? The vault is nearly impregnable," Swine said.

"The 'nearly' being the reason we carry insurance," Pimple-piss added.

"Why weren't there guards posted by the vault?" I asked.

"I had to make a decision in a circumstance that wasn't covered by ordinary protocols," Greenfield said. "The street-facing entrance to the bank is all windows; essentially a sheet of glass, and we were in the midst of what we understood might be a race riot. I decided to move all my security personnel to the front of the building to deter looters from trying to smash their way inside."

"And you left the vault unprotected?"

"No. I triggered the alarm, which was supposed to seal the vault. It should have been impossible to open. We can't figure out how the thief could have gotten into it."

"What sort of person could possibly do this?" Squidge said. "Who could take apart a state-of-the-art security system and unlock a sealed vault without ever being noticed?"

"Negroes," Greenfield answered without hesitation.

"Yes," I agreed. "When things like this happen, we generally assume Negroes are responsible."

The insurance man did not look pleased. "Detective, do you think you can recover the stolen funds?"

"I'll certainly do everything I can," I said. "But the truth is that I most likely will not be able to find the perpetrator. If thieves aren't caught in the act, and we don't have witnesses who can identify them, our best shot at capturing them comes when they try to fence the stolen goods. But thieves who steal cash don't need a fence, and it's hard to identify stolen money, even if we find it. We usually either catch bank robbers within minutes of the crime, or we don't catch them at all."

"That is bad," Sibilant said. "Very bad."

Here, the conversation paused as the secretary came in with my coffee. I took a sip, and it was very good. I almost felt guilty about dumping it out all over the rug.

"Oh, how clumsy of me," I said. "I'm so embarrassed."

I wasn't, really.

Greenfield pressed an intercom button on his desk and called the girl back in to try to clean up the mess. I felt awkward about having her on her hands and knees, rubbing the stain with a rag, so I dropped my cigarette on the carpet, ground it out with my heel, and then I bent down to help her.

"You don't need to do that, Detective," Greenfield said.

"Are you sure? I just feel so bad about this mess," I said.

"It's really not a problem," said the secretary.

"All right." I stood up, lit a cigarette with a wooden match, shook the match out, dropped it on the rug, and stepped on it.

After a very long and uncomfortable exchange of horrified glances among the three expensive suits, the conversation resumed.

"There is one silver lining — for you, I mean," Pissface said to the insurer. "The vault comes with fairly comprehensive guarantees from the manufacturer, and the security firm that installed it guarantees the work it performed as well. They promise to pay for any losses associated with the failure of the vault or the alarm mechanism."

"That is good news," said Swindler. "Detective, do you expect your report will find that the robbery occurred as a result of the vault failing to perform as promised?"

"I'll have to investigate further before I can say for sure," I said. "But that certainly seems to be what happened."

The lawyer seemed pleased by my willingness to oblige. "Obviously, we'll expect your firm to fully indemnify our loss as per the terms of the insurance agreement," he said to Shitball. "But you may then step into our shoes and attempt to recover on their guarantees, which should spread around the exposure a bit."

"I don't think this conversation is pertinent to my investigation," I said. If I had to listen to these assholes much longer, I was going to run out of cigarettes. "Maybe I had better go take a look at the vault."

"Certainly," Greenfield said with a dismissive wave. "Cartwright can show you anything you need to see."

Cartwright looked a little bit crestfallen to be kicked out of the high-level meeting, but he obediently followed me out of Greenfield's office.

Once we were in the elevator, he told me: "I think you pretty much destroyed his rug."

"That's a shame," I said. "It really tied the room together."

36
1965

"So the vault is just left open during business hours?"

"We keep two armed guards stationed on it," Cartwright said, gesturing at the two men standing by the open vault door. "But, yes. It would be quite unwieldy to have to open up this complex apparatus every time tellers needed to refill their cash drawers or a client wanted to access a safe-deposit box."

I examined the vault door. It was nearly two feet thick. I stepped through it and looked at it from the inside. Then I stepped out. I peered at the locking mechanism. I didn't know anything about vaults, but I figured cracking one open would involve drilling holes in it or something. The vault door did not appear to have any holes drilled in it. It didn't seem as if anyone had worked on it with acid or blowtorches or sledgehammers. As best I could tell, this door had not been tampered with.

"Could the guards have been in on it?"

One of the guards frowned at me.

"The men who guard our vaults each have at least fifteen years of professional experience, and an established record of trustworthiness," Cartwright said.

"A man's trustworthy only until you leave him alone with something that's worth more to him than his reputation," I said.

"Several of our guards have worked on armored truck crews, which routinely carry amounts in excess of a quarter-million dollars," he said. "Others have experience working security in larger banks than this; banks that always keep large amounts of cash on hand. These are good men. I hired most of them myself."

"I am not sure your word or anyone's reputation is good enough to eliminate all suspicion when so much money has been stolen," I said.

"Every member of the security team stayed on duty, guarding the front of the bank for hours after the lockdown," he protested. "I don't think any of them could possibly have been carrying all that cash on his person. And I don't recall any suspicious behavior from any of them, even after the robbery was discovered."

"Okay," I said. "So, for the moment, let's assume the guards are innocent."

I walked down the hallway to look at the security cage. It was made of a sturdy mesh that was too fine to stick a hand through, and too thick to cut easily, but there was no lock I could see on the inside of it; just a handle. "Do you need a key to open this?" I asked.

"Not from this side. Fire regulations prohibit having doors like this that lock from the inside."

I started to turn the handle.

"Don't do that, Detective. It isn't locked, but it's wired to the security mechanism, and if you open it, you will set off the alarm."

"So the exterior door at the end of the hall isn't locked, either?" I asked.

"It has a security bar, but the lock can be disengaged from the inside without a key."

"Seems like a pretty big hole in your impenetrable security system, if somebody can just walk right out the door after emptying your vault."

"We are a bank, not a prison. We want to keep people from getting in, not prevent them from getting out. Our security system assures that an alarm will be triggered and the vault will be sealed before a thief ever gets near it. Preventing an escape should never become a concern. And, of course, anything that would prevent a thief from escaping would also impede an emergency evacuation."

"The problem is that your security didn't work, and we need to figure out why," I said. "And it certainly wasn't helpful that the thief was able to walk right out the door after he cleaned out your vault."

"If he got out that way, I don't understand why the alarm didn't go off when he opened it."

"What if the alarm was going off already?"

Cartwright shrugged.

I turned to the guards. "Were either of you men guarding this vault the morning of the robbery?"

One of them nodded. "I was, until Mr. Greenfield moved all security staff to the lobby, to keep the rioters from smashing the windows."

"Were you standing here in front of the door when it sealed?"

He shook his head. "I was already up front. But I had only just gotten there. Mr. Greenfield called over the intercom and told us that we were to reinforce the street entrance, and then he activated the security system."

"Just so I've got this right: He moved you up front, and then he triggered the alarm, which sealed the vault."

"That's right."

"And the vault was open when you left it?"

"Yeah, but not for very long. Couple of minutes, at most. Nobody could have come in and robbed it before he set the alarm off."

I looked at the vault again, and then I looked at the security gate blocking the hallway. Then I looked at the ceiling.

"Is there a janitor here?" I asked Cartwright.

"Yeah, of course. Somebody's got to clean up."

"Have him come down here, and tell him to bring his broom."

Cartwright scurried off and fetched an elderly colored man in a faded blue jumpsuit.

"Were you here yesterday when the bank was robbed?" I asked the janitor.

"No, sir. I got sent home with the office staff. I was none too happy about it. You know, they all get salaries, but I get pay by the hour. If I ain't workin', I ain't eatin'."

I nodded. "Can I borrow your broom?" I asked.

"I'm gonna need it back," he said, but he

handed it to me.

I poked the ceiling with it.

Greenfield's office was covered in luxurious hardwood, and the grand lobby was made of pink limestone, but the guts of the bank, the parts the clients didn't see, were no-frills commercial office space. The walls were thin and felt like cardboard, the floors were cheap tile, and the ceilings were drop-in panels made of compressed sawdust and asbestos, held up by a grid of steel beams.

Using the broom, I lifted a panel out of place. There was an eighteen-inch gap between the panel and the concrete floor of the next story, and electrical wiring and heating ductwork filled most of that empty space. But I figured a man could fit up there, and the steel grid would support him, as long as he splayed himself out and spread his weight over several beams.

"Does the security cage stop at the panels, or does it go all the way up?" I asked.

"It's bolted to the concrete, and wired for alarms, if somebody tries to tamper with it. There is a gap in it for electrical, but it's far too small for a man to fit through."

I pushed the ceiling panel back into place, and then I gave the broom back to the janitor.

"So how did they beat the security alarms?" Cartwright asked. "How did they crack the vault?"

"I've got no idea," I said. Greenfield had clearly wanted to blame the security system so that the bank could collect on the guarantee. So, I said: "I guess the vault or the alarm must have malfunctioned."

And that's what it says in the official report, as attested by lead investigating officer, Det. Baruch Schatz: The vault was plundered during an episode of racial unrest, by perpetrators unknown, as a result of an as-yet-unidentified mechanical failure of the security system.

37
1965

The camp at Auschwitz was comprised of barracks where the prisoners slept and the parade ground where the roll calls were conducted. All of this was ringed by high walls and razor wire, and monitored from guard towers, to prevent any escapes. But Auschwitz was a work camp first, and imprisonment was only a secondary purpose. Every day, the prisoners marched through the gates to their various labor details, supervised only by a couple of armed guards.

Of course, those guards were vigilant, and there were no real restraints on their use of deadly force. If a prisoner ran, the guards would shoot him. If he somehow got past them, they'd hunt him with dogs.

Elijah got out of Auschwitz by bribing a guard to let him flee, and that guard taught Elijah his most important principle; the rule that guided his future endeavors and gave shape to whatever passed for his moral philosophy:

Every lock has a fatal weakness. No matter how complex or refined its mechanism; no matter how many pins and tumblers it has, no matter how many plates of steel you embed it in, every lock has a key. And that key is in the hands of a man.

A sophisticated lock can thwart the efforts of even the most talented safecracker, and a sturdy enough vault can withstand a power drill or a blowtorch or even dynamite.

But there's no technology that can reinforce the man with the key, and there's no way to increase the complexity of the urges that motivate him. So the best lock in the world can never be sturdier than some asshole's integrity.

The vault at the Cotton Planters Union Bank was a steel box with walls two feet thick, sunk into a block of concrete, protected by two armed guards, and rigged to a complex security alarm that would seal it at the first sign of a threat.

Six floors above the vault, Charles Greenfield sat in his lavish office, brooding. His career with the bank had been successful, but now he had climbed as high as he was ever going to get. He was an affluent man, but he was a servant to the truly rich; the people who owned everything. He had raised himself high enough to see over their walls and into their kingdom, but he would never dwell there.

He would never be one of them. And probably, he knew why that was; probably, he knew that even if his Tennessee drawl was spot-on perfect; even if he wore what they wore, and ate their deep-fried foods and sipped on sour mash whiskey, he'd always just be a Jew to them. Useful and servile and socially inferior.

He was a cog in a machine; an important cog, perhaps, but a cog, nonetheless. And below him, a small, sputtering inefficiency in the works was causing tens of thousands of dollars to pile up in his vault each week.

At precisely 10:30 in the morning on a Tuesday in late November, the protest outside Kluge erupted into violence. Elijah knew this would happen, because he'd paid Officer Len Weisskopf thirty-five hundred dollars to start busting skulls open at that specific time, on that specific day.

In response to these events, Greenfield moved all his guards to the front of the bank to protect the street-facing entrance, and then he pressed the alarm to seal and secure the vault.

If you review Greenfield's conduct during

the riot and the robbery, as a police detective or an insurance investigator might, there is nothing clearly wrong about any of the decisions he made. Except that the result of those decisions was that the vault was open and unattended for about ninety seconds, after the guards redeployed to the front of the bank, but before the alarm triggered.

And that was when Elijah slithered out of the ceiling, where he'd been hiding, splayed out on the steel beams. Greenfield probably stashed Elijah up there early in the morning, before the regular staff came in, when the premises were patrolled by only a single night guard.

It must have hurt like hell to perch up there, with his weight resting on a smashed kneecap and a crushed hand. But Elijah could deal with it; he'd survived worse.

And the payoff was worth it. He walked into the open vault and scooped all the cash into a bag and was out before Greenfield triggered the alarm.

The security cage and the alleyway door were wired to the alarm, but since the alarm was already going off, that didn't matter. Elijah just walked through the security cage and out of the bank, and then he disappeared into the crowd of white office workers fleeing the neighborhood. Meanwhile, since the vault was sealed by the alarm, nobody would even discover the theft for three hours.

I don't know how Elijah got to Greenfield, but the bank manager must have been in on it. There's no other way the scheme works.

But here's the thing: If that's the scheme, then what was Ari Plotkin's role? After I inspected the vault, I pulled Plotkin out of the lockup, put him in an interrogation room, and raked him over the coals again, just to see if I could rattle anything loose. I think, by then, he'd worked out that Elijah had set him up. If he knew anything, he probably would have snitched just for spite. But he didn't know anything other than what I'd already learned from his crew: They were supposed to walk in with guns and clean out the cages. He hadn't been involved in any plot to take the vault.

I went up to my desk, leaned back in my chair, lit a cigarette, and tried to figure out how the facts fit together.

I thought about how the department had taken the bank investigation away from Whit Pecker and dropped it on me. I'd busted a gang planning to rob the same bank just a few days earlier, and it seemed likely that the foiled plot was related to the successful theft. It made perfect sense that the department would tap me to run the investigation; I'd even go so far as to say it was a predictable outcome.

I thought about the first time I'd met Elijah; that meeting in the basement barroom full of river-stink and his five huge thugs. Why had he been looking for me, specifically? Perhaps because I was Jewish. But I had no reputation for corruption, and he had no reason to think I would be amenable to his offer. Why would he tell me he was planning a heist in Memphis; that he was trying to recruit a Jewish cop into his scheme? Why would he take the risk of even letting me know that he was in town?

I thought about Paul Schulman. If he hadn't run away when he saw me in front of the synagogue, I probably would have ignored him. But he ran, so I chased him.

And when I caught him, he'd given me two important clues: He told me that the plan was connected to the Kluge strike, and he told me that Plotkin was involved.

How had Schulman learned these things? He was a third-rate hustler, and Elijah was notoriously secretive. And why had Schulman run when he saw me? He wasn't one of the great intellects of his generation, but he had to know that I'd give chase if he fled. If I had to think of it, that outcome was predictable, too. Elijah had used Schulman to feed me that information.

When I held off on pursuing Plotkin and decided to try to stake out the bank instead, Elijah had shown up to provoke me. And I had responded in the most predictable way possible, by arresting the man that Elijah wanted me to arrest. And, because I'd arrested Plotkin, I ended up in charge of investigating the vault robbery.

In the end, any detective — maybe not Whit Pecker, but any competent detective — would have worked out that the vault was likely robbed during the ninety seconds it was open and unattended, and there was no way that could happen without help from somebody working in the bank.

Elijah and Greenfield wanted to be investigated by the one detective who had no desire to unravel their scheme; the one detective who would be unwilling to show the world how Jews in positions of trust and authority had betrayed society to enrich themselves.

I'd done exactly what they wanted me to do; I ran Weisskopf out of town before he spoke to the men investigating the Kluge massacre, and I covered up the ninety-second gap that Greenfield created for Elijah.

I don't know if what I did was the right thing, but I protected the Jews. I protected my family.

38
2009

"The weakness of every lock is the man with the key," said Rutledge. "So, if you want to get out of a concentration camp, you get to the guard. If you want to get into a bank vault, you get to the bank manager."

"And if you want to get into three different hidden caches of drug dealer money?" Clark asked.

"He had Carlo Cash's iPhone. As soon as he switched it on, Carlo could track him with the Find My iPhone application. Elijah wanted Carlo to find him," Rutledge said.

"But Elijah didn't switch it on until he was in police custody," I said. "He wanted to bring Cash directly into conflict with the police."

"And we responded to the attack on Andre Price with massive retaliation. We swept the streets clean of Carlo Cash's people. We've been doing somebody's dirty work. But whose?"

I shrugged. "The competition? Some underling who decided it was time to sit in the big chair? Personally, I think it was the Mexican suppliers. But I don't know these guys, and I don't care that much. I'm after my bank robber. The drug dealers are your problem. But if I had your job, I'd start with the assumption that whoever wanted Carlo Cash out of the picture was the same person who gave Elijah the address of the first stash house, six months ago."

Rutledge squatted down and looked at the bleached spot on the warehouse floor. It looked exactly like nothing at all.

"So, how does an eighty-year-old thief get past a bunch of armed thugs to rob Carlo Cash's locked-up stash?"

"My guess is, he buys the thugs off. Jacquarius Madison told me that Carlo's business only works for as long as his people stay loyal. Elijah sows disloyalty. It's how he works."

"But Jacques said that the guards were killed."

"Yeah, but how does he know? I asked him how they were killed, and he couldn't tell me. I asked him what happened to the bodies, and he didn't know. Most likely, the stash house was empty, and the guards were gone. Carlo told everyone his men had been killed, because he couldn't let anyone find out that his crew had betrayed and robbed him. But after that first robbery, Carlo's top lieutenants had to go with him to meet the Mexicans. And Carlo didn't have the money. Jacques told me those guys thought they were all going to be killed at that meeting. They had to be considering their long-term employment prospects — their long-term survival prospects — with Carlo Cash after that."

Rutledge took out his giant Internet cell phone and started jabbing at the screen with his finger. "And meanwhile, Carlo is scrambling to stack up twelve million dollars, while his people are thinking he looks weak, because he got robbed and is in debt to the Mexicans. It can't have been hard for Elijah to get to somebody close to him."

"I think Elijah got to everybody close to him," I said. "Jacques told me that no single person knew the location of all three stashes."

"How does he do that? How does he turn a drug-trafficking organization inside out like that?"

"Well, now we're entering a realm of speculation," I said.

Clark was looking very interested now. "Go ahead and speculate, Buck."

"You ever heard of a prisoner's dilemma?" I asked.

"Sure," said Rutledge. "It's one of the most basic interrogation techniques — I have two suspects, and I need a confession or I have to turn them both loose. I want to turn them against each other. So, I put them in separate interrogation rooms, and I tell each of them that the first one to confess gets a lenient deal, but his coconspirator will face serious charges. So they have to decide whether to keep silent, and hope their friend does as well, or confess and take the deal, at the friend's expense. I've tried it a few times, and one of them always confesses."

"Carlo created the same situation for his men," I said. "He felt it wasn't safe to put all his money in one place, so he had three different stashes. But he really couldn't afford to lose any of them. If he made it to the meeting with the Mexicans with all of the money to get even, and get his supply, then he was back on top, and he'd have fixed the damage the previous robbery had done to his organization. But if he went to the Mexicans without their money, it wasn't clear at all what would happen. Maybe the Mexicans would kill everybody."

"So Elijah goes to each of Carlo's lieutenants, and he tells them the others are already working with him. So the reward for loyalty is most likely the privilege of getting to go down with Carlo and his sinking ship."

"I figure Elijah showed up at each stash house with someone high up in Carlo's organization," I said. "He told the guards inside that they could either open the doors and get a share of the money, or they could have a gunfight. The benefits of protecting Carlo's interests were minimal, because if he lost any of the other stashes and couldn't pay the Mexicans, he'd be in no position to reward men who stayed loyal to him."

"That makes sense," Rutledge said. "When we take down a stash house, we send in a SWAT team. Those dudes roll in wearing full body armor and blow the doors in with plastic explosives. Then they fill the room with smoke grenades. The only way you break into a place like that is the loud way."

"Charles Greenfield told me something very similar about his bank vault."

"Even if the stashes were located in industrial areas, there's nowhere in the city where you could have a shoot-out with machine guns and shit, without police being alerted. You're probably right. The guys guarding the stashes must have just surrendered."

"Wait, so what is the point of the stolen iPhone?" Clark asked.

"The only way Elijah gets away clean is if he takes Carlo out," Rutledge said. "Carlo was in big trouble with the Mexicans because he lost the money, but if he got through that alive somehow, he'd be coming hard after everybody who crossed him."

"And Elijah is arrogant," I said. "It's not enough for him to get away with the loot. He has to find some kind of opponent, and make some kind of chess game out of it, and he has to gloat about winning it. I think that was what he was doing in the lobby at Greenfield's bank, the day I ran into him there. He needed to humiliate me; to force me to acknowledge that I couldn't kill him and I couldn't arrest him."

"But you dragged him into the bathroom and kicked the shit out of him," Rutledge said.

"Yeah. I don't think he anticipated that. But a beating doesn't change the way his mind works. He doesn't just want to steal something; he wants a sort of ideological triumph. He wants to unravel the social order."

"So, he got up in Carlo's face at some point, taunted him, and lifted the phone,"

Clark said. "He knew that Carlo would come after him in an irrational rage, like a wounded animal, as soon as he switched that phone on. So he switched it on when he was in the backseat of a police car. Carlo came after him, and inadvertently started a war with the police."

"Carlo thought he was bringing Elijah out to this warehouse to kill him, but really, Elijah was bringing Carlo, because Carlo's guys were secretly Elijah's guys," said Rutledge.

"Elijah forced those men to kill Carlo, by letting Carlo capture him," I said. "If Elijah confessed under torture, he'd expose them. Once Carlo knew what happened, he was too dangerous for anyone to let him live. And with the police out for payback, those men needed to get their money, get rid of Carlo, and get out of town."

"So, the stain on the floor is Carlo. I admire the intricacy of the scheme," Rutledge said. "I'd like to meet your friend Elijah. Preferably across an interrogation table. But I guess he'll have vanished by now, with the money."

"I don't know," I said. "There were plenty of ways he could have gotten himself into the back of a police car, but he chose to drag me into the mix. Whatever he thinks he and I are doing, I am not sure he's done with it yet."

Rutledge's giant cell phone buzzed. He looked at the screen. "Andre's new CAT scans are showing extensive brain damage. His parents are in a meeting with the hospital's chief surgical resident right now."

"Are they going to be able to save him?" I asked.

"No," Rutledge said. "They're talking about organ donation."

39
2009

When Rutledge dropped me off at Valhalla, Rose was waiting for me in our little apartment, looking at the television but not really watching it. She was fully wroth with indignation.

"I've been trying to reach you for hours. Your cell phone was going straight to voice mail."

I pulled it out of my pocket and flipped it open.

"I think the battery is dead," I said.

She took it out of my hand and pushed the big green button next to the keypad. The little screen lit up.

"It's just switched off. Someone must have switched it off at the hospital. We got you this thing three years ago. Why won't you learn how to use it?"

I took it back from her. "Don't see the point. Got along just fine for eighty years without any cell phone."

She slapped her hand to her forehead. "That's what you refuse to understand. Things aren't the same as they used to be. We aren't the same as we used to be. You need the phone to be charged up and switched on, because if you fall down, you can't get off the floor without calling somebody for help."

"I'm not too worried about that."

"Well, you should be. We had to move into this place because you got yourself horribly injured. I had to give up my home because of your stupid Nazi-hunting adventure. I told you not to go after the Nazi, but you had to do it anyway. You never even asked me how I felt about losing the house. All I wanted was to be surrounded, during my last few years, by things that gave me comfort. Now those things are all in storage, because we have to live here, because of you."

"I'm sorry," I said. "I'm sorry I gave you sixty-five good years, and now I am old and sick."

"We're not here because you are old and sick. We're here because you got shot fighting with desperadoes over treasure. Who the hell does that?"

I shrugged. "Sometimes I tussle with bad guys. You knew who I was when you married me."

"I thought I knew who you were. But you've changed. You've retreated into yourself. You've become someone different since Brian died."

"I've had a rough couple of days, Rose. Do we have to talk about Brian right now?"

"We've never talked about Brian. He's been gone seven years, and you can't even begin to deal with it. You want to know the difference between you and me?"

"Oh, I can't wait to hear this."

"I'm stronger than you. You can't deal with losing things. I've been preparing for it all my life. I spent the war worrying you were going to get yourself killed over there. A lot of girls had to worry about their men, so I couldn't complain about that. But those boys came back and settled into ordinary lives. You came back to me with a lot of scars and, for some reason, a taste for blood and danger."

"That's not true," I said. "You don't understand, because I never wanted to burden you with it. All I ever wanted was to protect my family."

"You didn't want to burden me? I spent thirty years worrying that something was going to happen to you. Every morning, you walked out the door, and I didn't know if you were going to come home or not. And when you worked late, you usually didn't even call to tell me you were all right. I just had to wait. So when Brian died, I had to handle it alone, because I was the only one who was prepared to handle loss. Your whole life, your only plan to deal with tragedy was to die first, except you could never bring yourself to even do that."

"My plan was to not ever need to endure tragedy. My plan was to take care of everyone. To keep you all safe."

"Buck, that is a stupid plan, and I think you know it. And you had no contingency to fall back on when your stupid plan failed. When you got hurt, I gave everything up to bring you here. That was a choice I made. If you were too weak to get up in the morning, I didn't have to move you someplace that could provide you with physical rehabilitation. I could have just left you in the bed and called in the hospice service."

"I'd have done the same thing for you."

"But you didn't. Four months ago, I fell down and had to go in the hospital. And you left me. You ran away to St. Louis with Tequila to go on your silly treasure hunt. And of course, you ended up getting hurt, because you're almost ninety years old, and you're trying to do things you're physically not capable of doing anymore. You insist on tussling with the bad guys, because you refuse to acknowledge the fact that you're frail and brittle."

"You don't understand," I said. "This is all I've got. I've lost my health, and I've lost my career, and I've lost my son, and some-day soon, I am going to lose my mind and my past. You say I can't deal with loss, but this is how I deal with it. By being who I am, for as long as I can. When I've got noth-ing else, I've got my integrity, and I've got my principles. And I don't leave things un-finished."

"You've got me. Does that even matter to you? Do you think about how it affects me, when you run off to engage in some prepos-terous struggle with some ancient foe who nobody has cared about for fifty years?"

"Of course you matter to me. You matter more than anything. But you can't ask me to be anything other than Buck Schatz. I'm much too old to change."

"I know who I am, too," she said, clench-ing her fists. "I am the one who has to get a phone call about how you're in the hospital because you got into a gunfight with drug dealers. What if you'd died?"

"What if I had? I'm going to die someday. Maybe someday soon."

"That doesn't mean you've got to go chasing after it."

"Is it worse to get a phone call than to just wake up one morning and find me cold? Or worse, to watch me die of something slow, like the dementia?"

"I had to lose my home because of you. That was our place, and we had to sell it to some faceless company that wanted it for an investment property."

This sounded familiar; sounded like something I might have written in a notebook at some point. But I'd forgotten about it.

"Wait. What company?" I asked.

"You know all about this. You were on the phone when William explained it."

"I don't remember that. Tell me who bought our house."

"It's a real estate trust that buys these properties as speculative investments."

I pushed my walker over to the rolltop desk in one corner of the room and started going through the drawer where we kept our important papers.

"What are you doing?" Rose said. "You can't just walk away from this conversation we're having right now."

I found the paper I was looking for: a record of the sale of our home to an entity called Fifth Cup Holdings. The fifth cup during the Passover seder was Elijah's cup. He had bought it. He had taken my house; he'd spent a hundred thousand dollars just to taunt me. Or to tell me something. Could it really be that simple?

"I have got to go," I said.

"What? You can't leave."

"I'll be back soon. I promise." I grabbed the keys to the Buick off the little peg on the wall where Rose hung them, because we hardly ever drove anymore.

"You can't drive now. It's nighttime. You don't drive at night."

"It's no big deal. I'll be back soon." I reached into the closet to get my .357.

"It's like you don't hear what I am saying to you."

"I hear you. I understand. But there are things a man needs to do."

She'd get over it. She always did.

40
2009

I still had a set of keys to the front door of the house, but somebody had changed out the locks, so I pushed my own doorbell and held it down.

He was here. I'd known it as soon as I spotted the Honda Accord parked in the driveway. It was exactly the car he'd drive, because it was a car that nobody would ever notice. It wasn't old enough to emit a memorable cloud of smoke, or to look remarkably boxy compared to the sleek edges of the latest models, but it wasn't new enough to attract the curiosity of owners of older Accords who might take some vague interest in the trim or features of a new model.

The color was the same as the color of every other car you look at the back of for three minutes at a stoplight and never remember having seen. You could look right at this Honda Accord and never notice it. It was the next best thing to being invisible.

It was riding low on the rear shocks, too. Like a couple of fat guys were sitting in the backseat. But there were no fat guys in that car.

Here is something you learn in thirty-five years as a police detective: A twenty-dollar bill, or any paper denomination of U.S. currency, weighs approximately one gram. If you work the math out, five million dollars in twenties in the trunk will weigh a car down on its rear shocks the same amount as a couple of fat guys sitting in the backseat. Most people who aren't drug dealers don't think of cash as being heavy, but most people who aren't drug dealers don't take the time to consider the implications of large amounts in small bills.

I didn't like that he'd parked the car in the driveway, though. He could easily have pulled it around the back of the house and parked in the garage, where it was out of sight. The driveway was the worst place to park it, because people on the street could see it and he couldn't, since the only window that looked out on that side of the house was completely blocked by a privacy hedge.

He'd have been better off parking it on the street, where he could at least keep an eye on it. I wondered why he'd parked it where he'd parked it. It seemed like a sign of extreme carelessness, or maybe arrogance.

Or else it was a signal; weird that a man hiding out after stealing millions from a drug dealer would want to signal his presence. But who would recognize this thoroughly inconspicuous Honda Accord as a message?

I had, so I supposed I would. It was a signal for me. Just as I'd known he'd be here, he knew I'd be coming. And he was waiting for me.

Elijah still hadn't answered, so I pushed the doorbell again.

Even though it was hot out, I was wearing the Members Only jacket that Brian had given me for my birthday in 1986. In the left-hand pocket, I was carrying a roll of silver duct tape. In the right pocket, I had my .357.

I thought of Longfellow Molloy lying on the pavement with his unblinking eye open and staring at me, and I thought of Andre Price lying in his hospital bed, hooked up to the ventilator. The check had come due, and it was time for Elijah to pay up.

I heard the lock click, but the door didn't open. I counted to ten, slowly, and then I turned the knob.

Inside, all the lights were off, and there was no sign of Elijah. I pushed my walker through the front door and trudged down a short hallway. The dining room opened to my right. We used to keep my mother's china in a glass-fronted cabinet in there. Now it was in a box in a storage locker someplace.

The wall to my left used to be covered with family photos. Of Rose and me when we were younger; of William as a baby; of Brian. Somebody had filled in the holes I'd nailed into the wall to hang the frames from, and then painted over the plaster.

The sturdy brick fireplace was the only remnant of my old den that hadn't been ripped out during the renovation. The carpeting was gone, and someone had waxed and polished the wood floor underneath. This place didn't look like home anymore. It didn't smell like us.

My family was here for sixty years, and a construction crew had eliminated every sign our habitation in a matter of days. Standing there, in the dark, in the den that used to be my den but wasn't anymore, I recognized the futility of all human endeavors. It didn't matter whether you tiptoed through the world invisibly like Elijah, or you stomped around bellowing and beating people with clubs; in the end, the sum total of your life amounted to nothing that couldn't be washed away or covered up with a dab of plaster and a coat of paint.

As years went by, you just got old, and then you vanished like a stone beneath the surface of a lake, and even as you gloated over the size of the splash you made, the waters stilled and everything went back to being exactly like it was before you appeared on the scene; exactly how it would have been if you'd never existed.

The kitchen where I used to eat breakfast with my family was to my right. The renovators had pulled up the cracked, dingy linoleum that Rose had been on my case for twenty years to do something about, and they'd laid down new tile. Stripped of its miniblinds, the window looked naked, but it was letting in a fair amount of light from the streetlamps outside, so I could see where I was going. I turned the other way and followed the hallway toward the bedrooms at the back of the house.

Along the way, I checked the guest room, where William used to sleep when his parents sent him here to get him out of their hair for a night or a weekend. The built-in bookshelves used to be lined with the thick, leather-bound photo albums that Rose had carefully maintained since before I married her. Now almost all of those albums were in the concrete self-storage locker we'd rented.

I checked the half bathroom in the hallway. I thought Elijah might be hiding in there, because it had no windows and was the darkest room in the house. I didn't miss that bathroom; it was not a well-considered architectural feature. When somebody took a shit in there, the smell had no place to go.

Anyway, he wasn't in there, which left two doors, across from each other at the end of the hallway. I put my hand on the door of the bedroom Rose and I had shared since Eisenhower was in office, and paused for a moment to think. Then I turned around, which was difficult to do with the walker in such a narrow space. I opened the other door and flipped the light switch.

Elijah was sitting in a metal folding chair in the middle of the room. Even the way he sat annoyed me: he crossed his legs with one knee on top of the other, like a woman. There was a large red duffel bag sitting on the floor next to him, and he had a black 9 mm pistol in his right hand.

"I'd halfway hoped you might fall down in the dark and die on the way in here," he said. "But it's good that we have a chance to talk."

41
2009

"If you hadn't wanted me to find you, you could have arranged to hide out pretty much anywhere else," I said.

His face bore no expression; just an indifferent mask. He looked like a melted wax dummy of the man I'd beat up fifty years before. "Yes, I suppose that's true, isn't it?" he said.

"So, whatever you want to say to me, how about you say it?"

He looked up; his eyes met mine. "This was your son's room, wasn't it?"

I flinched. "Yes," I said. "How'd you know?"

He waved the gun at me. "The master bedroom is across the hall. There are only three bedrooms in the house. It makes sense that you would put the child in the closest room."

"That's good," I said. "Impressive deduction."

Then I hit him with my walker.

Even though it only weighed about five pounds, I couldn't pick the thing up and swing it like I used to swing my truncheon. My legs weren't strong enough to support my body when I twisted my torso. All I could do was lift the legs of the thing off the ground and sort of push it forward at him.

But that was all I needed; he was surprised by the move, and he reflexively put his arm in front of him to block the blow, so I tangled him up in the legs of the walker and knocked the gun out of his hand.

I took a wobbly step back and disengaged the walker from him before he could grab hold of it, and then I swept the front wheels at the gun and sent it sliding across the floor.

I set the walker back down and then sagged against it, winded from the effort. Elijah rose to his feet, knocking over his folding chair.

"I can't believe you just did that," he said. "I can't imagine a more ridiculous or ineffectual thing for you to attempt. What else have you got planned? Are you going to spit your dentures at me?"

I smiled at him. "I've got all the original fixtures. You're the one with the false teeth."

"They're implant-supported bridges. Very

expensive, top-of-the-line orthodontic work, and they can't be spit out."

"Dentures is dentures," I said. "How did you get all that dental work done, anyway? Ain't you been living as a fugitive for fifty years?"

"I paid cash, like I do for all my medical care. And I paid extra to have the orthodontist destroy my dental records afterwards. Then I burned down his office, just to be safe." He took a step back to get outside the reach of the walker. "Did you think you were going to beat me again, the way you beat me when you caught me in the bank? You aren't strong anymore, Baruch. You're a goddamn invalid."

The demented part of my brain that still believed I was a detective was howling inside my skull; telling me I could break this man six different ways using only my hands. It was a lie. My hands weren't much good for breaking anything anymore. I could still break wind, but that was all.

"I wasn't trying to beat you," I said. "I just wanted to get the gun away from you."

"And then what? I can just walk over there and pick it up. You have to slowly, painfully shuffle across the room, and then you can't bend down to lift the thing off the floor without toppling over and busting your head open. There's no way you can get to it before I can. It appears you haven't considered this very carefully."

He took a step toward the gun.

"I wouldn't do that, if I was you," I said.

"Why not?"

I pulled the .357 out of my pocket and pointed it at him. "Because it appears my consideration is more careful than you realized, asshole. So, how about you sit down."

He started to pick up his folding chair.

"Not on that," I said. "On the floor." I pointed with my gun toward the corner of the room farthest from where his 9 mm had come to rest. He was right that I couldn't easily pick his gun up off the ground. But I was fine, as long as he couldn't get to it, either.

"Come on, Baruch," he said. "I have arthritic knees."

"I don't care. You can deal with the discomfort. Sit down."

"Of course you would be armed," he said. "I wouldn't have expected you to come after me, unless you were clutching your fetish object."

"I think it will probably afford me a little bit of protection, in the event our conversation devolves into gunplay."

"I don't think that's likely to happen,"

Elijah said.

"Well, maybe you and I have different plans."

"Do you think I would have hidden someplace you'd find me, if I didn't know exactly what was going to happen?"

He reached forward and grabbed the large duffel bag.

"Hold it," I said.

He let go. "I apologize. The contents of the bag are completely harmless, but I can understand why you might want to see what's inside before allowing me to handle it. You are perfectly welcome to examine it."

I paused. I couldn't unzip the bag while still keeping the gun trained on him, and bending over to open the thing up would put me in a fairly precarious position if he decided to lunge at me, even if I leaned against the walker for support.

"Unzip it, slowly. And don't reach inside. You may think you're fast, but all I have to do is squeeze this trigger to make you dead."

"I understand," he said. "You don't warn anyone twice." He pulled at the zipper and slowly opened the bag. It was stuffed with straps of twenty-dollar bills.

"What is that supposed to be?" I asked.

"Are you blind as well as crippled, Baruch? That's a million dollars."

"Yeah, but what's it for?"

"My plan was to give you a choice. You could either take the duffel bag full of cash, or we could have a pointless showdown. I guess, now that you've disarmed me, the proposition has changed slightly. You can either take the money and let me go, or you can kill me."

"Maybe I'll just kill you and take the money anyway," I said.

He shook his head. "Your house is in a nice, quiet neighborhood. The way your hand shakes, I think you'll need to fire several shots to kill me, and a 911 call about multiple gunshots fired here will result in a swift response. This bag weighs more than a hundred pounds, and from the moment you discharge a weapon, you'll probably have no more than four minutes before the police arrive. You won't be able to get away with the money in time."

"Maybe I'll just call the police and turn you in. Maybe the satisfaction of seeing you get what you deserve is worth more to me than the money."

"You'll have to kill me," he said. "I've got no intention of allowing the state to take me into custody. If you attempt to call the police, I shall attack you, and you will either have to shoot me, or else I will beat you to death with my bare hands, an outcome I'd find entirely satisfactory."

"Yeah, I don't like you, either. So, why do you want to give me a million dollars?"

"I'm not giving it to you. I'm buying something. When you take that bag and let me leave, you'll have given up something you treasure, and that's what I want. I don't care about the money." He was grinding his dentures as he spoke. "I've stolen more than I can ever spend. More than I can ever launder. I don't steal because I need to. I've buried shrink-wrapped bales of money in places I don't even remember how to find. I want you to sell the piece of yourself you think is too precious to be tainted by my muck. It's worth a million dollars to watch you stand there and do nothing as I walk out the door."

"You ass," I said. "You perfect, complete ass. I'm almost ninety years old. How can you think I am uncompromising, when I lead such a compromised existence? If there was any part of me that made it through thirty years of police work untainted, it got pretty damn tainted three years ago, which was the first time I had to take a shit and couldn't get to the toilet fast enough. Do you think I care about my dignity? I was cured of dignity a long time ago. During the last several months, I have performed every embarrassing bodily function in front of an audience of strangers.

"I was on the right side against the Nazis. I hope that's what people remember about me, if they remember me at all. And when I worked police, I went out of my way to get the bastards who liked hurting defenseless women and kids. But I know whose interests the police exist to protect, and I know who benefits most from the rule of law and social stability. I ain't one to romanticize police work. If I cared about rules, I might have done a better job of following them. If I cared much about the legal notions of right and wrong, I would never have let Charles Greenfield get away with his part of your bank robbery."

"You kept quiet about Greenfield because you feared unjust repercussions; and you worked for the people doing the repercussing. I forced you to confront the hypocrisy of your own position; the grotesque bigotry of your own establishment."

"I acknowledged it. And then I went on working as a cop for another twelve years, anyway," I said. "Nobody gets through life untainted. But my actions did not directly cause the deaths of three civil rights protesters. That is something that I would never want to carry on my conscience."

He grimaced. "I didn't cause that; I just made it happen at a time I found convenient," he said. "I didn't add a single ingredient to this city's acrid stew of hostility and bigotry, I just stirred the pot a little. The man I paid off didn't even discharge his weapon. Your organization killed those protesters. And the shooters weren't even punished."

"The investigators were never able to identify the officers responsible."

"How long did it take you to find the officer I bribed? Ten minutes? Did the investigators ever find him?"

"I ran him out of town."

"They could have tracked him down, if they'd wanted to. And they could have found the shooters. They could have just taken all the service weapons from the officers on the scene and smelled them, to see which ones had been recently fired."

There were reasons why that wouldn't have worked; I was sure of it. But I couldn't remember what those reasons were, so I said: "Maybe."

"And anyway, what if the Kluge strike hadn't broken down with police violence? Did you know that Kluge had replaced all the striking workers within three weeks? The few men protesting the work site were picketing a fully staffed facility. The strikers had already been fired. And the replacement workers were all blacks, working for the same wage the strikers were protesting. Eventually, the picketers would have had to give up. I rescued them from failure. I made them a symbol of something. Without my intervention, their cause was hopeless."

"I don't think Longfellow Molloy wanted to be a symbol."

"Who?"

"What about Andre Price?" I asked. "Do you remember who he was?"

"If it makes any difference, my heist this time tore down a massive, violent drug empire."

"Which will just be replaced, most likely by the people who tipped you off to the location of the first stash house."

His eyebrows lifted a little. He hadn't expected me to figure that part out. "You're a better detective than you ever let on. But, yes. When you take down bad guys, new bad guys pop up."

I nodded. "And when you take all the money out of a bank vault, they just fill it back up with more money."

He adjusted his legs on the floor and winced with pain as he bent them. "Glass is half empty; glass is half full."

"I just want to know one thing," I said. "Why me? Why did you drag me into this drug dealer nonsense?"

"Why not?" Elijah said. "The only reason I do anything these days is to be doing something. If you stop, you know, you stop. Also, I was curious to see what you'd do when Cash's crew showed up with their guns."

"I could have been killed."

He shrugged. "I don't care," he said. "I don't like you."

That made me laugh. "In some ways, you and I are weirdly similar," I told him.

"We're both old men," said Elijah. "You spent your life trying to be sturdy, and now you're crumbling. I spent my life trying to be smoke, and now I am dissipating. You spent your life trying to impose order on a disordered world, and I spent my life trying to take vengeance on a cruel world. The world is still disordered, and the world is still cruel, and we keep doing the same thing, because what we do is all we are. This, I think, is the way of things. So, are you going to kill me, or are you going to let me go?"

I couldn't see any way to bring him in alive, and he was no good to me dead. I wanted his story. I wanted the world to know what he'd done, and that I was the one who caught him. But maybe the world didn't care. The world didn't even know he existed. And in the end, his story wasn't really worth a million bucks.

"You were wrong about me, I think, when you told me that meanness doesn't weaken with age. There was a time when I'd have blown your goddamn head off on principle," I said.

"Meanness doesn't weaken," he replied. "But principle isn't quite so durable."

"Get the hell out of my house," I said. "And leave the bag."

42
2009

I listened for the sound of the Honda's little lawn mower engine, but when I didn't hear it for several minutes, I remembered that I'd gone slightly deaf and missed noises on the higher registers, so I pushed my walker down the hall and peeked out the front door.

The car was no longer in the driveway.

I called the main police switchboard at 201 Poplar from my cheap plastic cell phone and asked them to put me through to Rutledge, Narcotics.

"Rutledge, Narcotics," he said when he picked up the line.

"Did you lose something?"

"Yeah, motherfucker. I'm missing my goddamn cell phone. Did you steal it? Why would you steal my phone?"

The reason was pretty embarrassing. On the way back to Valhalla from the murder scene, I had been sitting in the passenger seat of Rutledge's unmarked vehicle, and he had been explaining to me in great detail why Quintin Tarantula was a better film director than Sam Peckinpah. I didn't give a shit what he thought about movies.

The phone was stuck in one of the cup holders between us, and I think I picked it up because I was trying to figure out how the thing worked; how one might dial a phone with no buttons. How it got Internets without any wires. I guess I got confused or distracted, and I absentmindedly stuck it in my pocket instead of setting it back in the cup holder.

Totally unintentional. Honest Injun.

But I still had it with me when I got in the Buick to go check out the old house, and it got me thinking about how Elijah had used an Internet phone to trick Cash into coming after him, and about what Tequila had told me people could do with computer programs. So, when I saw Elijah's getaway car parked in the driveway, exactly where I knew he couldn't see it from any of the windows, I realized that I obviously had to stick Rutledge's cell phone underneath the fender with duct tape, so Rutledge could track Elijah down if he slipped away from me.

It was not a coincidence that I had a roll

396

of duct tape in the Buick's glove compartment. I've always kept a roll of duct tape in my glove compartment. Duct tape is great. You can use it for everything from patching a ruptured fuel line to restraining a suspect.

What I said to Rutledge was: "Can you do that thing with the computer, where you trace it online?"

"I think so. I've got an Android, not an iPhone, but I have a similar app."

"I have no idea what any of those words mean," I said.

"I can probably track it."

"Maybe you should do that now."

"I'm kind of busy, Buck. Some folks walking in Riverside Park spotted a corpse floating out in the river, and I have to go look at it to see if it's Carlo Cash."

"Send somebody else, and go find your phone."

"Why?"

If I told Rutledge I'd let Elijah go, he would ask a whole bunch of questions that I wasn't sure how to answer without mentioning the million dollars.

Of course, even if I didn't tell Rutledge about the money, if the detective took the thief alive, chances were good that my payoff wouldn't stay secret, but at least, in that circumstance, Elijah would be alive, in custody, and talking.

I wasn't even sure Rutledge would go after Elijah if he had all the information. He could pin Carlo Cash's murder to one of any number of the drug dealer's former associates, and it was simpler to treat this as a straightforward drug killing than to explain to a jury what Elijah was. Some cops enjoyed the weird, intricate cases, but most just liked to be home in time for dinner.

"Trust me," I said. "You should hunt down your phone before you do anything else."

"All right, Buck."

"Seriously, Rutledge. I'm not crazy, and I'm only partway senile. I'm telling you this for a good reason."

"I'll take it under advisement."

"Track that phone, right now. Make it a priority."

"I'll get right on that. You take care, now."

And then he hung up.

I didn't know whether he was going to look for his phone or not, but I figured I'd done my part and earned my money.

43
2009

There was a time when I could have just dragged a duffel bag full of money out of the house and heaved it into my car, but I probably haven't been able to do anything like that for the last fifteen years.

I unpacked all the money out of the duffel bag, onto the floor. Then I sat down on Elijah's folding chair, and packed as much as I figured I could carry back into the bag. Then I carried the money out to my car, pushing the walker in front of me and leaning on it to help carry the weight. I unpacked the money in the trunk, and then went back in the house and repeated the process.

It took seven trips, which meant that I managed to carry about fifteen pounds at a time. I had to stop twice to rest and to smoke. Once all the money was in the trunk, I packed it back into the duffel bag.

There wasn't much, anymore, that I could

do with money. I didn't need any fancy cars, and wasn't looking to impress any glamorous women. I didn't care for technological gadgets or fine clothes. I wasn't going to travel the world; sitting in an airplane seat for a ten hour flight would probably give me blood clots, and I wasn't steady enough, even with the walker, to safely go for a stroll on the beach, or to maintain my footing on the slippery deck of a cruise ship.

Going back to the house didn't seem to make much sense. I needed daily therapy, and Valhalla had Cloudy-ah on site. And we were settled there. And the house wasn't really home, anymore.

If Medicare cut off the funding for the physical therapy, I supposed that Elijah's money might help pay Cloudy-ah. If I needed nursing care or hospice, I wouldn't have to worry about the cost. Beyond that, a million dollars didn't really change much for me.

But, hell, it was still a million dollars.

I had no choice but to leave it in the car overnight, since I had no idea how to lug it into Valhalla. It wasn't easy sleeping with all that money sitting outside in the trunk of the Buick, and it didn't help that Rose was refusing to talk to me. But the night passed without incident.

The next morning, I took the keys and went to a nearby Wells Fargo branch, where I asked for the largest kind of safe-deposit box they had. I paid the fee and arranged for my grandson to be allowed access to the box upon presentation of my death certificate.

A member of the bank staff hauled the heavy bag from my car into the private safe-deposit vault, and then he left me alone with the box. Nobody asked what was in the bag, because it was none of their business. When I was done, I closed the box and I called to the guy who was helping me. Then I carried the empty duffel bag out of the vault, and he locked up behind me.

I felt good about this resolution. After all, there is no safer place to stash a large amount of money than inside a modern bank vault.

Something I Don't Want to Forget:

I remember, on the day of Brian's bar mitzvah, I tied his necktie for him, because he didn't know how to do it himself. This is the speech he gave. I didn't help him write it, but I think maybe my wife did. Or else, the rabbi:

> Assembled friends, family, and congregants, Rabbi Abramsky, Mom and Dad:
>
> Today we celebrate my ascent into Jewish manhood, and I thank you all for being here to share this important moment with me. Today is a day of great joy, but it's also a solemn day, as I take on new obligations and responsibilities: to daven and to keep the mitzvoth.
>
> And as I shoulder the burdens of Jewish manhood, it is incumbent upon me to remember that this is not a joyous day for everyone. Three colored protesters who marched against their exploitative employer in hopes of winning a fairer wage and a better life are now lying in the hospital, shot full of holes and trying to cling to any kind of life at all. Three others are dead, at the hands of the police. Horrific punishments, inflicted upon these men for the crime of peace-

able assembly. Here in America. Here in Memphis.

The Torah portion we read today was *parsha Vayera,* which tells the story of how Abraham failed to dissuade God from burning down the ancient cities of Sodom and Gomorrah and killing everyone who lived there. So this is a good day to talk about justice, and what the idea of justice means to Jews.

Later this year, some other chazzan will sing to you the Song of Moses, the last divine words the greatest Jewish prophet delivered unto the Israelites before he wandered off into the desert to die.

In this last great speech, Moses explains God's philosophy of justice: "Vengeance is mine," God says. "And I will be satisfied. In due time, the feet of my enemies shall slip. Their day of calamity draws near, and what's coming down on them is coming down fast."

Because there is no god but HaShem! He makes life and He makes death. He wounds and He heals. And there is no force in heaven or on earth who can deliver the judged from His hands.

Today we're here in celebration, but we mustn't forget that our lives will not be comprised entirely — or even mostly — of *simchas*. The walls outside the sanctuary are covered with memorial plaques, each bearing the name and date of a family's loss; a family's tragedy. We celebrate today, because we know that soon we will suffer. Hopefully, our pain will never be as acute as that of our kinsmen in Europe who endured Nazi genocide, or that of the Negroes standing vigil over their wounded brethren today, but we will have pain nonetheless.

God is omnipotent and omniscient. He knows what's coming for us, and He has the power to stop it. But He doesn't; He looks on, and He allows us to suffer. How is that just? I think it is because, in our pain, we discover ourselves. It's only when we've been broken, when we've been stripped of the things we cherish, and the things we think define us, that we learn who we really are.

When Adam and Eve dwelt in the Garden of Eden, God gave them a life of plenty, and free of pain and death. And without suffering, they had no choices. They must have been incredibly bored.

The only act of agency available to them was to disobey the one rule God had laid down; that they must not eat the forbidden fruit. And so, of course, they ate it. What else could they do?

Do you think God, who knows all and sees all, was surprised when they transgressed? I don't think God is ever surprised.

And that brings us back to today's Torah portion. When God said He would spare Sodom if Abraham could find ten righteous men in the city, He wasn't sincerely offering to reconsider His decision to purge the city. He knew there weren't ten righteous men in Sodom, because He is God, and He knows everything.

God made that offer to show Abraham that the decision to purge the city was the right one. By going into Sodom and failing to find ten righteous men, Abraham saw the righteousness of God's judgment. There was nothing in Sodom worthy of salvation, and the city had to burn.

There are two lessons to take from this story: We should never question God's judgment, and we should try not to make Him angry. Although the destruction of Sodom took place in ancient times, the cities of the iniquitous still burn today. My great-great-grandfather Herschel Schatz bore witness when General Sherman put the torch to Atlanta in 1864. More recently, Allied bombers rained fire on the cities of Dresden and Hiroshima.

The lesson is clear: You can spite God for only so long, before your feet slip. The mistreatment of the Negro is an affront to the Lord, and someday soon, His patience may run out, and we may find that it is our day of calamity. We have got to repent. We have got to change. We have to be better than this.

Today, I am a man. God told Abraham that it takes ten righteous men to save a city from obliteration. I am going to try to be one. Let's hope there are nine more.

44
2009

William was returning that afternoon to New York to resume his prestigious internship that everyone was so impressed with. But he hadn't been back in town so close to the anniversary since he'd gone away for college, so he wanted to make a trip to the cemetery before his flight.

I didn't want to go to the damn cemetery. I figured I'd be spending plenty of time there soon enough. But I'd pushed Rose to her breaking point with my recent antics, and it seemed unwise to start a fight about this.

So I found myself looking at my son's grave for the second time in three days. It looked like every other grave. Being here was supposed to make me feel like I was close to him, but standing in front of the stone, he seemed just as far away as he did everywhere else.

My grandson had his arms crossed in

front of him, and I could see he was blinking back tears behind his sunglasses. His mother stood behind him, twisting the hem of her sweater with her hands.

"The worst thing about the funerals here is the concrete vaults," I said. "The water table is real high because we're close to the river, so they won't just let you put the box in the ground."

"We know, Buck. We've seen it," Rose said.

But for some reason, I couldn't stop talking.

"So they've got to drop the wood box they put you in into this bigger concrete box, and then the colored boys who work for the cemetery lower this heavy concrete lid down onto it with cloth straps. Takes four of them boys to put it down there, and they're strapping fellows. And then everybody has to shovel dirt onto the concrete."

"Enough, Buck," Rose said.

"Whenever I come here, that's all I can think about. The sound of concrete grinding on concrete. And you don't really return to the earth, I don't think, when you're buried in a thing like that. I reckon you just kind of molder in there."

Fran started sobbing.

"Are you happy with yourself?" Rose asked me. "Was that really necessary?"

I stuck my hands deep in the pockets of the Members Only jacket, which I was still wearing even though it was pretty hot out. "You've been saying you want me to talk about what I'm feeling. I'm just trying to explain it."

"This isn't feelings you're talking about. It's just horrible."

"I think so, too. That's why I usually try not to talk about it."

We stood there in silence for a few minutes. I looked at the little pile of rocks we'd put on the headstone and tried to remember what they were supposed to symbolize, but I couldn't recall.

"Why did you name him Brian?" Tequila said. "I never heard of a Jew named Brian."

"I think it's an Irish name," Fran said.

"That sounds right," Tequila said. "Why did you give your kid an Irish name?"

"Brian was a friend of mine who died," I said.

"A cop?" Tequila asked.

"No. He was in my unit. We went through basic together at Fort Benning, down in Georgia, and we were on the same landing craft when we hit Normandy. He was standing right next to me, and he caught one in the face."

"So you named your son after him?"

"Sure," I said. "Why not? He was a good guy. It was a fine name."

"Didn't your father die when you were young?"

"I was six." I pointed in the direction of the older section of the cemetery. "He's buried over there."

"What was his name?"

"Arnold."

"Why didn't you name your son after him?"

"Because I didn't want to have to think about my dead father every time I looked at him," I said. "Are you going to name your son after your father?"

"No," Tequila said. "I don't want my son to be the Jewish kid with the weird Irish name."

"You're real charming," I told him.

"You both are," said Rose.

Something I Don't Want to Forget:
By the way, this is why I am called Baruch:
It means "Blessed."

AUTHOR'S NOTE

My grandfather, Harold "Buddy" Friedman, died on October 8, 2013. He was 97. Buddy was a major inspiration for Buck Schatz, so I think readers of these books may be interested to know who he was.

Buddy was born in Memphis, Tennessee, and served in the Pacific during World War II. He worked as a traveling salesman for thirty years, and put two sons through graduate school. He was married to my grandmother, Margaret Friedman, for 72 years.

He was very generous with his time and devoted to charity. Well into his 90s, he was busy organizing a program to offer after-school tutoring to disadvantaged students, and badgering senior citizens at the Jewish Community Center into volunteering. But he would also make a point of letting you know if you'd gained five pounds since he'd last seen you.

My grandfather was a strong man, but nobody can be strong forever. He made his living on the road, and always took special pride in his cars. But, as his reflexes slowed, he had to give up his keys for his own safety.

Around the time he turned 90, he was still exercising regularly at the Jewish Community Center, but the last couple of years he was at a high risk of falling, and had to use a walker.

Pop-culture depictions of old age never seem to depict the price that people pay for longevity, the psychological burden that comes with burying everybody, the feeling of being imprisoned in a weakening body, the impositions on privacy and dignity that come with failing health, and the knowledge that things are likely to be worse tomorrow than they are today.

Buddy was a proud man who dealt with a difficult set of circumstances that millions of people face, but which popular narratives tend to gloss over with shopworn clichés and cowardly euphemisms. It was because of him that I wrote these books.

ABOUT THE AUTHOR

Daniel Friedman is a graduate of the University of Maryland and NYU School of Law. He lives in New York City. *Don't Ever Get Old* won a Macavity Award for Best First Novel.